The Gender War

Arthur Carey

What is most beautiful in virile men is something feminine; what is most beautiful in feminine women is something masculine.

Susan Sontag

Gender War Reviews

"Hard...hot..."

When the school bus lurched, I saw this book on the floor. I picked it up and took it home but the words are too hard and the type is too small, and my mom took one look at the cover and got really hot and threw it away.

Timmy Rawlings, 5th grade, Mirabelle, CA.

..."riveting..."

At first I thought the book was about Rosie the Riveter and the women who did riveting on ships in World War II, but it wasn't."

Alice Libramasky, Chugiak News-Herald

"Movie of the Week..."

This has "Movie of the Week" written all over it. Not necessarily "Novel of the Week," but at least during the dog days of summer TV reruns, I could see...

Marvin Newcombe, Entertainment Weakly

"They don't write books like this any more..."

They don't write books like this any more, which actually is a good thing because sexist, ageist parodies of traditional American values and institutions reflect the intellectual paucity and febrile approach to art of the current generation of commercial authors.

Andrew Durand, Les Lapins Literary Journal

"...blazing new literary star..."

The author may not be a blazing new literary star, but nobody thought Pet Rocks would be popular either.

Roland Petigrew, Channel 37, Schenectady, N.Y.

"OMG...! ROFL...! USBCA...!"

Oh, my God...Rolling on the floor laughing...Until something better comes along.

EtaoinShirdlu@Worldnet

Among those who helped make this book possible were my daughter Lisa and Gene Costello, both of whom bravely journeyed through the first draft and offered useful suggestions. Special thanks are due Karen Parker and Mike Cronk, who also provided encouragement and editorial insight.

Chpter I

Fortune can, for her pleasure, fools advance,
And toss them on the wheels of Chance.

JUVENAL

"They'll eat you alive," said Dale Seybold. The balding city editor gazed at Jack Kileen across a desk cluttered with computer printouts. "Mari O'Reilly and that woman professor will fillet you like the catch of the day before millions of television viewers."

"No, they won't," retorted Jack.

But the worry monster gnawed away at his vitals. When a producer from the nationally syndicated Mari O'Reilly Show had called to ask if he wanted to appear and plug his new book, 'Alpha Male, Pride of the Pride,' he had agreed quickly—perhaps too quickly. Would he flounder in flop sweat and make an ass of himself on TV?

Behind the editor and writer lay the diminished newsroom of the San Francisco Sun, monarch of the dailies–or at least monarch of the two daily newspapers still surviving in The City by the Bay. Like a vampire, the Internet had drained the paper of its lifeblood, advertising revenue. Now an economic meltdown was squeezing out the last few drops, shrinking the number of pages and the staff.

"What made you decide to appear on a women's TV program?" asked Seybold.

Jack's voice hardened. "Millions of people watch that program, people who actually pay money for books and don't scrounge them for nickels and dimes at library sales."

The editor scratched a narrow band of hairless skin on a finger that had once held a wedding ring. "Women are hard-wired as predators at birth. That's why the divorce rate is so high."

"I am man, hear me roar," said Jack. "I can hold my own in an argument, Seybold, anywhere, any time."

He received a pitying look. "You...roar? On national TV? With a hyped-up studio audience of women who've been standing in the hot sun for hours to get tickets? You'll be like Indiana Jones when he fell into the pit of vipers."

"But he got out, didn't he?" said Jack. Snakes...Indiana Jones...How did we...? He shook his head. "Besides, it's only a quickie appearance. They'll probably sandwich me between vitamin and hormone commercials and move on to drug addiction and infidelity."

Seybold shook his head. "You may regret your 15 minutes of fame." The editor looked puzzled. "Why is a women's talk show interested in a book for guys? It doesn't fit their demographic."

"Maybe they're trying to attract more male viewers," said Jack.

But he had another theory, one he wouldn't mention. Namely, that he had been selected like prime beef on the hoof, culled from the herd, and was about to be run to ground. For the past three days, the network had been promoting his appearance on the show along with that of a feminist Florida professor. It was being hyped as a clash between two authors trumpeting opposing views of male and female roles.

Jack shrugged. "How was I to know they'd bring in some professor with a book of her own and turn the interview into a debate?"

Seybold raised an eyebrow. "On the Mari O'Reilly Show? Where have you been, at an undisclosed location in Uzbekistan? The woman's got a reputation for skewering people Vlad the Impaler would have envied." He rubbed his chin. "What was the professor's name?"

Grudgingly, Jack pulled out a book half-hidden book under one arm. "Sanders...Dr. Laura Sanders. She's from Florida Southern University. Her book is a history of the women's movement, 'Saint to Siren to CEO: Changing Roles of American Women.'"

Seybold nodded approvingly. "Ah... sizing up the opposition! Good idea. You might survive longer in the pit with the vipers."

"Anyway, I'm on a red eye to New York tonight," Jack said. "I'll flip through the book on the way."

The editor's chair squeaked as he leaned back. "I like night flights. They turn out all the lights and shut off the movie. The drone of the engines is like a lullaby. You can doze right off." He paused, "Speaking of dozing off, what's this book of yours about again... male leadership, you said?"

Jack stiffened. "It's about traits like insight and sensitivity that real leaders possess. You might learn something from it," he added, the sarcasm unmistakable. "Actually, you might learn a lot."

The editor scratched the shiny oval at the top of his head. "I hate to buy new books—too expensive. Then they pile up around the house until the next garage sale." He brightened. "Any freebies? My brother-in-law has a birthday coming up. He might like to read something that isn't too challenging."

"I'll let you know." Not likely, pal.

Seybold held out a hand. "Let me see the lady professor's book."

Jack handed over the slim volume.

"Not a real looker," the editor mused, scrutinizing the photo on the dust cover. "But attractive, definitely attractive. She may have the few guys in the audience on her side as well as the women."

He studied Jack's worn blue shirt with frayed collar, hastily knotted tie, and tiny red nick on the chin from an unnoticed shaving mishap. "Lots of luck, Kileen, you'll need it."

Jack grabbed the book. "Thanks for the encouragement. See you next week."

At his desk, he trashed a used coffee cup and Dunkin' Donuts box and logged off on the computer.

Then he stopped. The unsmiling face of Dr. Laura Sanders stared back in no-nonsense black and white from the back of her book. She appeared intelligent, serious, and depressingly confident. He tried to push both her and the Mari O'Reilly Show out of his mind. It didn't work.

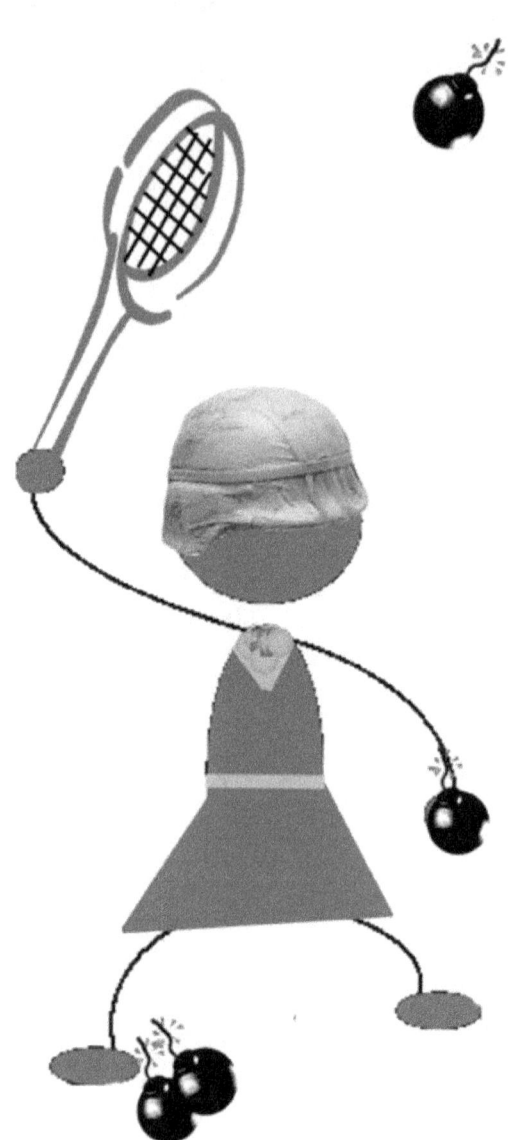

Chpter 2

Hope is a waking dream.

ARISTOTLE

Thunk! A ball of black and white fur exploded onto Laura's stomach. She threw back the bedcovers, arms flailing, shocked from deep sleep.

"Buffy!" Her voice rang with indignation, but the cat that had used her as a springboard to a table by the window contemplated her calmly.

Laura glanced at the alarm clock and sighed— 6:33 a.m. She had worked past midnight writing a monograph for an educational journal and had to fly to New York that afternoon. She never slept well on planes. Another half hour of rest would have helped.

The cat, which had slept at the foot of her bed, yawned and leaped to the floor, bound for the kitchen.

Laura dragged herself out of bed and pulled the drapes. Weak sunlight slanted through the blinds. She looked guiltily at the layer of dust devils on the curved plastic slats. Gotta do something about that, but not today.

She shrugged into a pair of shorts, a shirt, and sandals, and walked to the kitchen. A can of kitty tuna delight lay open in the refrigerator. She scooped it into Buffy's dish and replaced the cat's water. Buffy attacked the tuna greedily.

Laura sipped orange juice and polished off the remains of a cantaloupe while waiting for water to boil for tea. By the time bread had rocketed from the depths of the toaster, the water was hot. She made tea, waited for it to steep, and drank it without benefit of milk or sugar.

She pushed open the screen door to the backyard and picked up a bucket containing bird feed— black sunflower seeds and round-grained millet. The sky was pearly blue and cloudless, holding the promise of another hot day. Breathing in the cool air, she made her way along a gravel path through unrestrained grass, weeds, shrubs, and wildflowers to a tray sitting on a post four feet above the ground. There she scooped out the seed with a small hand trowel and spread it about generously. "Good luck, guys," she said, "the bully of the backyard will be here soon."

She had barely reached the kitchen before the first vigilant sparrows and finches swooped down for breakfast. Laura watched out the window. Within minutes, they scattered as an aggressive Florida scrub jay arrived to take over the feeder. Typical male.

The morning's coolness had dissipated when she arrived on the Fort Myers campus of the university.

Palm fronds dangled listlessly in the torpid air. In the distance, the muffled whine of a leaf blower leaked through single-pane glass in the Humanities Building.

"Laura!"

She stopped and turned.

Dean Morris Evander bustled up to her, a stack of manila folders under one arm.

"Hi, Morris."

She noticed the dean's crisp, white shirt had wilted in his walk from the faculty parking lot to the air-conditioned refuge indoors. His tie, ocean blue flecked with red triangles, was knotted tightly at the neck of a spare, trim body honed by hours on the squash court.

Evander supervised the graduate studies department at Florida Southern, home of the Fighting Sea Slugs. "Just wanted to wish you well on the Mari O'Reilly Show, Laura," he said. "We're all rooting for you." He paused, struggling for a thought. "What's that expression...break a leg?"

She laughed. "That's for people in show business, Morris, not professors of women's studies."

"Well, whatever. We know you'll do us proud."

Laura's grin faded. She had hoped to slide under the radar in appearing on the Mari O'Reilly Show, but it wasn't going to happen. The campus newspaper had carried a picture and story about her on the front page. She breathed in Evander's cologne and her heart fluttered. Silly!

He glanced at his watch. "Oops...late for a meeting."

"I know the feeling. I've got an exam to give," she said, wishing again she could pin him down for a glass of wine or at least a cup of coffee. "See you later." She watched him hurry off and headed for her classroom.

An hour later, Laura looked up from the book she had been trying to read, her mind elsewhere. A sea of bowed heads faced her, students scratching away thoughtfully, or desperately, in bluebooks. Occasionally, one would glance up and stare straight ahead, blank faced, as if inspiration lay hidden in the wall behind her. It reminded her of descriptions of the 10,000-yard stare of infantrymen who had been in combat too long. Exams created stress, too.

Laura sympathized with her students. She knew what it was like to lose sleep studying, to work part-time at mind-deadening jobs for peanuts, and to take out crushing loans to survive. And then it got worse, graduating into the real world where failure wasn't measured by a disappointing grade.

One of the students sneezed loudly, dragging her thoughts back to the classroom. She wore a white blouse, jeans accenting a willowy figure, and tennis shoes. That was one of the nice things about teaching: Every day was casual dress day. Peach lipstick, lightly applied, was her only concession to cosmetic enhancement. People who met her for the first time often were disconcerted by unblinking hazel eyes that assessed them analytically as if they were butterflies pinned under glass.

When the clock at the rear of the room read 11:50 a.m., she delivered the bad news: "Time's up. Turn in your papers."

Sighs and rustling greeted the words. Students shifted in their seats and stretched to work the kinks out of stiff muscles. They began organizing bluebooks, putting away pens, collecting backpacks. Some looked relieved, others unhappy. They had finished the midterm exam in English 203, Gender in Modern Literature. The class had an extensive reading list, and it wasn't dumbed down to the level of pop culture paperbacks.

"Remember, there's no class Monday," she warned, voice rising above the murmurs and scraping of chairs. "We'll be back in session Wednesday as usual." The students, mostly female with a sprinkling of males, began trickling out the door.

"Hey, doc, I'll be looking for you on Mari," boomed a boy with sun-bleached hair. He wore a polo shirt, ripped shorts, and leather sandals. "I'm working that afternoon, but I'm TiVoing the show. Aren't you nervous about being on the Mari O'Reilly Show? She's a tough lady."

"A little," Laura admitted.

He added his blue book to the growing pile on her desk. "Don't be! You'll be killer!" He slouched off, the ring in his left eyebrow twitching.

Laura rose, brushed brown hair back from her eyes, and began stuffing the pile of bluebooks into a worn leather briefcase. She felt guilty canceling a class, but who could turn down a chance to appear on the Mari O'Reilly Show? It could be a huge push for her new book. After dashing to the airport, she'd have the weekend in New York to get some publicity for her book and to prepare for the show. After a last glance about the deserted classroom, she picked up her briefcase, switched off the lights, and walked out into the humid air.

Ch*ter 3

*Happiness is the interval between periods
of unhappiness.*

DON MARQUIS

Mari O'Reilly waved and smiled warmly at the camera. "Have a great weekend," she said, "but be sure to join us on Monday for a terrific show! We'll see who makes the better leaders, men or women!"

The applause sign lit up, and members of the largely female audience began clapping on cue. They began to file out slowly, loath to leave the air-conditioned studio. Outside, New York City simmered in a late spring heat wave.

Mari yanked off her earpiece, thrust it wordlessly at a technician, and stalked off the set.

Waiting in the wings was Cliff Hansen, the program's producer. He handed her a bottle of chilled water. "Great show, Mari!"

Laser-like green eyes drilled him. "Oh? I thought it sucked. The guests bored even me," she replied. "I didn't connect with any of them, and neither did the audience." She took a swallow of water. "Is the Monday schedule locked up?"

Hansen consulted his clipboard. "Yeah. We've got a really funny parrot act. They ride bicycles. Can you imagine? Then there's Reena Winslow, just out of rehab again. She'll be plugging her new movie, 'Love, Love, Love!'" He paused, "Oh, and the two writers we've been pushing in promos, the newspaper guy from San Francisco and the woman professor from Florida." Hansen tried to pump enthusiasm into his voice. "The prof is a women's libber, and the guy's your basic Neanderthal. Should be oil and water, Mari."

She gave him a look that could reverse global warming. "Bird tricks? A pill-popping, B-film actress? A couple of no-name writers pushing books nobody will buy?" She pointed the water bottle at him as if it were a gun. "We need guests who'll make housewives in Dubuque and Petoskey stop ironing and say 'wow'! Our ratings are in the crapper, Cliffy."

Hansen masked his irritation. She knew he hated the name. He'd hated it growing up in Waterloo, Iowa, when neighborhood kids taunted him with it, and he hated it now.

She cocked her head. "How about the guy who got voted out on Idol, the puppy dog tenor with the Beatles haircut? Did you get him?"

Hansen looked unhappy. "I tried. He's already booked on another program."

She raked him with her eyes again. "I can't make it all happen by myself, Cliffy. Hit your Rolodex and line up some A-list guests, people whose names the audience recognizes. Or someone else will!" The threat lingered in the air between them.

He swallowed without replying.

She tapped him on the chest with the bottle. "Have the driver bring around my limo."

Hansen watched her walk away. Bitch! He chewed his lower lip. It was late to dump the two no-name authors for Monday because the promos had run. Oh, well, it could get exciting. If anyone could manipulate people into blowing their cool before millions of viewers, it was Mari. He put aside thoughts about Monday's show and began worrying about Tuesday's.

If it was sunny and warm in New York, a storm was brewing in Chicago, and it wasn't blowing in off Lake Michigan. Roland Ebert, publisher of Glimpse (The Magazine That Tells You What Others Don't Dare!) eyed the picture of a half-man, half-fish on the cover of his publication with mounting irritation. Nor did the headline "Merman Discovered in Seattle Sewer!" lessen his displeasure.

"Helen..." he rumbled, his voice echoing beyond the spacious office, "tell Larry Clayton to get up here... now!"

His secretary, a thin, gray-haired woman, stuck her head through the open door. "Intercom not working, boss?" she asked pointedly.

Ebert picked up on the implied criticism. "I keep pushing the wrong button when I'm ticked off," he said sheepishly.

She nodded "O...kay." They had been through that before.

Roland Ebert had become a multi-millionaire after dropping out of college and starting a mountain biking magazine with $5,000 borrowed from his father, who was glad to get him out of the house. He now owned a string of other slick publications devoted to auto detailing, physical fitness, outdoor living, and entertainment, including *Glimpse.* He lived behind locked gates in a 15-room mansion in an exclusive Chicago enclave where homes listed in the $7-million range. His wife donated five figures to the symphony society annually in the hope she would be selected to head the annual charity drive. Fat chance. That was as likely to happen as Osama bin Laden being awarded the Nobel Peace Prize. Despite its three million devoted readers, *Glimpse,* flagship of her husband's publishing empire, was a sleazy tabloid. Symphony society members didn't get their fiction fix from sensationalistic magazines picked up at supermarket checkout counters.

"You wanted to see me R.E.?" Larry Clayton, the magazine's managing editor, stood in the doorway, slightly out of breath, awaiting an invitation to enter. A thin, nervous man in his late fifties, owlish in thick glasses, he tried to project the barest hint of impatience. Clayton hoped to convey the impression he was extremely busy and interruptions had better be important, publisher or not.

"Yeah." Ebert gestured toward a seat. The publisher sorted through a pile of magazines on his massive teak desk, selected one, and pursed his lips. "*Epic* suggests the fix was in for the guy who won a million bucks on that TV survival show *Win Out!* He dropped the magazine and picked up another. "I see that the *National*

Examiner has a block-buster story about erectile dysfunction drugs being linked to cancer." He shuffled other publications. "Ah, here it is...the *Insider* says the CIA has discovered an al Qaeda base on Mars." He leaned forward. "Do you know what that is, Clayton?"

Clayton glanced about the room as if looking for an answer. He scanned the framed magazine covers and plaques lauding *Glimpse Magazine's* sponsorship of Little League baseball, pee-wee football, and girls' soccer. His eyes came to rest on a picture of Ebert shaking the hand of a Republican congressman recently indicted for accepting bribes. He swallowed. "No, boss. What is it?"

"It is brilliant, Clayton. It is ab-so-lute-ly brilliant. A home run! It combines images of terrorists blowing up the Statue of Liberty with the mystery of the Red Planet, which, by the way, our previous President wanted us to visit in a decade or so at a cost of a few hundred million bucks. It's as good as sex, sin, and celebrity, all wrapped up in one package. And what do we have?" He picked up the current issue of *Glimpse* and waved it at Clayton. "A guy with a fish's tail! Haven't we done this before?"

"Well...not exactly...."

Ebert's eyes, agate-hard orbs tented by bushy eyebrows, narrowed. "I remember something like this. What...a year...two years ago?"

Clayton sorted through mental images of *Glimpse* covers, real, semi-real, and totally fabricated. "You might be thinking of the dog-faced girl." He remembered that one: the face of an English bulldog Photo shopped onto the curvaceous body of a Hollywood star. The story had sucked, but so what?

Ebert sneered. "You're wrapping the same fish in different paper."

Clayton shifted in the plush leather chair, confidence draining from his voice. "It'll be new to most of our readers."

Ebert shook his head. He leaned menacingly across the desk and slammed his right hand down, sending papers flying. Clayton flinched.

Damn, thought Ebert, that really works! He had been reading an article on M.B.I. (Management by Intimidation) and had wanted to try it out. He waved the copy of *Glimpse* again. "Our readers don't *like* recycled stories, art or no art. Some of them have been reading this crap for years. They remember stories. They remember pictures. They write letters. They want new stories. *I* want new stories."

Clayton nodded. He got the message and groaned to himself. Did this guy have any idea how hard it was to come up with stories about flesh-eating viruses, clairvoyants, dying movie stars, and new sightings of Elvis every week? "Right. I'll get on it, R.E."

The publisher gazed out the window at early commute traffic limping along the freeway and turned back. "Find me something new, Clayton... something big... something hot...something with legs!"

Abruptly, he changed the subject. That was another technique of Management By Intimidation, keeping your employees off balance. "How's the new hire working out?"

Clayton blinked as he switched gears mentally. "Ashford Sloan? Great!" he said enthusiastically. "I've got him working on a story about an 85-year-old woman who had identical twins."

Ebert smiled. He had great hopes for Ashford Sloan. For all the Ashford Sloans. Fresh talent kept readers thumbing through copies of the magazine at check-out counters and adding them to shopping carts. He loved impulse sales. "Okay." He dismissed the sweating editor with a curt nod.

Clayton shuffled out, biting his lip. Where could he find the next red-hot read? Police reports on weirdos? Spaced-out bloggers on the Internet? He decided to get a cup of coffee and took the elevator down to the second floor lunchroom. As he entered it, the flickering images on a TV set caught his eye. Two women were screaming at each other while a man tried to separate them. Clayton paused. Why not TV? Who knows? One of the guest wackos on a talk show might make a story. He smiled. It was always reassuring to have a plan.

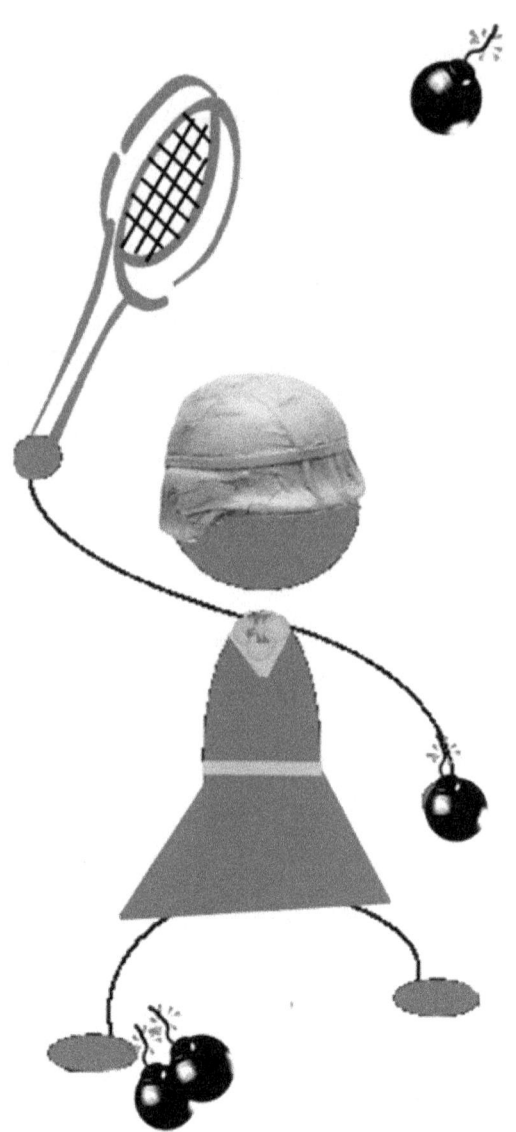

 Chapter 4

"New York, New York, it's a wonderful town...."

"ON THE TOWN"

"... morning, Manhattan! Time to fly with the Eye in the Sky on WXTP A.M. radio! If you're on the road this beautiful Saturday morning, be careful! Here's how your ride is shaping up on what promises to be a warm spring..."

Jack surfaced from beneath the covers with a groan and backhanded the clock radio beside the bed. But not before Larry, high in the Eye in the Sky, delivered the morning's good news for weekend drivers: a four-car pileup on the Henry Hudson, a blocked tunnel leading into New York City, and more construction on the East River Drive. It took three tries and a bruised hand before there was silence. Well, almost silence. From 44th Street, 10 stories below, the muffled sounds of a city grudgingly coming to life rose in the cool morning air.

He had flown in late the night before from San Francisco to promote "Alpha Male." Several days of radio and television interviews plus book signings lay ahead. Shrugging into a fluffy white hotel bathrobe, he unbolted the door. With luck, the newspaper outside wouldn't be *USA Today*, starved staple of the nation's motels and inns. He expected the Algonquin Hotel to do better. It had. A copy of the *New York Times* he had requested lay by the door.

After scanning the breakfast menu, he reached for the telephone. "Hello... This is Jack Kileen in..." Damn... what was the number? His room card lay on the table by the bed, but it had no number for security purposes.

"Oh, you know the number? Okay, send up some orange juice, toast, a poached egg, and coffee. Make that in 20 minutes, please." Four bucks for a small glass of orange juice? At least *he* wouldn't be paying for it; his publisher would.

Stepping to the desk, he flipped open his Apple laptop and brought up the calendar. Today's schedule featured a radio interview at 9:30 a.m. and a book signing his publisher's publicist, Jessica Longley, had lined up. On Sunday, he had an early morning TV appearance. And on Monday he was scheduled for THE BIG ONE—the *Mari O'Reilly Show*.

Stripping off pajamas, Jack turned on the shower. He eyed the scale distrustfully, finally yielding to guilt and stepping up to truth. The digits spun and stabilized at 182. Not bad for a 43-year-old guy whose usual daily exercise involved punching computer keys. After a quick shower, he examined himself critically. Love handles had started to jell above his hips. "Stomach in, chest out," he ordered the image in the mirror. It worked until he exhaled. He saw the face he displayed to the world: unruly sandy hair, thinning slightly into a widow's peak; brown eyes, not-quite-straight nose, the result of contact with a knee while playing sand-lot football, and a firm mouth anchored by a square chin. He stepped into the glass enclosure, showered quickly, and shaved after rubbing clear a circle of fogged glass.

He dressed quickly: gray, open-necked sport shirt; charcoal pants; black sport coat, and black shoes. Nobody would see him on the radio, of course, but he had an image to create. Publicity revealed all, and authors who hoped to crack the New York Times best-seller list couldn't dress like dweebs. And, this being New York, the funereal look was always in.

Breakfast arrived. Sipping hot coffee before spread-ing congealed butter on room-temperature toast, he scanned the headlines. After checking the weather in San Francisco (cool, with a chance of showers), he turned to the sports section for the really important news. The Giants were building suntans and signing autographs in spring training. The Oakland A's, whose relief pitchers usually only gave relief to the oppos-ing team, had already settled into a rut of one-game losses in Cactus League play.

The Algonquin Hotel, a few blocks from Times Square and the theater district, lacked the glitz and glamour of some of the newer hotels, but it had its own cachet: literary tradition. Dorothy Parker, Robert Bench-ley, and Edna Ferber had made it their pied-à-terre in the 1930s. Whenever he thought of the worn, polished wood table in the library room downstairs, Jack imag-ined himself sipping martinis and exchanging clever bon mots with the other Round Table habitués.

He drained the cup of coffee, checked for his room card and wallet, waited for the door to click shut behind him, and walked to the elevator. It came too quickly to enjoy more than a few of the James Thurber cartoons on the wallpaper.

Sunlight exploded as he emerged, blinking, onto 44th Street and flagged down a taxi. After providing the address of WBXT radio, Jack sat back and studied the unsmiling photo of his driver, Ramon, on the plasti-cized identification card attached to the sun visor. The oniony odor of a breakfast taco lingered in the cab. The sounds of bleating horns and pounding jackhammers seeped through closed windows. Ramon ignored the "Don't Block the Box" signs and aggressively pushed forward into intersections on yellow lights while hum-ming along with Latin music on the radio. He scanned adjoining streets for police cars with the wariness of a gazelle approaching a lion-infested waterhole.

As the taxi jerked through the morning traffic, Jack imagined himself on a felucca, floating down the Nile. His riverbanks were crowded sidewalks, registering as brief images flashing by in a computer slide show. Along both shores passed the natives of New York as they began the weekend: latte-seeking young couples; mothers pushing bulky strollers and dragging young children; darting riders on bicycles, helmets bobbing up and down in the metallic current; expression-less old men peering from café windows, doers become watchers; sullen-faced boys in drab baggy pants and in-your-face t-shirts, their heads wrapped in do rags or wearing baseball caps; vendors, licensed and unli-censed, hawking Italian ice, hot nuts, marijuana t-shirts, fake Rolexes, and Ground Zero memorabilia from side-walk tables and carts. But unlike a real river, this one stopped and started on signal, flowing between towering slabs of concrete and steel and glass that imprisoned the sunlight in narrow, dusty shafts.

The Big Apple.

After Ramon delivered him to the WXBT studios, Jack waited, tense and jittery. Through a thick glass window, he could see his host, Brad Lamar, talking animatedly into a microphone, occasionally eyeing a large clock.

First up today for Jack was an interview in the book slot of a weekend show called "Eye Opener." Would Lamar have read the book? Like it mattered. Jack's publicist had prepared an interview kit consisting of a brief summary of "Alpha Male—Pride of the Pride" and a list of five questions. All of the information had been printed on two 3x5 cards in 14-point Geneva bold caps for easy reading.

Jack studied his soon-to-be interrogator. He hoped Lamar was having a good day. Like most newspaper writers, Jack felt much more comfortable asking questions than answering them.

As it turned out, Lamar wasn't having a good day. He had just checked his 401K stock portfolios on a PDA and discovered the NASDAQ had ended the week below the life support level again. Lamar wasn't really Lamar, of course; that was his on-air name, and it wasn't listed in any phone book. No calls from irate listeners who might be packing heat. His real name was Stanley Polchowski, and he had been born in Muskegon, Michigan; but he had come a long way from spinning discs in store promotions at suburban malls. WXBT cranked out 50,000 watts of "all news, all talk, all day and night."

During a commercial break, Jack sat down opposite a microphone and donned a headset. When they went live, Lamar nodded and said warmly, "Jack Kileen, author of 'Alpha Male—Pride of the Pride' is with us this morning." He looked past Jack and waved at someone walking past in the hall. "I must admit the testosterone level of your book almost kept me awake! " Lamar's eyes flicked down to a 3x5 card. "In an age of political correctness, aren't you stepping into a potential minefield here?"

Jack smiled and tried to look earnest while responding to a fat man in sunglasses sipping a Diet Coke and wearing a "Drilling is for Dentists!" t-shirt.

"Well, Lamar..." he began.

Fifteen minutes later, he was out of the studio, unscathed. The radio interview had been a piece of cake. He was on a roll.

Who needs April in Paris when you can have April in New York without the trauma of changing dollars into Euros? Jack decided to stroll the half dozen blocks from the radio station to the Broadway Bookery where he'd be signing copies of "Alpha Male—Pride of the Pride." Interviews on radio and TV set his stomach muscles twitching; but the worse thing that could happen at a book signing was getting writer's cramp, an affliction he had never experienced.

New Yorkers, pale of face after winter's enforced hibernation, thronged the streets in sunglasses, baseball caps, and shorts. Trees brandished new greenery. Dusky finches and sparrows sang with renewed exuberance, voices mingling with the drumming of traffic.

First-time visitors to the Broadway Bookery got a surprise. The store wasn't on Broadway, and it didn't appear to be a bookery, at least not what the word suggested. Jack had expected a small, intimate refuge steeped in silence that invited readers to dawdle while browsing its treasures. Instead, he found a two-story concrete box with a cold, cavernous interior. No gourmet coffee shop enticed customers to pick up a double latte and plunk down in a comfortable chair to sample the wares.

Still, the Broadway Bookery had included a small (very small) picture of him in its Sunday ad in the *New York Times Book Review*, informing readers Jack Kileen, author of "Alpha Male—Pride of the Pride," would be in residence from 10 a.m. to 1 p.m. to autograph copies of his new book. He wandered around, getting a feel for the place. The green screens of strategically placed computers customers could use to locate books contrasted with the '50s ambiance. He walked up to the central purchasing desk.

"Hi, I'm Jack Kileen. I'm here for the book signing."

The clerk, a thin, mousy-looking young woman in jeans, wore large round glasses secured with a cord around her neck. She continued sorting books and spoke over her shoulder without looking up.

"Derek… author to see you!"

Behind her, a man in rumpled cord pants and a dark sweater broke off entering numbers on a computer and walked over.

"Mr. Killian? I'm Derek Jones, assistant manager. We're all set up for you."

"Kileen," replied Jack.

The man blinked. "Oh, sorry." He led Jack to a table near the gardening section. A white board next to it announced "Jack Killian—here today!" Eraser marks showed where a previous name had been rubbed out and Jack's written in. He handed Jack a marking pen.

"It's a little slow," he said apologetically, "but I'm sure the traffic will pick up soon. We're having a sale on the Peter Barret boy vampire books. Very popular now, especially with teen-age girls."

Jack nodded noncommittally. He had never heard of Peter Barrett and mentally linked vampires with old Bela Lugosi movies. He picked up an eraser, rubbed out "Killian," wrote "Kileen" in large, block letters, and sat down.

Time crawled by. Most of the Broadway Bookery's customers knew what they wanted and either found it or didn't, leaving quickly. Few browsed. Jack didn't blame them. The air conditioning hadn't been turned on yet, and harsh fluorescent lights revealed cracks in the painted over brick walls. What had the building been used for before? A brewery? A warehouse? He signed a few books and tried to look warm and fuzzy in case any potential buyers were shy about approaching him.

An elderly woman in a sweater adorned with hummingbirds approached his table tentatively. She squinted through bifocal glasses as he scrawled his signature on the book she offered. "To Emily," he wrote, "One of my favorite readers!"

"Thank you," she said, in a high-pitched, quavering voice. "I'm looking forward to reading 'Alpha Male.'

I just love animal books, especially about big cats. I watch them whenever I can on 'Discovery Channel.'"

Jack smiled. "So do I."

He started the *Times* crossword puzzle. A scruffy, bearded young man wearing a torn Yankees sweatshirt interrupted him while he pondered 27 across. Tiny gold bands hung from the man's ears, and Jack wondered if he also had nipple rings because of twin bumps under the sweatshirt. The man thrust a copy of "Alpha Male" at Jack and looked at him expectantly.

"How shall I sign it?" asked Jack. "What's your name?"

"Not my name, man! Just sign it 'To Rollie.' It's for my mom's boyfriend. He's into this macho bullshit, and she said I had to get him something for his birthday. What I'd like to get him is his own shower in the morning," he said bitterly.

"Of course." Jack signed with a flourish. "I hope that he enjoys reading this macho bullshit as much as I enjoyed writing it."

The young man grabbed the book. "He'd better, man. Seventeen bucks plus tax! I should have waited for a 2-for-1 sale. This looks like an overweight comic book."

"Oh, I don't know," Jack murmured. "Think of it as acquiring a signed first edition."

As the morning wore on, he autographed seven more books and resumed working the crossword puzzle until stumped by 51 down, a four-letter word for a Revolutionary War general whose first name was Thomas. He decided to cheat and look up the answer, only to find the answers provided were for yesterday's puzzle. Today's answers were obtainable, but only on the telephone at $1.20 a minute. He decided that he could wait to find out. At 1 p.m., the assistant manager appeared with an armful of books and a slightly disheveled, wild-eyed, impatient man. The books had lurid red covers and pictures of flying saucers hovering over a city at night. The manager explained another book signing had been scheduled for that afternoon. As he yielded his place at the table, Jack said, "Tell me, are there alpha males among aliens from space?"

The author looked at him blankly as if he were from another planet.

Chpter 5

Revenge is a Dish Best Served Cold.

ANON.

Laura took a sip of chardonnay and let the cool liquid trickle slowly down her throat. She began to unwind. She wished she could slip off her shoes, but decided an expensive New York restaurant probably wasn't the place. About her, the buzz of conversation and tinkle of glass and silverware provided soothing background music.

She had flown into JFK the day before, taken a taxi into Manhattan, and registered at the Excelsior Hotel, too late for high tea. After a restless night, she had met her publisher's press agent, Bob Wingate, and worked through a radio interview, a brief talk at a women's writer's club meeting, and a book signing session.

But then Wingate had pulled a surprise. He suggested a late lunch at the Z, a fashionable restaurant off Fifth Avenue. Their lunch companion was to be another of the publisher's authors, a former Broadway actor who had just written a telltale memoir about life on The Great White Way. The actor, evidently into several martinis when they had arrived at the restaurant, was introduced as Rodney Randall. The name hadn't rung a bell with Laura. But she remembered his clammy handshake that never seemed to end. He had once been a handsome man, she decided, probably a matinee idol basking in the glow of the footlights and the applause that rang from beyond them. But now bleary blue eyes gazed at her from a deeply lined face. Spider-like lines radiated along a reddened nose, the sign of a dedicated drinker.

As the conversation between Wingate and Randall, droned on, she tried to avoid yawning. But then she jerked upright. Something had nudged her shoe, lightly at first and then more insistently. *A foot!* Clawing fingers settled over one of her kneecaps and squeezed. She flinched and turned startled eyes to the aging Broadway actor sitting next to her. She watched as he swallowed an olive with a loud sucking sound and winked at her. The grip on her knee tightened.

"Excuse me," she blurted, "I have to use the restroom." Laura shoved back her chair and bolted from the room, leaving a puzzled press agent and a disappointed actor in her wake. Once in the women's restroom, she collapsed into a chair in front of a mirror and waited for her heart to stop racing. *Damn...it had gone so well up to now! Why did this have to happen?*

She tossed her purse against the mirror and seethed. Not again! Not after Victor Slansky! The image of Rodney Randall faded in her mind, replaced by another, that of a smirking, middle-aged man, stomach barely constrained by ugly red suspenders. She shut her eyes but the memory remained.

Detroit, December 1999—Laura shoved the empty cart into a corner, muttering an unlady-like expletive. Delivering the mail wasn't part of her job description at Barnaby & Fitch Advertising Agency; but the high school dropout whose job it was had taken yet another sick day. *Maybe he's polishing his brass,* she thought bitterly. The kid had rings in his ears, lips, and nose, and probably more in places that she didn't want to think about.

She decided not to wait for the elevator and dashed up the stairs to the Creative Department, where she had a desk and a title: Assistant Manager, Dairy Consumables. Big deal. That meant answering the phone, double-checking billings, and doing whatever else her sleazy boss, Victor Slansky, the manager of the milk, cheese and ice cream accounts, wanted done. When she had graduated two months earlier at the University of Michigan with a bachelor's degree in English Literature, she hadn't even known that Michigan was a dairy state. She did now.

Laura glanced at the clock: 12:15. Lunchtime. She picked up a copy of the Detroit Free Press and a brochure that had come in the mail about a graduate program in Women's Studies at Florida State University and headed for the lunchroom on the 4th floor. After pawing through the refrigerator to find the paper bag with *Laura's!* scrawled in black ink, she found a seat at a table and pulled out a container of banana yogurt and an apple. Auburn hair spilled onto freckled shoulders, framing an alert, intelligent face. Thanks to yogurt lunches and Jazzercise classes, she weighed only three pounds more than she had as a college freshman. She unpeeled the yogurt lid and began reading the brochure. At 12:45, she returned to her desk.

"The laser printer is about out of toner, Laura, dear. Would you get some from the supply room?" Victor Slansky leaned over her desk, his shoulder brushing hers, peppermint breath soft on her cheek.

Laura drew back without speaking. Her boss, in the words of a co-worker, was a "turd" nicknamed "the groper," who hit on all the new female hires—if they were single and attractive. Slansky made her feel uncomfortable, but she didn't know what to do about it. Complain to management? Not as a probationary employee. Slansky had begun making off-color remarks to her from day one. At first they were sly little compliments about how "fine" she looked. Then they escalated to questions about how her weekend had been spent and finally to her love life. She ignored them.

She went to the supply room and started hunting for the toner on shelves filled with ink cartridges and paper. She heard the door open and close quietly behind her. Two hands fondled her breasts and a hoarse, familiar voice breathed raggedly in an ear.

"Let me go!" she gasped. "I'll scream!"

"Oh, go ahead, darling, no one will hear you anyway," the voice said.

Unable to break free, she flung her head back and felt it connect with something soft. She heard a loud groan and the hands fell away. Laura twisted around and brought her right knee up sharply between her assailant's legs. The groan changed to a whimper. She pushed past her boss and opened the door. Heart pounding, she ran to the women's room and locked herself in a stall, fighting the urge to be sick. When her stomach stabilized and her breathing had returned to normal, she went back to her desk and sat there, twisting a paper clip in her fingers, unsure of what to do next.

"Where have you *been*, girl? You don't know what you missed!" She looked up into the grinning face of Mandy Simpson, one of her co-workers. Mandy's coalblack eyes gleamed and the gold bracelets on her wrists jingle-jangled in excitement. "The Groper just staggered out of the supply room clutching his ding dongs, blood all over his white shirt. He grabbed his coat and dashed out of the office!"

Laura nodded dully. The tension drained out of her slowly, like air from a leaking tire. Then the relief gave way to anger.

The creep shouldn't get off that easily! She bent the paper clip back into its original shape. *He wouldn't! But she wouldn't just file a complaint that could be ignored. No...her revenge would be more creative.*

When Victor Slansky walked stiffly into the department the next morning, his nose concealed behind a patchwork of white tape, he stopped abruptly. The door to his office was ringed with pictures—pictures of Porky Pig. Porky pig in a top hat... Porky holding a parasol... Porky laughing. And in the center of the pictures, he saw an enormous "No. 1," cut out of red paper. He tore the pictures and the number down angrily while the women in the office pretended to be engrossed in work. Throwing Laura a dirty glance, Slansky stormed into his office without a word and slammed the door.

That evening, Laura stood by the window of her apartment, watching wind-blown snowflakes dance in the gathering dusk. Blurred patches of yellow appeared in the indistinct shapes of buildings across the street. She still had a job at the advertising agency—at least for now. But what about tomorrow or the day after that? She thought about the brochure from Florida State University, the one with the pictures of white sandy beaches and palm trees under an azure sky. *I wonder if the mosquitoes are as bad as people say?*

Victor Slansky's face faded from her mind. Laura sat upright in the restaurant restroom and gazed into the mirror, willing the anger to go away. Tight lines eased at the corners of her mouth and she felt her pulse return to normal. When she had regained her composure, she rose and returned to the table.

The press agent sensed the tension in the air. He studied the faces of his two companions nervously. "Well, are we ready to order?"

"As soon as I get another martoooni," laughed the actor, dragging out the slurred syllables.

Laura felt warm pressure on her knee again. She reached down, grasped a finger and bent it straight back until the owner yelped. Then she leaned over and hissed in Randall's ear. "Touch me again, and I'll break them off, one at a time." She released her grip and turned to the press agent. "Yes, I'm famished. Let's order."

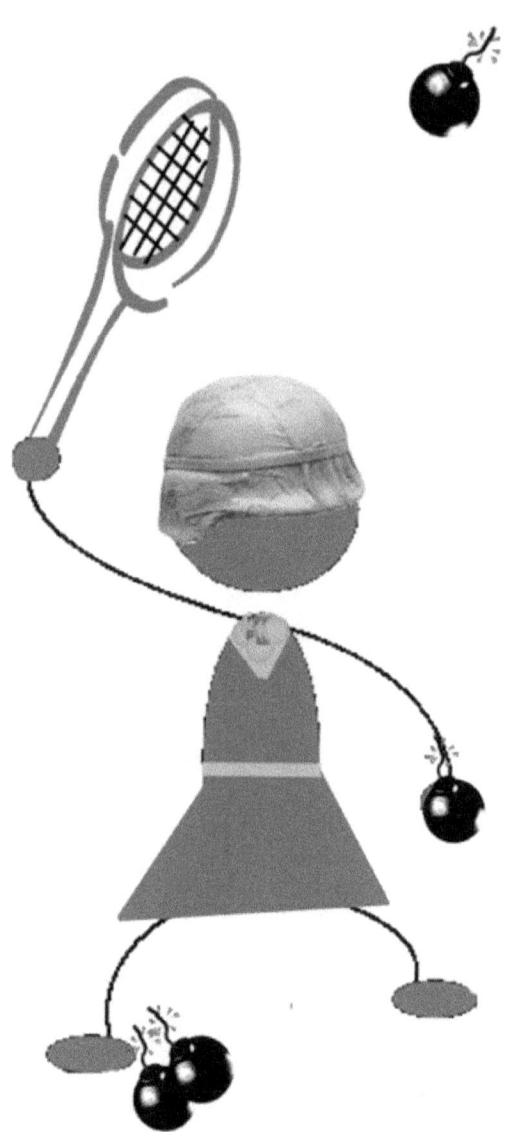

Chpter 6

Death will be a great relief. No more interviews.

KATHERINE HEPBURN

Even if he hadn't checked the calendar, Jack would have known it was Sunday from the size of the New York Times. Double banded and fat despite the recession, it still contained a week's worth of reading. After a hurried breakfast, he caught a cab to the WXDX TV studio for his first live, on-camera interview. Mid-morning, he decided, was a reasonable hour for a weekend television program. Jessica Longley sat next to Jack on a lumpy couch. A skyscraper scene with puffy clouds provided a backdrop for "Weekend, New York!" Cozy armchairs, tables, and monogrammed coffee cups for the two hosts conveyed a "we're in your home and you're in ours" message. The hosts were Warren Baxter, an amiable man with great hair and an all-year tan, and Allie Storm, a stunning blonde who had been Miss New York Transit System. Baxter nodded to Jack and smiled. Allie ignored him.

Jack's first hint the show might be better called "Lost Weekend!" came as the first guest, Janice Nowicki, a pudgy, badly dressed woman with fluttery hands and a nervous smile, stumbled off the set in tears during a commercial break. She had been honored as "New York Adoptive Parent of the Year" for taking disabled children into her heart and home. She had left ashen, dabbing at her eyes, after merciless probing by Allie: Why didn't she have children of her own? Didn't she realize that her life of sacrifice might be merely a means of fulfilling unmet emotional needs? Did her husband leave her before or after she held open house for the kids? Jack decided the frigid atmosphere in the studio was due to more than over-amped air conditioning.

"The coffee is cold!" Allie snapped. The camera had shifted to an adjacent set at which the weather guy made clouds and showers appear and disappear magically on a map. "Can't I even get a hot cup of coffee this morning!" A young woman scurried over with a fresh cup. Allie turned to Baxter, who studied his cue cards. "You ran over one of my lines, again," she accused. "And you're hogging the responses as usual."

Baxter glanced up and smiled apologetically. "Sorry."

Jack turned to Jessica. "What's going on?" Jessica cupped her hand and whispered in his ear. "I read an item in a gossip column in the *Post* this morning. Both of them signed new contracts, but Baxter's is for $35,000 a year more than Allie's. She's pissed at her agent, but he isn't around now. Baxter is." Her shoulders tightened. "Women always get screwed over."

A floor techie counted down and a camera blinked. "We're back," said Allie with a ravishing smile. "And our next guest is a San Francisco author who has written a new book suggesting men are superior to women!" She cocked her head knowingly and flashed a "we'll see about that" wink. "Please welcome Jack Kileen!"

He took a seat and smiled. It was his last smile. Allie held up Jack's book and then put it down before the cameraman could move in for a close-up.

"Do alpha males think that women should be paid less than men?" she demanded.

"Of course not..." Jack said only to be interrupted in mid-sentence.

"Would you deny that a male-dominated marketplace has left women in virtual servitude in many areas, including television?" She sniffed and threw a withering glance at her co-host, who smiled wanly.

"I'm not an economist..." Jack began, "my book..."

"Your book perpetuates the myth of male entitlement, doesn't it?"

"N-o-o-o... It..."

Relentlessly, she continued the attack. "But it suggests that males are basically superior to females, doesn't it?"

"Men have some different characteristics, certainly, than women, but I wouldn't agree that..."

"Really!" she flared. "Do you discuss alpha females in your book?"

"That's a good point," Baxter broke in jovially. "I think..."

"We're more interested in what Mr. Kileen thinks," she said, cutting him off abruptly.

Baxter looked wounded and retreated into sullen silence. He pretended to sip cold coffee.

"Well, do you discuss alpha females? They do exist, don't they?" she continued.

"Yes," Jack conceded, "but the book is more about male roles and..."

"Then you ignore female leadership and concentrate on the old cliché of male dominance?"

He had no idea how to respond without digging a deeper hole.

The verbal onslaught continued, with Allie powering vicious forehands over the net and Jack hitting weak backhands in response. Mercifully, she was interrupted by a commercial for Pare the Pounds, a revolutionary new weight loss drug. The commercial ended with the announcer cautioning, "side effects may include nausea, respiratory problems, motor imbalance, impaired sphincter control, and hair loss."

Jack braced for another onslaught, but Allie glanced at the clock on the wall and thanked him abruptly for being a guest on the show. She looked guilelessly at the camera.

"And the book" (she didn't mention the title and held it too briefly to read the title) "is $17.95. My, that sounds like a lot for only 311 pages, doesn't it?" she asked innocently. The dazzling, high voltage smile reappeared. "But if you hold off buying until there's a sale, the price may be reduced."

Jack winced.

As they left the studio, Jessica said, "Gee, I need a drink, and it's not even noon." She looked guilty, Jack thought, probably like the Indian scout who had led Custer to the Little Bighorn.

"Wow!" she continued, "I've never seen anything like that. You might need a rabies shot. Are you okay? You could have used a flak jacket in there."

Jack shrugged.

"I'm tied up for the rest of the day," she continued. "Tomorrow is the *Mari O'Reilly Show,* and you'll be on your own. They only let guests into the green room. I'll catch the show at work. Break a leg!"

"Oh..." she eyed him critically. "Lose the sports jacket and tie tomorrow. Do the macho thing: jeans, leather jacket, boots... whatever. Don't shave. Left Coast writers aren't supposed to look like high school principals."

"That's never been hard for me," he replied.

They parted on Fifth Avenue, Jessica to return to her office and hope she could retrieve the video of "Weekend" before her boss saw it. Jack decided to stop in a drugstore and pick up some aspirin.

Chpter 7

Television? The word is half Latin and half Greek.
No good can come of it.

C.P. SCOTT

Laura arrived at the *Mari O'Reilly Show* studio the next day, well before the show was to start. After a brief trip to makeup, she was ushered into the waiting room. Pictures lined the pale green walls. They showed Mari greeting guests, laughing, and hugging people in the audience. A large-screen TV tuned to an empty set dominated one corner of the room. The green room had roses, a large bowl of mixed fruit, and a refrigerator containing bottled water and fruit juice. Coffee burbled in a pot.

Mari popped in, chatted briefly about Laura's book, and vanished.

Then a young woman in jeans and sneakers appeared holding a clipboard. "You're the second interview after the opening segment, professor, so you've got awhile." After she left, Laura opened her briefcase and pulled out some bluebooks. *Might as well get some papers graded.*

She had barely gotten started when Cliff Hansen turned up and welcomed her to the show all over again. "Where's your fellow debater?" he asked.

"I don't know," she said.

"Let's hope he's here soon or you'll be doing a solo act," Hansen joked. "You'll be fine. See you later."

Laura returned to grading papers, her eyes drifting periodically to the increased activity on the TV set. Stagehands appeared and positioned furniture. Lighting was tested.

Finally, the show began. Mari sat behind a desk that held her notes and a monogrammed coffee cup. An indigo blue backdrop, with *Mari* gracefully illuminated in italic gold script, loomed behind her.

Mari smiled gamely at a bearded man seated next to her who held a blue and green parrot on one arm. The bird squawked, fluffed its feathers, and left a suspicious dark spot on his arm.

Laura stopped watching and grabbed a bluebook.

The door opened and Jack entered, wearing jeans and a black turtleneck sweater. He looked about the green room and paused. The only other occupant was a slender woman in a blue blazer, white blouse, and gray skirt. He judged her to be in her 30s, despite the granny glasses with old-fashioned frames she wore. A scuffed leather brief case lay on the floor beside her.

Recognition came. *Ah...the woman on the back of the book jacket!*

Spotting the bowl of fruit, he walked over and took a red apple.

"Prof. Sanders, I presume," said Jack.

"Dr. Sanders, yes."

"Jack Kileen. I guess we're up next in the lioness's den. Sorry I'm late, the taxi driver dropped me off two blocks away. Horrendous traffic. Then I got here and they tried to make me look pretty." He took a single bite out of the apple, made a face, and tossed it toward a wastebasket. It rattled in. "Two points!"

She inspected him as if he were a fleck of dandruff just discovered on a shoulder.

"Sorry," he apologized. "I'm just nervous, I guess. This is my first time on TV."

She looked at him without smiling. "Why? An audience is an audience, whether it's in a classroom or on a stage or before television cameras. I suppose it's different for newspaper writers." She returned to making red marks in the blue booklets.

B-r-r-r-r. I guess we won't need air conditioning. He started to say something and stopped. The worry monster in his stomach growled.

The young woman in jeans and sneakers poked her head through the door. She had streaked blonde hair and a harried look. "Three minutes, Mr. Kileen," she said.

Jack gestured toward Laura. "I thought we were going to be on together."

"You're on first," the young woman said and shut the door.

On the television monitor, Mari laughed as two parrots on bicycles raced around a circular track. "Isn't that something" she gushed. "We'll be back in a moment," she confided to the camera with an inviting smile, "with the author of a book that I think you'll find interesting and provocative."

The door opened again, and the young woman reappeared. "You're up, Mr. Kileen." He rose and took a last nervous glance in the mirror by the door and followed her.

Jack took a seat where she directed. Mari was nowhere in sight, having bolted to the restroom during a commercial. But the audience remained, murmuring behind the glare of the lights like a restless animal. Technicians bustled about the cameras and the set. Jack crossed his legs, cleared his throat, and wondered if the Christians had felt this way when led into the Colosseum in Rome. At least there were no roars from the crowd—yet.

Mari swept in and plopped down behind the desk. "Hi," she said brightly. "Ready to sell some books?" She reached under the desk and pulled out a book. It was his. "We'll have about 15 minutes or so," she explained. "Maybe more, maybe less, depending on how the audience reacts. Just relax and have fun."

Jack forced a smile. *Like that's going to happen.*

A man wearing a headset caught her attention. "Thirty seconds." Time froze, and then the man glanced at his watch and began counting down from 10. Mari faced the camera. The applause sign blinked and the audience came alive. "We're back," Mari said, "and with me is Jack Kileen, author of 'Alpha Male—Pride of the Pride.'" There was a scattering of applause, and

Jack noticed the studio audience tended to be heavily female and young, with a sprinkling of bored-looking men, probably boyfriends and husbands.

Mari leaned forward. "What made you decide to write a book with a title like 'Alpha Male'?" she asked. "An alpha male is the top animal in a pack isn't it?"

Jack nodded. "Yes, although pride refers to lions, of course; but wolf packs are also led by alpha males. I wrote the book, Mari, because too many male traits—leadership, courage, aggressiveness, competitiveness—are being compromised and weakened in a society that values accommodation over confrontation and feeling good over doing good."

"And the result is...?"

"A climate in which men no longer take pride in the mental and physical strengths that led them out of caves and into condos."

"Can you give us some examples?"

"Sure," he replied, warming up. "Critics praise male actors who cry in films and on TV. Kids on losing teams get sports trophies so their feelings won't be hurt.

"Some of it's due to political correctness," he resumed. "Social pressure forced the Navy to put women on ships and in jet aircraft. And Title 9 made colleges eliminate men's sports that drew crowds and replace them with women's sports that don't draw flies."

"Wait a minute," Mari jumped in. "Title 9 is about equal rights. You don't object to women having equal rights, do you?" Muttering rose from the audience.

"Of course not," he said reasonably, "but access to legal and political rights shouldn't be carried across the whole cultural spectrum. Men don't get pregnant on aircraft carriers and if I were overcome by smoke in a 14th-floor apartment, I'd hate to wait for a woman firefighter to try and sling me over her shoulder and carry me down the stairs to safety."

He paused, eyeing Mari nervously, wondering if he'd gone too far. "That's what my book tries to say: Men shouldn't be apologetic about what sets them apart, what makes them men."

Mari looked doubtfully at the audience and shook her head. "You're not suggesting that because a woman can't carry you down 14 flights of stairs that she isn't as good as a man?"

Jack squirmed in his chair. He had a bad feeling where the discussion was headed. "No, of course not. But there are areas in which men are superior to women." *Damn, why did I say that?* "And areas in which women are superior to men," he added hastily.

"So how *are* men superior to women?" She zeroed in on the first part of his statement, ignoring the second.

"Well, certainly not in a social sense" began Jack. "When it comes to things like nurturing…"

Hisses rolled from the audience.

"But in terms of physical ability… intelligence… creativity…" she said, maneuvering for a kill shot.

"If you're talking about strength or speed, men clearly have an edge," he said carefully. "They also have larger brains, bigger hearts, and weigh more. Creativity? There are areas that women excel in, I suppose, like literature; but let's face it, even from an intellectual standpoint, most Nobel Prize winners are male."

Boos began to drown out the hisses.

Jack half expected Mari to disagree with him. He was surprised when she didn't.

Instead, she turned to the audience. "I think we need another opinion, at this point, don't you?" A roar of approval rose from the audience. She swiveled and faced another camera.

"Let's welcome our next guest, Dr. Laura Sanders, professor of women's studies at Florida Southwestern University, who may have another perspective as author of a new book, "Saint to Siren to CEO: Changing Roles for American Women."

The applause sign blinked to life again as Laura walked on stage. Laura Sanders walked on the set and smiled warmly at Mari. She favored Jack with a frosty glance as if she had read the script and knew what was going to happen on the next page.

He shivered inside.

The clapping trailed off and Laura took a seat next to him. He caught a brief whiff of lilac. She sank into the couch, crossing her legs demurely. She looked at him the way that a butcher might look at a loin of pork before reaching for a sharp knife.

I think I've been sandbagged. He corrected himself. *No, I know that I've been sandbagged. Time to suck it up. Too late to worry now.*

"Dr. Sanders," Mari said, holding up a copy of "Saint to Siren to CEO" for a close-up, "How would you describe your book?"

"Well, Mari," Laura began, "it's about the evolution from the early idealization of women—putting them on pedestals—to their perceived threat as sexual seductresses—to the role that they fill today, often as chief executives of important companies. It's also a response to some of those books by stay-at-home soccer moms who feel their only role in life is cooking, cleaning, baby sitting, and satisfying their husbands' physical and emotional needs. We can do so much more."

Murmurs of approval drifted from the audience.

"Too often," she continued, "women have been held back from realizing their true potential by sexism and economic persecution. We don't have to be the caregivers all the time. Regardless of what Mr. Kileen says, I think it's great that women fly jets in combat." She paused, waiting for the applause to die, and looked directly at Jack. "And it doesn't matter how big your brain and heart are. What matters is how you use them."

"You go, girl!" a large African-American woman in the front row shouted, elbowing the thin, uncomfortable looking man next to her.

"Mr. Kileen, what do you think about that?" asked Mari.

"I'm not going to defend sexism," Jack began, "any more than I would defend unequal wage scales. But they exist. Modern society, heck, any society, rewards those who make the greatest contributions."

Although thirsty, Jack didn't reach for a glass of water, afraid that he would gulp it down and appear even more nervous.

He went on the attack. "If you are the most successful hunter in your cave, or grew the most beautiful tulips in Holland in the 17th century, or design the best computer system, cream rises, and it knows no gender," he continued gamely.

"But achievement depends on opportunity, wouldn't you say?" Laura countered. "Women in Afghanistan who leave school after the fourth grade and have to wear those stifling burquas all day aren't going to have much chance to become a Bill Gates or a Mari, are they?"

Ouch, thought Jack. Mari beamed and the clapping continued.

"Certainly, achievement depends upon opportunity," he agreed, "but you've picked a bad example. What about when there are equal opportunities? How about in Western Europe or Canada or the United States? What's the excuse then? Women head less than 15 per cent of the corporations in this country." He spoke more confidently, tapping the alpha male within.

"The best chefs are male. If women's sports attracted as many female fans as men's sports attract male fans, there would be a female equivalent of the Super Bowl."

Hisses, catcalls, and boos rained down.

"There's a glass ceiling," Laura replied heatedly. "And it's not just at the corporate level. It applies to women's roles in general. Women vote for men, but men won't vote for women. Why do you think the U.S. Senate is overwhelmingly male? Because women don't understand politics?"

"No," said Jack curtly, "it's because women aren't aggressive enough, persistent enough, and willing enough to get down in the trenches and fight for what they want. Politics is a nasty business. But it's not because society discriminates. Let's face it, even in a society like ours that offers educational, legal, political, and social advantages, women play a secondary role."

Mari broke in over the uproar. "We'll pause at this point for an important message," she said. "Don't go away!"

Jack hastily sipped some water and avoided making eye contact with anyone. He tried to ignore the muttering and hostile stares from the audience. The man with the headset reappeared. "Thirty seconds," he said.

The applause sign lit up and so did Mari. "We're back," she said, "with a provocative discussion between writer Jack Kileen, author of "Alpha Male—Pride of the Pride," and Dr. Laura Sanders, educator and author of "Saint to Siren to CEO: Changing Roles of American Women."

"Dr. Sanders," she said, "would you agree that, overall, men are superior to women?"

"I never said..." began Jack, but he was overridden quickly.

"Absolutely not," Laura replied. "This is the smartest, best educated, most productive generation of women ever. Women are prime ministers, college presidents, helicopter pilots, and brain surgeons. And if men are so superior physically, why do women live longer? And that's despite the physical, mental, and emotional stress of having children. The most stress many men face is deciding when to get up and get another beer during a football game."

She smiled at Jack patronizingly.

"Women today have more expanded roles than they did in the past," he conceded. "But let's face it. If you were to drop a man and a woman in the jungle or on an island or in a forest, the man would adapt and survive, and the woman would become a meal for the nearest predator with sharp teeth."

"Perhaps in a jungle" objected Laura, "where brawn and muscle are all that's needed, but not in Manhattan or Paris or Sydney. Not where civilized skills come into play. Modern life isn't 'Jurassic Park.'"

Jack shook his head. He began to speak but was interrupted.

"Perhaps there is one way to settle the question," Mari suggested.

"What question?" asked Jack.

"The question of whether men or women are superior."

He shook his head. "It's not a question of..."

"How?" Laura broke in.

"We could have a contest," Mari said, "and announce the results right on this show."

"Contest?" said Jack. "What contest?"

"Survival skills," Mari continued, enthusiastically. "But not just physical skills like muscular strength." She paused, as if thinking. "No, I'm thinking of the types of abilities people need to flourish in a modern urban society—intellectual, cultural, and social abilities. We'll let our viewers decide which ones are important. They can send in their ideas for competition, and we'll have a blue-ribbon panel pick the best types of challenges."

"I agree, a competition should be mental as well as physical," commented Laura. "Most women wouldn't carry Mr. Kileen down 14 floors in a fire even if they could." Her smile had a sharp edge. "The challenges of living in the 21st century require brains more than brawn."

This was going way, way too fast for Jack. "Whoa... First, I never said men were superior to women," he objected. "And the whole question—which is dumb, really dumb—is to complex to be resolved by competition."

Mari laughed. "I disagree. I think a contest could go a long way to settle the question of sexual supremacy in the modern world. Sort of a civilized 'Survivors.'" She stood and walked to the front of the set. "What do you think, audience?"

Shouts. Cheers. Bedlam. The studio rocked.

"But no male vs. female teams," she continued. "What's that Spanish expression men like to use, 'mano a mano,' sexist though it is? We'll do it one-on-one. You and Dr. Sanders can compete. You can represent alpha males, Mr. Kileen, and Laura—Dr. Sanders—can represent the women who want to be CEOs." She smiled. "Unless, of course, you're afraid...."

Mari beamed. Laura appeared thoughtful. Jack sank back speechless. *I don't believe this!*

But he would.

Chapter 8

A wise man will make more opportunities than he finds.

SIR FRANCIS BACON

Larry Clayton clicked off the TV in his office at *Glimpse Magazine* with a thoughtful expression. He punched a button on the intercom.

"Helen, is the kid in the office?" When she replied in the affirmative, he said, "send him in."

The "kid" was Ashford Sloan, "Asher" to his friends, and "Ash Hole" to his non-friends. He had a guileless face and blond hair that fell boyishly over blue eyes. People, especially women disarmed by his shy smile and friendly manner, often revealed their deepest secrets to him in interviews—to their lasting regret.

Ashford Sloan had shown up at the *Glimpse* office one nasty winter morning three months earlier looking for a job, the ink barely dry on his journalism degree from Ohio State University. He had lots of clips heavy on colorful verbs and adverbial modifiers.

Sloan had been thawing out in Clayton's outer office for 30 minutes. He had arrived half frozen after a six-block walk. A polar air stream, attacking from the northwest, bombarded pedestrians with bursts of snow off Lake Michigan, whipped by gusts of wind up to 20 miles an hour. Wind chill? He was afraid to ask. He appreciated why Chicago was called the Windy City.

Job-hunting hadn't been going well for Sloan. In fact, it hadn't been going at all. The Chicago Tribune had a hiring freeze. The Sun Times was laying off seasoned reporters. Metro Star Magazine was overstocked with interns willing to work for bus fare, a place to sit, and a few college credits. *Glimpse Magazine* was his last hope.

"Why come here?" Clayton asked bluntly, when Sloan was ushered in to his office. "First, we don't hire inexperienced writers, and second, we're near the bottom on the journalistic food chain. Too sensational."

"I like the magazine's free-wheeling, pull-no-punches style," Sloan lied promptly. "Who wants to write club notices and obits? Besides, you pay your writers more than union scale." (He didn't mention another reason, the $7,852 in student loans he had accumulated because he had no intention of paying them off.)

That was true, Clayton mused. If it weren't for the fat paychecks, he wouldn't have a staff cranking out stories about alien visitations or bribing underpaid hospital attendants to take photos of aging former movie and TV stars. Instead, they'd be aspiring to win Pulitzer Prizes on mainstream newspapers.

Still not impressed, he shook his head. "Sorry, kid..."

"I also took creative writing," Sloan blurted out in desperation. "I'm very good at writing fiction."

That had sealed it for the managing editor. He liked writers who didn't bullshit themselves about what they did, especially when he could get them at a starting salary that was half of what he paid experienced staffers.

"You wanted to see me, boss?" Sloan stood expectantly in the open doorway.

Clayton waved him in. "I was just watching the *Mari O'Reilly Show*. She's launching some kind of crazy contest to determine sexual superiority. It pits a guy from San Francisco and a female professor from Fort Myers, Fla. Think of it as an urbane 'Survivor.'" He waited to see if Sloan picked up on the pun.

Sloan grinned.

"Not that kind of sexual superiority, unfortunately," Clayton added dryly. "They haven't worked out the details, but the challenges will be intellectual and cultural as well as physical.

The grin faded. "Sounds like a yawner to me. Just another quiz show."

"Maybe, maybe not," Clayton replied, rolling the idea around in his mind. "I have a hunch it could get a lot of ink and airtime. Spring...sex... This thing could develop real legs." *It had better. I need a hot read and soon.*

"So?"

"We'll give it a few days to simmer. If it generates press, I want you to fly down to Florida and get some more education." He smiled at the surprised expression on the young writer's face. "The woman's name is Sanders. Sign up for one of her classes. Dig around. Turn over a few rocks. You know."

Sloan cocked his head. "Gotcha." He visualized himself lying on the beach, a pina cola in hand, soaking up some rays.

"Oh," Clayton said as an afterthought. "I wouldn't try to pad the expense account. The accounting department has seen every trick in the book."

"Of course not!" exclaimed Sloan, trying to look hurt at the suggestion.

That evening, one of the objects of their discussion, Dr. Laura Sanders, engaged in her favorite form of psychotherapy, bubble baths. Dunks in the tub are soothing. Muscles unwind. Sensory apparatus goes into standby mode. The mind filters out worries, at least in theory. Not this time. She was back at home in the 1940s bungalow with peeling paint she lived in on Sanibel Island, linked to Fort Myers by a causeway. As she soaked up to her shoulders in bubbles and troubles, she brooded, replaying the final moments of the *Mari O'Reilly Show*.

She had been living on the island for three years, partly because it was near the beach and only a 12-minute drive to where she taught. The funky old bungalow, which had been in her family for decades, was on a potholed back road, almost hidden in trees. A screened front porch kept most, but not all, of the mosquitoes at bay. At least the house still had an old-fashioned bathtub. Standing on claw-like legs with chipped gold paint, the tub was a throwback to the age of relaxed living before showers, when ritual Saturday baths preceded church on Sunday. Kids could push pretend boats about in a porcelain-lined sea, and their frazzled parents could unwind after long hours in the factory, farm, or kitchen.

A shrink might suggest this pleasure evoked primal memories of man's descendants crawling laboriously from the sea to experiment with life on terra firma; but for most people, it represented a simple, practical luxury. Best of all, Laura's bathtub had a sloping back designed for comfort and the room to stretch out, almost fully submerged. As a graduate student sharing an apartment, she had hated the straight-backed, midget-sized bathtubs shoehorned into modern apartment buildings to save space and cut builders' costs.

She frowned. *Why had she let a talk show host persuade her to get involved in a silly contest that probably would prove nothing? Who cared if some arrogant West Coast writer thought that men were better than women?* The *Mari O'Reilly Show* had been a great opportunity to plug her book, but all that she wanted to do was get back into the classroom and educate the next generation of female leaders.

Perhaps she shouldn't have appeared on the show in the first place? Ha! Like that was an option. Writers who wanted their books to sell had to sell themselves. Her publisher wasn't pleased that she hadn't developed a website and a presence on Facebook and Twitter.

The telephone rang in the next room, but she ignored it. Her answering machine had overloaded with calls. Some came from friends and colleagues who had seen or heard about the television show. But others were from reporters, agents hustling business, and anonymous males excoriating her in four-and five-letter words, the nicest of which had five letters and was better applied to female dogs.

Laura scrunched down and manipulated the hot water tap with her right foot. *Perhaps this contest idea will all fizzle out,* she thought. *Maybe Mari O'Reilly will drop the whole thing and it will be forgotten. Then life can return to normal.*

But back in New York, in the almost deserted network offices from which the *Mari O'Reilly Show* originated, a frazzled Cindy Martinez wouldn't have agreed. Sure, it was exciting being the personal secretary to a television personality like Mari O'Reilly. Cool guys gave her a second glance. When she met people for the first time and mentioned casually what she did for a living, their eyes widened and she knew lots of questions would be forthcoming. Another perk was that friends, relatives, and high school rat-packers wanted tickets to the show, which she doled out selectively. She rewarded those who had been nice to her on the way up and stiffed those who hadn't. She couldn't believe Billy Krantz had had the cojones to ask for show tickets for his pregnant wife and her mother. Not after the way he had jumped her bones and then dumped her following that memorable evening in the rear seat of his '92 Ford Taurus after the senior prom. But now Cindy was 24, an honors graduate of Dr. Martin Luther King High School, proud graduate of the secretarial skills track, and there'd be no tickets, not even freebies, for a rat like Billy Krantz.

But this... She glanced in dismay about the cluttered office. In addition to the e-mails that had filled the message box, three piles of snail mail, faxes, and yellow slips representing telephone calls spilled over a banged-up gray metal table. Mari would answer the calls from network news shows and major metropolitan newspapers, but she herself would get the job of calling the others back and saying "no, she's too busy." Cindy sighed. Even show business had a down side.

Chapter 9

*You will do foolish things, but
do them with enthusiasm.*

COLETTE

"Okay," Mari said crisply, "where were we?" It was almost show time. She eyed her features critically in the dressing-room mirror and reached for the lipstick again. Mascara was a little heavy, but she could live with it. Eyebrows needed some work. Should she call makeup back? What was that new girl's name? Crissy? Kirstie? Why did Irma, her regular makeup person, have to get pregnant?

Cliff Hansen, sitting in a corner, cleared his throat.

"Have we settled on a name for the contest yet?" she asked impatiently. Hansen shook his head and rubbed his receding hairline thoughtfully before answering. He wore a rumpled, second-day white shirt with a gaudy purple tie. Pudgy from too many donuts and countless cups of coffee, he accepted his fate as the ringmaster of a five-day-a-week circus that attracted bored housewives, the unemployed, high school kids cutting classes, sensation seekers, and lots of the type of viewers who had inspired the industry's L.O.P. theory: People, desperate for SOMETHING to watch on TV, will view the Least Objectionable Program. When he had been a hotshot graduate student in the Television-Radio Program at Syracuse University, Hansen had produced a prize-winning documentary titled "Our Crowded Skies," which pointed with alarm (most TV documentaries point with alarm) to the dangers of proliferating air travel. Naively, he had thought his career would be spent doing similar documentaries and newscasts. Now he knew better.

"Marketing has come up with a couple of possibilities," he said, flipping the pages of his clipboard. "Let's see, Man vs. Woman…"

"Too blah," she said.

"The Gender War…"

"Too obtuse. Gender sounds like a term from a biology class."

He reached the end of the list. "Battle of the Sexes?"

"Been done." Mari chewed the end of a mascara brush, reflecting.

"It needs to be more 'wow!'"

"Wow!"?

She kept chewing. "I've got it! Let's call it 'Challenge of the Sexes.'"

The producer made a note on the clipboard.

"Plug it on every show this week," she continued. "Get some mail and e-mail addresses to flash on screen. We'll ask for suggestions from viewers for contest events."

His head bobbed affirmatively.

"As soon as we sign up the volunteers for the national panel to choose the contest events, we can turn over some of the suggestions to them. Is anyone writing in to suggest people for the panel?"

Hansen didn't bother to check the clipboard. "Yesterday? Dozens. Today? Hundreds. Tomorrow? Who knows? The mail kid is threatening to put in a disability claim for a back problem from lifting mail sacks."

"This should ramp up the ratings," Mari reflected, fiddling with an errant curl. "And it'll get better when we announce the panel and the contests they pick."

"Nielsen city," he agreed. "But what about the contest events? What if the panel picks boring brainteasers? And what if the guy steamrollers the professor?"

Mari turned back to the mirror. "Well, we'll just have to see it doesn't happen, won't we?"

"You don't mean fix the competition in favor of the woman, do you?" Hansen wanted the situation made perfectly clear, not because he had ethical concerns, but because he had learned long ago that it was easier to play cover your ass when everyone was reading from the same page of the script at the same time.

"Fix the competition, of course not!" Mari snapped. "That would be dishonest." She shook her head. "No, I'm going to pick the people who pick the events and let them fix the competition." *Oops, shouldn't have said that. But let the sexist jerk from the Left Coast win? No way! Not if I have anything to do with it.*

Cliff hesitated. "Uh, Mari, we still need to talk about my contract. It ran out last month, remember?" He had been producing the show from the start and thought, not unreasonably, that he deserved a raise. So did his wife, who reminded him about it frequently.

Mari decided to lighten the mascara after all. "Not now, Cliff. Let's get this thing going and then we can talk about it. *But not for a while.* Mari liked to keep her employees twisting slowly in the wind from time to time. She owned the show, having incorporated, and more money in Hansen's pocket was money out of hers. *Let him wait.*

Unfortunately, as Mari soon discovered, lots of people wanted a say in picking the people who would decide the events. And they let her know it. By phone (the switchboard went nuts; by e-mail (her box overflowed); by snail mail (the mail clerk decided that he needed an assistant and one of those re-enforced back support belts), and in person.

Her hairdresser suggested an aging soap opera lothario. A guard at the studio entrance voted for an acerbic right-wing Congressman. And Mari's mother joined in. Her choice was Oprah, whose show she never missed. (She also told Mari she needed to do something about her hair, which she said looked like a rat's nest on TV). Mari's agent, whom she thought did damned little to justify his 15 per cent, opted for Mother Teresa, and was surprised to discover she wasn't available due to death. Mari's trainer, a crew-cut, muscle-bound hunk named Rick, badgered her between sit-ups to pick NBA basketball player turned sports show provocateur Charles Barkley. "He tells it like it is, Mari," Rick argued, holding her ankles while Mari rose and fell, grunting and wheezing. "Takes no prisoners, you know?"

But after her minister had left a telephone message recommending Desmond Tutu, Mari decided she had had enough. After the show, she summoned Cliff and Cindy to her office and ordered up two large white boards. They began listing possibilities, keeping age, sex, race, religion, ethnicity, education, and public image (if any) in mind. When they were done, she added to the list the president of WRN (Women's Rights Now!), the pit bull of women's organizations, and a player from the Women's National Basketball Association.

"Why can't we just draw the names out of a hat," complained Cindy. It was 2 a.m. and they had been adding and subtracting names on the white boards for hours. Yes, she decided again, there definitely was a downside to the entertainment business.

"I told you," snapped Mari. "This has to be done right. The panel has to be diversified." It also had to be carefully manipulated, but she didn't intend to get into *that*.

Slowly, the list took shape. She had decided on 15 people who would represent heartland America. There was a minister from Kansas to please the Bible Belters, together with carefully selected African-American, Asian, and Hispanic representatives. There was even one person of trans-gender to satisfy the switch-hitters. By 3:32 a.m., Mari was satisfied. Like the NCAA basketball pairings, the panel wouldn't please everyone. But, she reflected, glancing at Cliff Hansen, who was snoring loudly on a couch, breathing through a deviated septum, it really didn't have to please everyone. Just her.

Once chosen, panel members were flown to New York City, sipping champagne and munching hot hors d'oeuvres in first class while the paying prisoners in coach fought for space in the overhead luggage bins and shelled out for Cokes and snack packs. Upon arrival, limos whisked the panelists to the studio where they debuted with great fanfare on the *Mari O'Reilly Show*.

The panel consisted of a 16-year-old high school senior from Newark, N.J.; the Montana state schools superintendent; a regional vice president for the American Association of Retired Persons, based in Washington, D.C.; a laid off dot.com worker from San Jose, Ca; the Grand Rapids, Mich., president of the League of Women Voters; a personnel manager for Krispy Kreme donuts in San Diego; the point guard for the Dallas Lobos of the WNBA; a retired elementary school teacher from Phoenix; a long-haul truck driver from Mississippi, and the executive director of Women's Rights Now! Joining them were a Marine Corps sergeant; a minister from Kansas; the mayor of Gold Harbor, Ore.; a Minot, N.D., plumber, and Cindy's sister-in-law Rose, a surprise but unopposed selection, nominated at 3:31 a.m. Eight of the 15 members were women and six were men. The sex of the other would be a frequently discussed topic.

Following a group picture with Mari, the clapping of the studio audience still ringing in their ears, all 15 received a complimentary box lunch of stringy roast beef sandwiches, stale potato chips, rock-hard apples, and warm Pepsi. They were then hustled off to a hotel and sequestered to begin their deliberations. Just like a real jury.

"Have they got the suggestions yet?" Cliff Hansen asked, as two mini-buses pulled out of the studio parking lot, bound for the hotel. (First class treatment had ended with show time.)

"Delivered by van this morning," Cindy said. "Saw to it myself. Seven boxes. E-mails, letters, phone messages, and a coconut."

"A coconut?"

"Right. Some guy in Hawaii hollowed one out, put his suggestions inside, taped it shut, and Fed-Exed it."

Hansen unfocused and refocused his eyes wearily. "That should get noticed, I guess."

"I'm sure it will," Cindy agreed.

"Now we can get back to what we actually do for a living."

"I can't wait," she said fervently.

Why do some things catch the public's interest (think American Idol, White House pets, and iPads) and others (think NFL Wednesday Morning Football, Balloon Boy, and One Leg Barstools) appear and vanish almost overnight? What could have piqued the interest of the media and then the public to notice a contest spawned by an afternoon TV show? Whatever the reason, the impending male vs. female brouhaha pushed the right buttons.

A national magazine created a clever graphic showing Laura and Jack in a boxing ring, face-to-face and glove-to-glove.

A network anchorman ended the evening news with a wry comment and a raised eyebrow.

A late-night talk show host tossed off a one-liner in his monologue.

An unauthorized "Party With Jack and Laura" porno site turned up on the Internet.

Meanwhile, on the 17th floor of a mid-town Manhattan hotel, the panel members began sorting through boxes of suggestions for contest events. Thousands of suggestions. Some were physical. Some were intellectual. Some were off the wall.

A survivalist in Wyoming suggested disassembling and reassembling an M14 rifle in a speed contest while blindfolded.

A dairy farmer in Wisconsin wanted a contest milking cows by hand. ("Udder fun," snickered the Oregon mayor.)

A teacher in Maine thought it would be educational to find out who could remember the most states in reverse alphabetical order.

A bartender in Alaska wanted to see who could drink the most Denali Dive-Bombers (his recipe) and walk a straight line.

A gambler in Minnesota saw a challenge in handicapping the 5th race at Santa Anita Park for one week.

A Boy Scout in Mississippi wanted to see someone catch, clean, and cook a catfish. (It was assumed he was working on a merit badge in fishing.)

Others were more prosaic:

Give a cat a bath.

Decipher a California election ballot.

Find a vacant metered parking place in lower Manhattan in mid-morning.

One that nobody could figure out involved a two-party sexual encounter with a toilet plunger, two oranges, and a plastic funnel.

Some were discarded out of hand:

Using a cell phone. (Too easy.)

Programming a DVD to do multiple timed recordings on different channels. (Too hard.)

Riding a bicycle "no hands." (Too dangerous.)

Explaining the infield fly rule. (Too arcane.)

Mixing a pousse-café cocktail without screwing up the layers. (Too frustrating.)

Watching 24 hours of reruns of "Gilligan's Island." (Too painful.)

Deciphering an insurance policy disclaimer. (Impossible.)

Getting two mid-court tickets to the NCAA Final Four Men's Basketball game and paying face value. (Get real.)

The panel slogged on. The minister said grace after every delivery of food from room service. The Marine sergeant suggested last rites might be more appropriate.

They had four white boards delivered, and two people with illegible handwriting immediately volunteered to record ideas. And so it went.

"I think," said the point guard from the Lobos on the third day, "that we need a new game plan." Discarded boxes and scattered papers covered the floor. The white boards bore scrawled suggestions, many unreadable. Remnants of a spaghetti dinner with day-old French bread, yellowing apple cores, and stiffening brownies awaited pickup outside the door.

"Let's try using management-by-objectives," offered the executive from Krispy Kreme. The collar on his white shirt needed ironing, and he had discarded a brown sports jacket, which drooped from the back of a chair.

"Meaning..." broke in the long-haul truck driver, a beefy woman with close-cropped red hair and a tattoo on a sun-tanned left arm. She wore a sweatshirt that read "Amelia Earhart Would Be Alive Today If She'd Ridden With a Teamster."

"Figure out just what it is we're trying to accomplish first and go from there," responded Krispy Kreme wearily. "Are we trying to determine who's smartest, strongest, quickest, toughest, or who can cook the best spinach quiche?"

The high school student forgot and waved her hand vigorously to get attention. They had told her to knock it off because everyone thought she wanted to use the bathroom. (The Oregon mayor, who had a prostate problem, was using it frequently.)

"On the SAT, the questions are organized into categories," the high schooler enthused. "Why not do it that way?"

"Like…" the Marine sergeant asked, glad he wasn't drilling recruits in the hot sun at Parris Island but unwilling to admit that he didn't have an idea what sort of questions were on an SAT… let alone what an SAT was.

"Well," responded the teenager, "how about setting up these categories: physical, mental, and emotional?"

They chewed on that for a while, arguing over emotion, which the AARP person pointed out could combine physical and mental states. "Okay," said the retired teacher, "what about a cultural literacy test instead, one with three broad groupings? Almost any type of test would fall into one category or the other."

The high school student smiled. She had been hoping to parlay this committee thing, which her friends thought was really, really lame, into at least a scholarship at a state teachers college; but now she saw other vistas opening up. The Ivy League might be in reach. Dartmouth?

And it came to pass that on the fifth day, the panel actually reached agreement on the contest events. (No one except the Marine sergeant wanted to endure a weekend in the hotel. The sergeant, however, if they finished, could look forward to spending it sleeping in a tent in South Carolina, worrying about the West Nile virus and dreaming of cold beer.)

The teenager's original suggestion had been expanded. The revised list divided tests in the following categories: physical, mental, technical, practical, and lifestylical. (There was no such *word* as lifestylical, of course, but the retired teacher, being big on parallel structure in writing, had created it. Everyone else was too frazzled to object.) They divided into subcommittees to fine tune contest events.

"Okay, here's what we have for the mental challenge," the VP from AARP said after the subcommittees had finished their work. "We wanted to get beyond just being able to name the capital of New York or know who was the second president of the United States.

"New York City and Thomas Jefferson?" asked the ex-dot.com worker, who had majored in computer technology in tech school.

"No, Albany and John Adams," corrected the high schooler. Why start with Princeton. What's wrong with Yale or Harvard?

"Any way," the VP continued, "one part of the test measures urban survival skills. First, the contestants have to make a last-minute airline reservation and fly to an unfamiliar city. We'll equalize the flying times. Then they rent a car and drive to an unfamiliar location. That tests map reading, route planning, concentration, and driving skills. Fastest time wins."

"What city?" asked the trucker.

"St. Louis. We drew the name out of a hat."

"Then," the VP resumed, "the second part will test their candle power with a nasty, broad-based cultural literacy test. We ruled out the U.S. citizenship exam. Too easy." He sat down.

The point guard stepped up. "The first part of the physical challenge is simple—running a mile to test fitness. Again, best time wins." She smiled. "But the second part is completing a segment of an adventure race like the "Eco Challenge" that tests stamina, skill, and strategy."

The minister outlined the technical test. It would involve logging onto the Internet and doing research. And, since *they* didn't have to do it), the subcommittee added the challenge of filling out a federal Form 1040 tax form—unassisted.

The truck driver reported the mechanical skills to be demonstrated in the practical test: "Painting a room, giving a dog a bath, and fixing a flat tire."

Finally, the lifestylical test was announced, with the male members of the subcommittee dissenting. It was cooking a five-course dinner with an appropriate wine selection.

Scores in all events would be decided by speed and/or quality of performance.

"I think that we've got a winner," beamed the executive director of Women's Rights Now! "Intelligence always trumps brawn."

"I feel sorry for the poor schmuck," the Oregon mayor, a bachelor, whispered to the Marine. "I can't heat canned spaghetti without burning it."

The high school student started collecting names, e-mail addresses, and telephone numbers. She decided to start with Mari in requesting recommendations for Dartmouth and then work her way up the Ivy League food chain.

Their work completed, the panelists hurried to their rooms to make last-minute airline reservations, pack, and get on with their lives. The Marine sergeant wandered down to the hotel gift shop to see if it sold mosquito repellent.

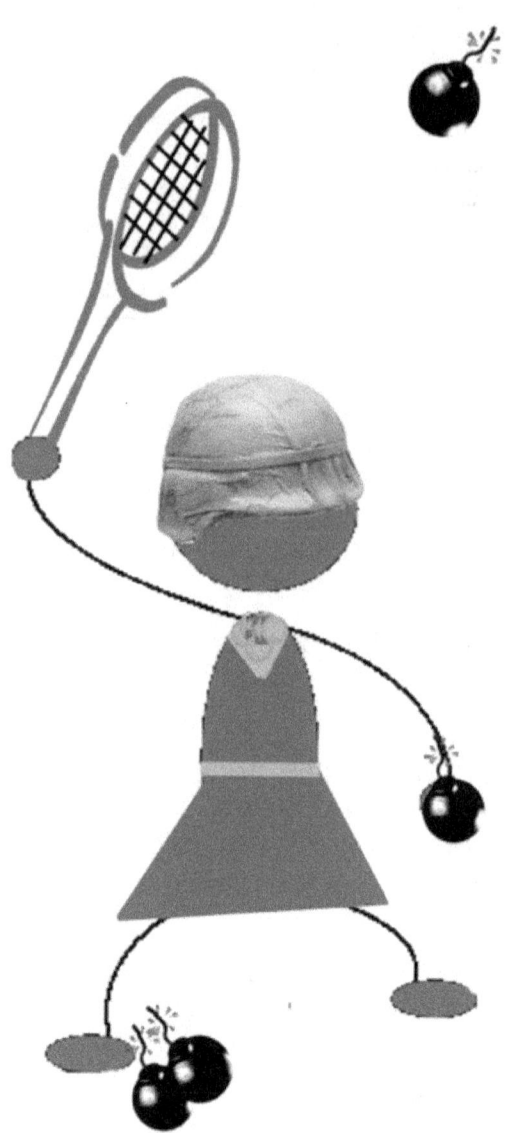

Chapter 10

There are moments when everything goes well;
don't be frightened, it won't last.

JULES RENARD

Jack looked out the window of his Lombard Street apartment. Did he have time for a quick stroll? He glanced at his bag by the door and ruefully decided there wasn't. Damn... He needed to unwind, and a walk down the street to the Marina on the bay usually did the trick.

His neighborhood was called Cow Hollow although the cows were long gone. People, cars, trucks, and motorcycles had supplanted them, all jostling for space in a city with too little of it. But he loved San Francisco, nonetheless. Apartment rents? Too high. Home prices? Don't ask. Parking? A never-ending nightmare. But when he walked out the front door and glanced toward the Marina, San Francisco Bay always drew his eyes like a magnet. It shimmered, metallic and mysterious, stretching to the Golden Gate before vanishing in the rolling vastness of the Pacific Ocean.

On weekends, Jack dragged his scratched blue and white trail bike out of the basement and set off down Fillmore Street to the Marina, drawn by its close-cropped patches of green that overflowed with pic-nickers, Frisbee-throwers, dog walkers, and running, laughing, tumbling children. On even the coldest days, hardy swimmers flutter-kicked paths back and forth in Aquatic Park as if on horizontal treadmills. From a dis-tance, their rubber caps looked like tiny dots bobbing up and down amid the whitecaps.

If it were one of those bright, sunny days in which the light takes on a crystalline clarity and Alcatraz Island loomed so close it seemed you could reach out and touch it, he would pedal along the waterfront. And on Sunday afternoons when banks of fog imprisoned the Golden Gate Bridge in a gauzy gray veil, Jack sometimes wheeled over to the Presidio, locked up his bike, and strolled along bark-strewn paths, inhaling the fragrant odor of eucalyptus.

But today he had no time for nature's beauty. The first test loomed. He had received a telephone call 48 hours earlier, informing him he was to be at the San Francisco International Airport at 8 a.m. Saturday where he'd be met at the Trans-America Airlines coun-ter by a man holding up a sign bearing his name. At that time, he'd get an airline ticket and find out where the driver navigation contest would be held. A rental car would be waiting for him when he landed.

Saturday dawned gray and overcast. He waited nervously outside his apartment building, shifting from foot to foot, peering up the street for the taxi he had called. Miraculously, it arrived on time. Before ducking his head and jumping in the backseat, Jack looked suspiciously at the puffy clouds hanging low over the ocean.

Rain was forecast. But, he hoped fervently, anything but heavy rain or fog! Rain was more likely than fog. But when fog came, fog didn't tiptoe in on little cat's feet; it clomped in on hiking boots with waffle-stompers, creating massive puffy walls that obliterated most of the Golden Gate Bridge or made it look as if the upper spires floated on whipped cream. But even rain could choke the life out of San Francisco International Airport. Because two runways had been designed too close together, the airport often shut one down in bad weather, delaying takeoffs and landings and snarling the travel plans of air travelers. Local television stations loved foggy days, of course, because they gave reporters the chance to sympathetically interview frustrated passengers who weren't going to be in Cincinnati or Boston or Dallas for mom's birthday or a business meeting or to connect for a flight elsewhere. The airport concessionaires loved bad weather and delays because they sold more under heated, tasteless food at inflated prices.

Jack offered up a prayer to the weather god: no rain or fog, please! But when he got to the airport, the skies had opened. His heart sank as he hurried inside the domestic terminal and read the departure board listing for a string of departures: *Flight Delayed.*

At the Trans-America Airlines counter, he spotted a young woman in jeans holding up a sign with his name. He hurried over.

"I'm Jack Kileen."

"I.D.?" she said.

He fumbled with his driver's license.

She scanned it. "Okay." She handed him a boarding pass for a flight to St. Louis. "You'll get instructions about where you're going at the rental car counter." With that, she left.

Resigned, he took a seat in the waiting area outside his departure gate. Usually, he liked airports. Not the process of flying, of course, with unpredictable waits, worries about lost luggage, and plastic-wrapped $7 sandwiches with wilted lettuce and limp cheese. No, the airports themselves—solid, familiar, classic examples of the architectural dictum that form follows function. Like the hubs of wagon wheels, terminals push out spokes lined with restaurants, bars, souvenir shops, news kiosks, and restrooms. At the end of each spoke, numbered gates await, orifices to accept or eject streams of passengers. Airports also forced you to slow down, to decompress, to accept a timetable not of your own design.

Resigned to being punished by the weather god, Jack hauled out the copy of "Saint to Siren to CEO." He found the usual laudatory blurbs: "exciting new voice… significant contribution to women's literature… powerful and forceful…."

Other women writers, he noticed, had written all of the truncated tributes. He wondered if anyone had created an award like an Oscar or Emmy for writers who wrote the best over-inflated puff piece for another writer's work. Or was it a "you scratch my back and I'll scratch yours" type of thing? The blurbs on his books, he liked to think, were justified by the quality of the reporting and writing.

The back cover noted Dr. Laura Sanders had been born in Missoula, Mont., and had graduated from the University of Michigan with a Phi Beta Kappa key. He frowned. Phi Beta Kappa? That alone was intimidating. After earning a doctorate in American Studies at Florida State University, she had joined the faculty of Florida Southwestern University where she was currently a full professor of Women's Studies. Author of numerous magazine and journal articles, and two books on the changing role of women in modern society, she enjoyed biking, collecting sea shells, and had a cat named "Buffy." He scanned the chapter headings, and began reading the one titled "Time for Action." But by the third or fourth time the words "denial, entitlement, and empowerment" cropped up, he yawned and put the book down. He doubted if there would be any interesting references to sex other than in terms of discrimination. Several hours later, the weather god relented, and TransAmerica Flight 203 lifted off the runway for St. Louis.

Laura caught an early morning Delta flight out of Fort Myers, arriving at Lambert-St. Louis Airport after changing planes in Atlanta. The flight was a tedious, seven-hour affair, but it gave her a chance to grade some class projects. The boy with the earring who had wished her well in New York had earned a "B," which surprised her.

She had never been in St. Louis before and connected the city with images of big horses pulling sleds at Christmas and an arch that reminded her of a fast food chain. Since she was traveling light and didn't have to wait for luggage, she went directly to the car rental.

"Hi, you have a reservation for Dr. Laura Sanders. Is a hybrid car available?"

The clerk, a young woman in a blue jacket, consulted a computer. "No, sorry, no hybrids."

"How about a car with GPS?"

The clerk smiled. "Sorry. Not permitted. After she checked Laura's driver's license and credit card, she handed her an envelope. In it Laura found a card with a single sentence: *Using the rental car company map provided, drive to the Stanley G. Goldstein Museum at 3364 Merrit Way. Your driving time begins when you are given keys to the car.* Laura took the keys and began studying the map. She plotted a route and marked it with pen.

St. Louis, according to the airline magazine stuffed in the back of the seat in front of Jack, had been founded in 1765. It enjoyed a rich historical past, stretching from early fur trapping days to the computer age, highlighted by a world-famous brewery (Anheiser-Busch), a storied baseball team (the Cardinals), and a towering arch (not to be confused with McDonald's). Indeed, a handful of Fortune 500 companies were headquartered there, and how many cities can claim to have been governed under three flags—Spanish, English, and French—in one year, 1803? History lesson over, Jack stuffed the magazine back in the seat pocket and looked out the window at the rows of houses rising toward him.

As soon as the plane landed, he pushed his way up the ramp and sprinted to the car rental, where he nervously chewed a knuckle while waiting in line.

"Kileen, Jack" he said when he reached the counter.

The clerk punched some keys on the computer. "You were due in on TransAmerica 203 two hours ago," she said.

"The flight was delayed in San Francisco. Rain. Happens often. Only two runways, and some idiot put them too close together." He waited.

The clerk wore a large button on her blue jacket that read: "You're always No. 1 with us!"

"Can I get a car with one of those navigation systems?"

Her mouth tightened. "No, I'm sorry."

"Okay. Okay. I'll take whatever you have. I'm going to the Stanley G. Goldstein Museum."

She looked up. "Oh, that's where that other lady said she was going."

"Oh," said Jack. "When?"

"About an hour ago."

She checked Jack's information and handed him an envelope and a map.

He was relieved to find that being late wouldn't be a handicap. Now the map... He scanned it quickly and headed for the parking garage.

The car in space No. 14 turned out to be an economy subcompact, and he swore as he banged his head squeezing inside. He turned the key in the ignition, put the car in gear, and lurched off. Signs led him to the interstate. He had barely gotten started when he saw a string of red lights stretching out ahead of him. Jack grimaced. Freeway accident! A time killer! He decided to get off the freeway and use local streets. At the third interchange, he exited and headed across town.

Soon the business district gave way to the inner city. The neighborhood deteriorated rapidly. Actually, it had already deteriorated. Worse, he was lost in it. Uncollected garbage poked up from cans, gusts of wind disturbed discarded newspapers and rattled discarded cans in gutters. The white-frosted windows of abandoned stores stood out against facades of red brick, spray-painted with gang symbols. Knots of men congregated on corners drinking out of brown paper bags. He was lost. Jack spotted two young African-American men sitting on a graffiti-decorated bench at a bus stop and pulled the car over.

He rolled down the window. "Can you give me some directions?" he asked. "I'm looking for the Stanley G. Goldstein Museum on Merrit Way and I'm lost."

One of the young men, wearing a leather jacket and toting a backpack, sauntered over.

"Where you say you goin'?" he asked. Jack repeated his destination.

The young man nodded. "Yeah, that's easy," he said. "You only minutes away on the freeway."

"Great!" said Jack. He waited.

"Cost you $10."

"What!" Jack exploded. "That's outrageous!"

"Thass up to you. I ain't lost, honky." He shrugged and turned back to the bench.

"Wait!" Jack fumbled for his wallet.

The young man waited. "Only fair," he said conversationally.

"What do you mean fair," Jack sputtered. "It's robbery!"

He got no sympathy. "You heard about consultants, man. Guys in $500 suits gettin' thousands of bucks a day to give advice. Well, I'm a motorvational consultant."

"Motivational," Jack corrected automatically.

The young man grinned. "No, motorvational. You pay for my geographical expertise and then you motor on out of here, dude."

Jack stifled a comment and handed over two Lincolns.

Leather jacket accepted them without expression. "Turn around, head two blocks back the way you came. Look for 13th Street and turn right. Follow that about four blocks to Camden and turn left. Take you back to the freeway. Head north. Look for the museum sign about three miles down the road."

"You mean that I could have stayed on the freeway and just followed the signs?" Jack groaned.

The young man looked critically at Jack's car. "Was I you, I'd get me a better car next time. This one a piece of shit. Dude gets lost like you needs a ve-hickle with one of those GPS things."

"All right," lamented Jack, "but $10 is still a rip-off."

"That isn't what my economics instructor would call it," said the young man. This time there was with no trace of street jargon. "Think of it as the invisible hand of the marketplace at work."

Maybe it was, Jack thought as he drove away, *maybe it was. But more like the invisible finger.*

The young man returned to the bus stop and looked up the street hopefully.

"What's with the ghetto jive?" asked his companion. "Honky? That is so-o-o '70s."

"Well, that's what he expected. Why disappoint him?"

"And holding him up for $10? He was right. It's outrageous."

The motorvational adviser pulled the two $5 bills out of his jacket pocket and carefully inserted them in his wallet. "I look on it as two specials du jour in the college cafeteria."

His friend considered that briefly. "I withdraw my objection." He glanced up the street. "Here comes the bus. We don't want to be late for acting class again."

After almost driving the wrong way up a one-way street, Jack saw a sign for the freeway. *North or south!* He couldn't remember. Three miles further, he realized he was going the wrong way. He got off the freeway at the first exit and turned around, proceeding until he saw a sign for the museum. *Twelve more minutes lost!* He pulled into the museum's parking lot and looked at his watch. It was 4:45 p.m. It had taken 56 minutes to get to the museum from the airport. Perhaps the Dragon Lady—that was how he now thought of Dr. Laura Sanders—had been delayed, too.

Jack had been instructed to go to the information desk, where his time of arrival would be noted. A uniformed guard sat behind the counter, reading the St. Louis Post-Dispatch sports section.

"Excuse me," Jack wheezed. "I'm here. Jack Kileen."

The guard looked up, sighed, closed the paper, and reached for a note pad.

"Driver's license." he said.

Jack fumbled for his wallet, masking irritation. "Here" He handed over the small, plastic card.

The guard compared the name and photograph and grunted unintelligibly. He made a notation on the note pad. "Okay, you're logged in." He handed back the driver's license and picked up the paper.

"Mr. Kileen! We meet again." He turned at the sound of a familiar voice. A slender woman in jeans, a white canvas jacket, and tennis shoes approached him, smiling. "There's a lovely Degas exhibit in the main gallery. You must make time to see it." She held a museum program.

"Dr. Sanders" he said glumly. "Did you have any trouble finding the place?"

"Oh no," she said. "Traffic was light on the freeway. It only took 37 minutes."

He noticed group of people hurrying toward them. Several carried cameras.

"Oh," she said, "Did I mention the press is here? I was nervous at first, but then you're used to interviews, aren't you?"

C*h*apter 11

There are three ingredients in the good life:
learning, earning, and yearning.

CHRISTOPHER MORLEY

Laura arrived home tired but exhilarated. She flew into Southwest Florida International Airport, picked up her '96 Honda, and drove through light traffic over the causeway to Sanibel Island, the lights of Fort Myers shrinking in the rear view mirror. Unwilling to face the telephone answering machine, she poured a glass of Chardonnay and sat down, trying to unwind.

Buffy, still in a snit at being left alone for several days with tepid water, dry food, and a rapidly filling litter box, sulked in hiding.

Laura eased into a vinyl lounger and put her feet up on a hassock. Ah...it's good to be home.

Sanibel Island was twelve miles long and three miles wide. It was linked to Fort Myers by a ribbon of roadway. During the tourist season, the population quadrupled to about 20,000 people. They came for bright sun, sandy beaches, and great seashell gathering, putting up with traffic jams and difficult parking.

But living on Sanibel was expensive. Laura felt spectacularly lucky to have inherited a summer cottage, now renovated, that had been passed down through three generations of family. The lot on which the house stood was worth far more than the original structure. Aside from the traffic, summer temperatures in the '80s, and the humidity, there were more pluses than minuses to island living. Miles of beaches for walking and shelling and ocean watching were only minutes away. She doubted if she'd be happy living in a big city, especially in snow country.

Hers was a low-key, self-contained lifestyle. She filled it with work, writing, listening to her Beethoven CD's, and gardening. She played bridge on Wednesdays at a community center and subscribed to the university's lecture and discussion series. She rarely dated, but she had a career, weeds to pull, and a cat to keep her company. Dull? Probably for a lot of people, but enough for her. Except... she had found to her surprise and dismay she had enjoyed jousting with that arrogant San Francisco newsman and besting him in their first test.

Jack got an inkling of what lay in store shortly after pulling up to the gate at the Sun's employee parking lot the next morning. He had slept badly after the late flight back to San Francisco. Now, depressed and jet-lagged, he faced a return to work. Rasheed "Downtown" Jones stepped out of the parking shack and smiled. No mere parking attendant, he had once led Riordan High School to a city Catholic League championship in basketball by scoring 26 points and hauling down 13 rebounds.

Jack rolled down the window and yawned. "Morning, D.T."

"Good morning, Mr. Kileen," came the respectful reply. "May I show you to a parking space and direct you to the employee entrance?"

Jack winced. "Aw, come on! I don't need that kind of crap this early in the morning!"

"Down Town's" smile widened. "Glad to see you found your way home okay." He turned away chuckling, and Jack drove to his assigned parking space. There was a sheet of paper with a large black arrow taped to the wall above it pointing to the employee entrance. Under it were the words "This Way, Jack!"

He groaned. How had he gotten suckered into being in a crazy contest to determine which sex is superior? He tore the arrow down and went inside. Happily, no one in the busy newsroom looked up as he walked to his desk. An Automobile Association of California map of San Francisco had been taped to it. An impressive black X and the words "You are here!" stood out boldly.

A ripple of laughter reached his ears and a quick glance told him a number of writers and editors had stopped work to see how he would take the joke.

He picked up the map and waved it over his head. "All right, people. I'll report to Rand McNally for remedial work. OK?"

He folded the map, stuffed it into a desk drawer, and turned to his phone messages. After that, Jack thumbed through snail mail, consigning most of it to the circular file. But when he logged onto the computer and checked the first of his e-mail messages, he swore softly and hurried to the desk of Dale Seybold.

"Why me?" he asked plaintively. "What did I do to deserve this? It isn't because of that stupid contest, is it?"

"No," said the editor. He leaned back, arms crossed, an ever-so-faint smile wrinkling the corners of his mouth. Jack ran through a mental list of his most likely other failings: A threatened libel suit? Expenses red-flagged by accounting? Forgetting to use the spell checker again and misspelling "judgment" or "accommodate" and thus ticking off the copy desk?

None of the above. And then...

"It was the poker game, wasn't it, Seybold?" he growled. "The hand when I had four nines and you had a full house."

"A flush," corrected the editor. "No, it wasn't the poker game. It was the managing editor's mother-in-law. The cat lady."

"The managing editor's mother-in-law...the cat..."

"You know," Seybold said helpfully, "the nice lady who called with the idea for a story about a roller-skating cat."

"The cat that... Oh, *that* cat. How was I to know she was the managing editor's mother-in-law?" objected Jack. "Besides, nobody's interested in reading about a roller-skating cat. It's not news."

The editor cocked his head. "Of course, it's news. Anything the managing editor says is news *is* news. You know that."

"Okay, okay, I know that," Jack conceded, "but give the story to Carla. She's good at soft stuff."

"Sure she is," Seybold agreed. "But Carla hates soft stuff. Wants hard stuff. Wants to be like the guys and cover the cop shop. Do I look like I need a sexual discrimination complaint?"

He handed a slip of paper to Jack. "The cat's owner lives in the Sunset. Here's the address. Pick up a photographer. Take Mickey. He's good at shooting animals."

As Jack started to turn away, Seybold said, "Oh... better let Mickey drive. I wouldn't want you to get lost."

Actually, Mickey was good at shooting animals. As they pulled out of the parking lot, Mickey behind the wheel, he described how he had bagged a deer in the Sierra Nevada Mountains the previous fall. He described with gusto the artful stalking... breathless aiming... explosive firing. He relived the moment, peering from behind a Jeffrey pine tree, heart thumping, having become one with nature in his gray, brown, and green mottled hunting outfit.

Jack imagined the scene. Mickey... just another faded fall shrub with black boots, pasty white face, and shiny .30-06 rifle. He sank lower in the seat. That must have been one dumb deer.

Escaping the congested downtown traffic, they headed west toward the Sunset District. Jack had been a writer for the *Sun* (The *Sun* Always Rises for San Francisco!) for seven years. A graduate of UC Berkeley, he had begun his reporting career in the hot Central Valley, working his way up to the *Sun* and its union pay scale. After a year of covering budget overruns, liquor store holdups, and rubber chicken Kiwanis luncheons, he graduated to feature writing. He discovered a talent for writing perceptive, colorful stories about people. Not cats—people.

It had to be the poker game, he thought glumly. He settled back and zoned out, nodding occasionally at tales of Mickey's vendetta against California wildlife.

Clauson Street was old San Francisco, lined with narrow two-and three-story wood Victorian houses butting directly onto the sidewalk. At No. 46, chipped concrete steps led up to a front door opened to catch the ozone-tinged breeze. Jack rang the bell. An unshaven old man in a frayed red bathrobe came to the door and looked at them questioningly through thick bifocals.

"Mr. Mariucci? We're from the *Sun*," Jack said. "I'm Jack Kileen and this is Mickey Nolan, our photographer."

Recognition came slowly to the old man's face, and when it did, he blinked.

"Oh, you're here to write about Dancer! Come in." He ushered them into a musty living room. Half-opened blinds filtered thin bands of pale light. Fringed cushions lay haphazardly on a sofa, and magazines and newspapers overflowed a coffee table. Tarnished oval frames held black and white pictures of unsmiling men in round bowler hats and women in long dark skirts with their hair piled high atop their heads.

"Just a minute. I'll get Dancer," the old man said. He came back with an obese cat cradled in his arms. The cat's eyes, yellow slits in a black mask, looked at the two strangers with suspicion.

"This is Dancer," he said. "My wife named him when he was a kitten. She's gone now."

No one spoke for a moment.

"Nice cat," said Mickey, breaking the silence. He unslung his shoulder bag and rummaged through it, pulling out a digital camera with flash.

They followed the old man into the kitchen. Stacks of unwashed dishes overflowed a chipped porcelain sink.

Jack glanced at his watch. "Okay, can we see the cat roller skating?"

The old man opened a drawer and removed four tiny metal skates with felt straps. "I made these myself," he said.

Nolan moved about the tiny kitchen, taking pictures from different angles as the old man fastened the skates to the feet of the squirming animal and lowered it to the floor. Legs quivering, Dancer struggled to stay upright.

Jack shook his head. "How is it going to skate? It can barely stand up."

"Oh, you'll see," the old man assured them. "Now you stand over here." He positioned Jack at one end of the kitchen. Jack squatted for a cat's-eye view. Then the old man picked up Dancer and walked the length of the kitchen until he leaned against the back door. "Get ready," he said.

"Ready for what?" Jack glanced up just as the old man grasped the cat tightly, his right hand firmly under its belly, brought his arm forward, and launched the animal like a bowling ball across the worn linoleum floor.

"Catch him!" he called. Feet flailing, wheels spinning, Dancer became a feline projectile. The cat careened across the floor toward Jack, meowing wildly, eyes wide with terror. Before he could react, the cat was upon him. Too late, Jack put up his hands to ward off the animal. Dancer crashed into his stomach, and he tumbled backward. Momentum halted, the frantic cat slid off its human cushion—but not before leaving a large, damp stain on Jack's left pant leg.

"See, I told you Dancer could roller skate!" the old man said, picking up the frightened animal. "Good kitty! Good kitty!" He nuzzled the cat with a whiskered chin and began to remove the skates.

Jack struggled to his feet. "Did you get that?" he asked the photographer.

"Oh, yeah," Mickey replied, stifling laughter. "Oh, yeah...I got it."

Jack looked about the kitchen for his assailant. Dancer lay under the kitchen table, calmly licking a paw.

At the *Sun*, the newsroom buzzed with energy as the deadline for the home edition neared.

Seybold looked up. "How did it go?" His eyes dropped to the dark stain on Jack's pants.

"It'll be the first cat story to win the Pulitzer Prize," snapped Jack. Ignoring the curious glances of co-workers, he walked rapidly to his desk, a folded newspaper held awkwardly at waist level.

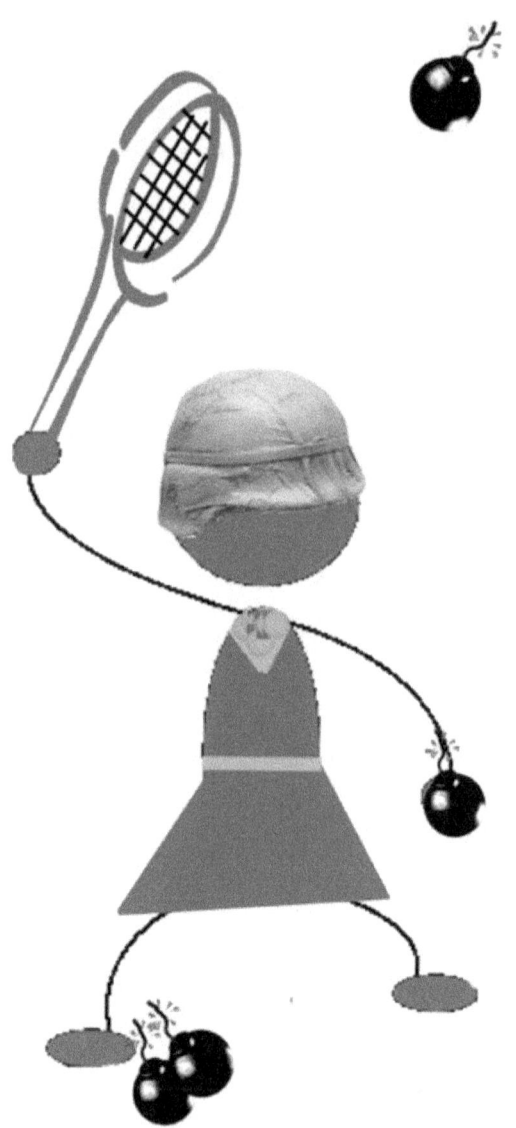

Chpter 12

There is no such thing as an underestimate
of average intelligence.

HENRY JAMES

Light rain off Lake Michigan pinged the window. Larry Clayton looked up in surprise and some trepidation as Roland Ebert strolled into his office unannounced.

"How's the next issue shaping up?" asked the publisher.

Clayton fumbled with some papers on his desk. "Good...good... We've leading with a story about a faith healer who says he can cure AIDS by immersion in a secret rejuvenation juice."

Ebert nodded. "That should kick up circulation after that crappy Merman story."

Clayton flinched.

"Oh..." The publisher paused as if struck by a sudden thought. That was another tactic of Management by Intimidation—making your employees dread the unexpected. "You know Bill Hadley will be retiring as editor in a few months. You could be on the short list of candidates to replace him." He paused to let the words sink in. He'd given the same speech to half a dozen other editors on the magazine, so his timing had improved. Competition kept people on their toes. He changed gears again. "How are we doing on this battle of the sexes thing?"

"Ashford Sloan is busy developing something right now," Clayton replied.

The publisher nodded and left to mention the future job opening to the magazine's graphics editor.

It turned out to be an embarrassing week for Jack as the loser du jour. Newspapers, his own included, joined magazines in pestering him for interviews. Pitting sex against sex touched primal nerve endings and the story, as Larry Clayton had foreseen, developed legs, lots of legs. Browsing magazine stands and surfing the Internet, Jack discovered just how many.

The N.Y. Times

> Woman wins first
> 'Challenge' test
> in St. Louis race

Le Monde

> Elle gagne!

Sydney Morning Herald

> Read a map, mate!

Newsweek

> Late, Lost, and Last

Variety

> Boffo Beginning for Babe

Glimpse

> <u>Exclusive!</u>
> "Challenge of Sexes"
> Contestants Target
> Of Terrorists?

Outdoor Living

> Map Reading Skills Can Save Your Life!

Popular Mechanics

> GPS Technology: The Future Now

Working Women's Wear

> Right Sweater, Blouse Combo Can Make You a Winner, Too!

Still, for all of that, it was good to be back, asking, not answering, questions. Jack considered himself a private, if not a shy, person. Women had told him it was one of his appealing traits, vulnerability with a tinge of awkwardness. Although he was a journalist, asking personal questions in interviews still made Jack uncomfortable. His other two books, "Eight Who Dared," a tribute to men like Arctic survivor Ernest Shackleton and Dr. Martin Luther King, and "Inside the Subprime Meltdown," a scathing indictment of the role of banks in the housing collapse, had involved research more than contact with people. Neither book had been a commercial success. He hoped the recent publicity, bad as it was, might boost sales of "Alpha Male."

But in New York, book sales weren't on Mari's mind as she took a swig of Evian water and relaxed. Cliff Hansen, sitting across the desk from her, clipboard in hand, relaxed, too. Yesterday's program had gone well. A Hollywood leading man, starring in a just-released action film, had admitted under badgering that yes, he had fathered a child with a script girl years before and continued to pay her child support on the condition she remain silent. On the lighter side, the head chef at one of Manhattan's best restaurants had successfully prepared a flaming cherries jubilee on camera without burning the studio down.

She frowned. Something.... "Too bad we didn't have a camera on Kileen when he got lost in St. Louis," she said.

"Right," agreed Hansen.

Mari frowned. "Let's do it from now on. Assign a camera crew—they have to be unobtrusive—to both of them. We can air clips of the tape on the air."

Another thought struck. "Cliff, when I announced that Laura Sanders had beaten Jack Kileen, how did the audience react?"

"Clapping...shouting...pandemonium, Mari."

"How long?

"How long? I don't know three, four minutes, we could..."

Mari fixed him with an unforgiving glance. "They forgot about it five minutes later," she pointed out. "We need something to remind them and the TV audience about the contest."

He pursed his lips. "You mean like a sign or something?"

"No. A scoreboard. One of those thermometer thingies they use on those boring weekend fund-raising drives for charities everybody forgets about as soon as the program is over."

Hansen pursed his lips as if deep in thought. It was never a good idea to admit you were clueless around Mari. "Oh, yeah. Let me see what I can come up with."

And he did come up with something. When she arrived at the studio two days later, something new had been added to the set. A twenty-foot tall, perpendicular prop loomed next to her desk. It held two backlit columns of red liquid. Graduated numbers from 100 to 1,050 rose along the sides. Inside one column floated the figure of a woman; in the other, that of a man. They looked suspiciously like larger versions of the little plastic figures on wedding cakes. The woman bobbed above the man at the 150 level. Large bulbs in red, white, and blue framed the display, and strobe lights flashed in the background.

"Who said that nothing succeeds like excess?" said Hansen proudly.

"Actually, I think it's somewhat understated," observed Mari.

Back on Sanibel Island, Laura puttered about the house until late afternoon, leafed through some professional journals, and waited for traffic on the causeway to subside. Then she fed and put a protesting Buffy outside, evading a clawed protest, and drove to Fort Myers.

Florida Southwestern University sat on the landward side of the city, a collection of sun-bleached two-and three-story buildings built around interior courtyards and separated by flower-lined concrete walkways with ferns and palms. Walled off from ocean breezes by the city's business center, the campus stifled in the heat. Laura hurried into the cool relief of the Archibald L. Wentworth Undergraduate Library, named after an early pioneer in Florida beachfront development who had had the foresight to leave the college $6 million with the sole proviso that a building bear his name. He would have been less than pleased to discover that students usually referred to his undergraduate library as the UGLI.

Laura walked through the library (she had needed an air-conditioning fix) and exited, crossing a walkway to the Humanities Building, where she had her office. As she passed the office of the Morris Evander, she peeked in.

Evander sat reading, a ballpoint pen in one hand tapping the desk. Most faculty members knew him as a reasonable, efficient administrator, not as a Chaucer scholar and authority on Florida Marlins' batting averages, which he also was. A bachelor, he had abandoned the classroom to administer the college's literature, foreign language, and specialty programs, which included Laura's. He was also, as some of the older married secretaries noted over coffee, "a hunk." Laura had tried, without luck, to catch his eye, even inviting him out to lunch under the guise of getting his opinion on new classes.

He saw her and waved her into his office. "Well done! Well done! Have you got a minute? Come in."

Laura glanced at her watch. Damn! Why couldn't he want to chat after class, over a drink, for instance?

"Only a minute, Morris," she said regretfully. "I've got a seminar to prepare."

"Of course, of course." He gestured for her to sit down and leaned forward in a leather chair behind a cluttered desk. His office window was open to catch the evening breeze and she detected a scurrying in the palm tree outside. Probably rats.

"You're becoming famous, you know. It's all over campus. There's a story in the *Blade* this afternoon," the dean said.

She set her briefcase down. "I was afraid of that. I can't wait to get a call from the campus newspaper."

He grinned. "You already have. They called me, too." She leaned forward with a smile and crossed her legs, body language designed to show receptivity. Perhaps now he'd ask her out if only to talk about "The Challenge of the Sexes."

No such luck. "I won't keep you long," Evander said, all business. "This contest may be a pain for you, but it's good news for the university. Positive publicity. More students. When you get a chance, let's talk about your idea for a class on sex, politics, and social change."

Laura yielded to the inevitable. Something is better than nothing.

"Yes, let's do that," she said, rising. Outside the birds quieted as pale, yellow light faded and shadows deepened. "I've got to go. My Leadership Roles of Women seminar is at 7 p.m., and this is the second week. We're still getting organized."

He rose. "I hope you can add a few more students tonight. Enrollment is low."

"So do I," she said, picking up her briefcase. "So do I."

It was her favorite class, a small seminar in her area of expertise and interest, female leadership. It met once a week on Tuesday nights, and usually attracted eight to ten seniors or graduate students who fancied themselves the leaders of tomorrow. Sometimes they were right. One of her former students was a youthful dean of admissions at a private college in Georgia; another, tired of lectures, inflated grades, and having to teach summers to make ends meet, had abandoned teaching and joined the business world. Recently, she had been promoted to vice-president of a credit union.

Laura spent fifteen minutes in her office, checking phone messages, scanning mail, and brushing up on lecture notes before leaving for her seminar. When she walked into the room, eight women sat around a table, notebooks and pens ready, backpacks with water bottles hanging from chairs or stuffed beneath them.

"Hi," Laura said, setting her briefcase on the table. She didn't bother taking attendance; she knew them all by name. Most had been in previous classes. The door opened behind her.

"Sorry, I'm late" came a tentative and apologetic voice. It belonged to a young man in neatly pressed jeans, blue pullover, and white shirt. He handed her a registration slip and squeezed past the women to a seat at the end of the table.

Several of the women rolled their eyes and studied the newcomer with clear hostility.

Laura looked at the name on the slip. "Mr. Linderman..."

He nodded.

"Welcome to the class. It's rare to find a man in a seminar on women's leadership. May I ask why you're interested in the class?"

"Toby," he replied. "Call me Toby. I'm here, Dr. Sanders, because my sister, who was a high school guidance counselor, recently died after a lingering illness. She mentored troubled young women." He looked down at the brown table top, scarred with coffee cup and bottle rings, and paused. "Before Addie died, she asked me to do what I could to continue her efforts in helping people. I run a small business, and I want to help the women who work for me to prepare for management positions and better themselves, even if it's with other companies."

One of the women, who had been clearly resentful of a male intruder moments before, swallowed and looked at him sympathetically.

"That's an excellent reason to be in the class," said Laura approvingly.

"Thank you," whispered Ashford Sloan.

Chpter 13

Fame is a fickle food upon a shifting plate.

EMILY DICKINSON

Applause ringing in her ears, Mari unclipped her mike and refocused her eyes as the spotlights bathing the set winked out. Another show in the can. How many was that? She had lost count.

The audience filed obediently toward the exits. A hopeful few hung back, hoping for autographs. No way. She waved, smiled, and strode off the set, bound for her dressing room where a cup of tea and an aspirin awaited. Not all shows are winners and this one had been one of the losers. Her main guest was to have been a "No Guts, No Glory" reality show contestant who had been kicked out of the sandbox due to an abrasive personality and underdeveloped politicking skills. The woman had agreed to appear on the show, but had bailed at the last moment. Her replacement, a handsome but incredibly dumb and inarticulate TV comedy star, had bombed badly. Mari debated taking two aspirins.

Cliff Hansen was waiting, a sympathetic expression on his face. "There's always tomorrow," he said philosophically. "You'll knock 'em dead." When they had first teamed up, he had made the mistake of saying "We'll knock 'em dead." She had corrected the pronoun use quickly. Only Mari knocked 'em dead.

"We'd better, Cliffy. Did you find out what happened to that loser from 'No Guts, No Glory'?"

"Y...e...s..."

"Well...?"

He looked unhappy. "Her agent called and said she decided at the last minute to be on the Jerry Elkins Show."

"Elkins...Elkins...Oh, the new guy on United Broadcasting?" She pretended not to recognize the name.

"Right. I taped the show for you, just in case..." He placed a videotape on her desk.

Mari collapsed in a chair. "This Elkins...what's he like?"

"The usual," Hansen said. "Nothing to worry about." But he was thinking, not unless a bright, smart guy who's chopping you off at the knees by stealing your guests would keep you lying awake at night.

She poured some tea and swallowed an aspirin. And then another. Her headache was worse.

Although she wouldn't admit it, Mari had been reading about Elkins in newspaper entertainment columns. Elkins was the bright new star twinkling in the firmament of afternoon television. He had started out as a slick, two-timing doctor in a soap opera, "Psychiatric Hospital." But when the writers had rashly let the star, who played a nurse, smoke him with a .32 after his affair with her 17-year-old sister, thousands of outraged female viewers had written in to protest. He had been miraculously brought back to life in the operating room. From there, Elkins had moved to a game show. There he mastered the art of smiling a lot, and went on to his big break, a talk show that featured over-the-middle-of-the-plate, slow pitch questions to TV and film stars about their latest projects, favorite charities, and pets. "Meet the Press" it wasn't.

Mari moved on.

"Did you line up some judges?"

Hansen nodded. Once again, he had anticipated a problem and solved it. Would Mari give him credit for it? Hah! The driving test in St. Louis had been easy. But who was going to decide the details of the other challenges? Who was going to solve the techie problems for the computer test...choose a menu for the dinner... award points if there were irregularities or ties? Not him. They needed another panel, one composed of dedicated, objective people who would oversee the competition and make sure that it was run efficiently before Dr. Laura Sanders won. In return for ironing out the details of the contests, making the arrangements for travel and monitoring, and settling any disputes, the lucky panel members would each get an honorarium of $1,000. Plus, they would appear in the final spectacular finale on TV and get a program DVD, autographed by Mari herself.

"I've got about a dozen possibilities here," he began. "We need an odd number to break ties. How

about four men and three women? Would that do?"
Having lit the fuse, Hansen awaited the reaction. Seeing Mari explode made his day if he wasn't the target.

She said nothing; but the look she gave him said it
all.

"Okay, then how about four women and three
men?"

"Who?"

"Four professors, a doctor, a nonprofit executive,
and a rabbi."

"Is one of the professors from the Ivy League?"

He nodded. That went without saying. How could
you have a distinguished panel of experts without
someone from an Ivy League school? "Good." Mari's
headache had receded to a dull throb.

Hansen shifted gears. "Look, Mari, could we talk
about my contract now?"

"I promise you we'll get to it, Cliff; but now isn't a
good time. Soon."

He stifled a comment. He had worked with Mari
long enough so that he could read her feelings as well
as he could read his wife's. She wasn't thinking about
his contract or the panel of experts. The worry lines in
her forehead meant she was thinking of something
else. And he knew what it was.

"Don't worry about this guy Elkins," he said. "They
come and they go. Why should this one be different?
A little competition is healthy."

Mari forced a confident smile and the worry lines smoothed out. "Of course it is." As soon as he left the office, she picked up the tape.

Several days later, Jack got an e-mail at the office. He scanned the contents rapidly. It was from the panel of experts, which he noted had a female majority. He had begun to get the feeling that gender equity might not apply where he was concerned.

The message contained a blueprint and timetable for the contests. Events would come at roughly four-week intervals. The next would test practical skills, followed by a part of the physical competition, a one-mile run, then a cultural literacy competition, and a computer challenge. After that, he could look forward to a cook-off, tax preparation, and adventure racing, the final leg of the physical challenge. It sounded doable. He'd be okay on most of the practical skills, and certainly ace the mile run, tax preparation, and adventure racing. He'd bomb on the cook-off, but he had a shot at cultural literacy and the computer test. "I've got the edge," he gloated aloud.

"You've got the what?"

He looked up to find Maggie Bauer standing before the desk.

"I've got the edge in the Challenge of the Sexes, Maggie, my love." He pushed over the message for her to read.

She read it quickly, scanning for content, skipping over the definite and indefinite articles and prepositions, concentrating on the nouns and verbs. She thrust it back.

"I think you're in deep doo-doo, sport."

Jack grinned. "The lovely Dr. Laura Sanders isn't like you, Mags. She's a lady. Lacks your killer instinct and feral cunning."

Maggie took no offense at the inference that she, herself, might not be considered a lady. He could join the crowd on that one. Despite their ages (she was pushing retirement age from the other side), Maggie and Jack were buds. Both considered being reporters on a Pulitzer Prize-winning newspaper that gave them some elbowroom as having won the lottery of work-a-day. They also shared an appreciation for the craft of writing, which, unlike most of their colleagues, they never stopped trying to master. Over drinks at McGinty's, a favorite watering hole of the newspaper's ink-stained wretches, they had quickly discovered they both despised bureaucracy, even when it paid their salaries.

Maggie's gray-flecked, thinning brown hair hung in unruly bangs over a furrowed forehead. Sharp blue eyes, her most striking feature, sank in a sea of wrinkles and ridges revealing her age. She did nothing to disguise it. Years of nicotine exposure had stained the fingers of her right hand a weak saffron color. She usually wore uncomplimentary, often ill-matched slacks and blouses that looked as if they had come from a discount store sale. Some had.

She got away with it because she had been a sports writer for decades, an institution in a male-dominated field that had only grudgingly admitted women to the inner circle. Gruff, sometimes foul-mouthed and always aggressive, she was accepted by athletes as a reporter who couldn't be intimidated. It didn't hurt that she admitted and corrected mistakes, rare though they were.

Maggie had attained anecdotal status one day in the spring of 1978 when she had been assigned to cover the San Francisco Oakies baseball team, only to find herself barred from the men-only dressing room after a game. Furious, she found an open window in the rear of the building, climbed through it, and appeared in the dressing the room to stunned silence. Finally, Charlie Haslet, a center fielder who would last only two years in the bigs due to an affinity for bourbon on the rocks and a tendency to swing at low, outside pitches, stood. He unknotted the towel about his waist and let it drop to the floor.

"Hey, Maggie, is this what you wanted to see?" She looked down, considered the question, and replied. "No, Charlie. My eight-year-old nephew has a weenie like that. I wanted to see the kind grown-ups have." From then on, Maggie Bauer went where she wanted.

She coughed and looked for a place on Jack's desk to extinguish her cigarette. "Where's your ashtray?"

"I don't have one, Mags. I don't smoke, remember?"

"Oh, right." She ground out the cigarette on the inside of the wastepaper basket. Jack hoped it wouldn't start a fire. The newsroom was a no-smoking zone, but Maggie was Maggie.

She waggled a finger at him. "I've got two tickets for the Quakes tonight in San Jose. Want to drive up?"

He shook his head. "Can't do it tonight. Besides, I don't get the same thrill out of seeing guys running around in shorts that you do. I'll take a rain check."

She guffawed.

Jack had never enjoyed the unpredictability of soccer. He considered grown men who vied to let hard-kicked balls bounce off the tops of their heads as being less than bright.

"Okay. Next time," she said regretfully. "Maybe I can catch it on the tube." He knew Maggie didn't like to drive at night. She claimed that on-coming headlights attracted her like a moth to a flame. He supposed that she didn't want to fight post-game traffic on I-280, either.

"Where are you going to lose next," she needled.

Jack looked at the letter again. "Nowhere. I get to paint an apartment, change a tire, and give a dog a bath right here in San Francisco."

"Well, at least the apartment and tire won't suffer permanent damage. I can't say the same for the dog. Had your rabies shots?" Maggie chuckled and walked away, leaving Jack thinking. Rabies?

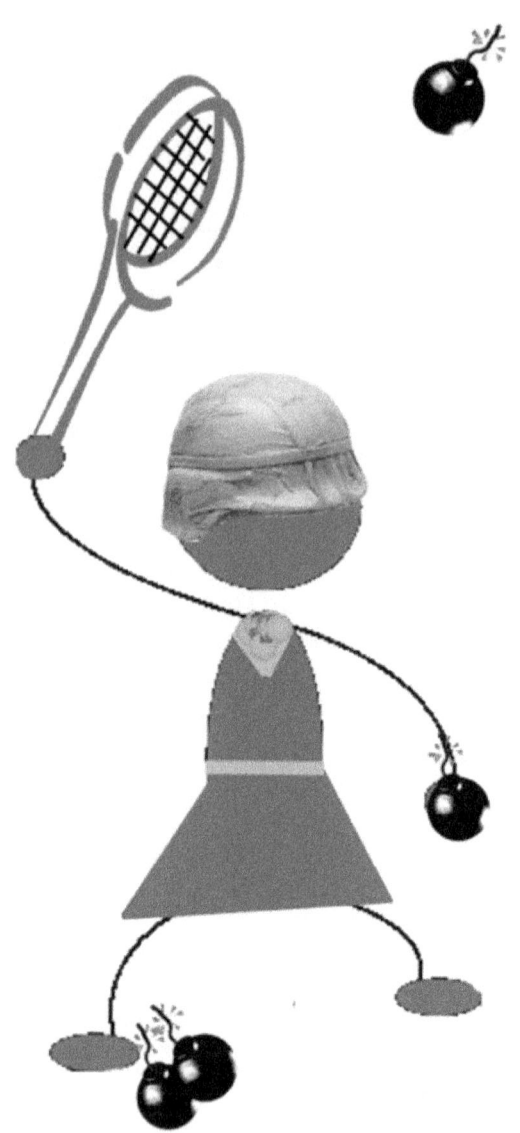

Chapter 14

Do not do what you would undo if caught.

LEAH ARENDT

The next contest would be held in Fort Myers and San Francisco simultaneously. That came about because both Jack and Laura rebelled against the network's idea that they should make themselves available for the next few months to travel around the world. Both pointed out they had jobs and lives apart from television. So the network prevailed upon the now-named Committee of Seven to schedule most of the contests in Florida and California to save airfare. The cultural literacy competition would be done on closed circuit TV, and the adventure-racing event, still undecided, would be an exception, staged at some exotic foreign site to drum up excitement for the big finale. Of course, that left open the question of who would ensure the fairness of the contests at each site. Cliff Hansen, veteran problem solver, suggested that Jack and Laura each pick a representative to monitor the other's performance. He suggested each monitor be paid $5,000 plus expenses.

Laura racked her brain, trying to remember the name of anyone that she knew living in the San Francisco Bay area. Then she had an epiphany. She had saved the program from every professional conference she had ever attended on the off chance she might need to contact someone whom she had met at a workshop, seminar, speech, or reception. Opening a shoebox stuffed high above her bedroom closet (Laura's information retrieval system didn't limit itself to computer storage), she began pouring over old conference programs. Soon, she struck pay dirt. Among her co-panelists at a seminar on "Changing Legal Rights for Women" at Western Michigan University in Kalamazoo, Mich., four years ago, she found the name of Patricia Rossi. Rossi was an English instructor at Arroyo Community College in Union City, which, she found out from a map, was in commuting distance of San Francisco.

"Patricia Rossi..." Laura murmured. Buffy, who had been dozing on the bed, opened her eyes at the sound of Laura's voice, and decided there were no emergencies or opportunities for food that required her immediate attention, and went back to sleep.

Laura tried to recall what she knew about Patricia Rossi. Ah... Rossi was the panelist from Arroyo College who had given an impassioned call for the enforcement of alimony and child support payment. That meant she was likely a) divorced and b) a parent. She just might be willing to help another put-upon female, especially when she learned the payoff would be $5,000. Laura scooped up the telephone book, found the area code for Union City, California, and picked up the phone.

Meanwhile, Jack was having even less luck. He quickly gave up trying to remember anyone that he knew in Fort Myers, "population 48,000 plus and grow-ing!" and tried to remember the names of other Florida cities, none of which he had ever visited. In desperation, he turned to the only person that he knew with contacts rivaling those of Homeland Security or the CIA: Maggie.

She listened to his problem in silence. "Let me check my Florida file on the computer when I get home."

"You've got an address book broken down by states?"

She raised an eyebrow. "Sure. That's one of the things I do to kill the evenings. Otherwise, I'd drink myself to death faster. I'll get back to you."

Jack punched computer keys for the next hour, finishing up the profile of an 87-year-old golfer who claimed he could have been the first Tiger Woods if only things had been different in Ben Hogan's era. Then he grabbed lunch at a nearby taqueria, got a haircut, and returned to the office. The message light on his phone blinked. He listened and returned the call.

"Maggie? Jack. Have you got something for me?"

"Do koala bears like eucalyptus leaves?"

That set him back. Conversations with Maggie often began and ended weirdly. "I don't know, do they?"

"Of course, they do," she said in exasperation. "Don't you ever watch 'Animal Planet' on TV?"

"I'll make a point of it tonight."

"Anyway," she resumed, "I've got a name for you: 'Cracker' Marion Sally. He lives in Naples, an easy drive from Fort Myers."

"Marion Sally... Isn't he the guy who..."

She chortled. "Did he ever! Played pro football for seven years with the Jets and Lions, including one Pro Bowl. Then on the day he retired he held a news conference and..."

"...came out of the closet," said Jack. "But why is he doing you—and me—a favor?"

"He owes me one. I was covering Stanford football the year he was a senior and an all-Pac Ten linebacker in that "walk don't run" defense. Stanford was to play Tennessee in the FedEx Bowl when I got an anonymous telephone call that Sally was gay. What a story! I called him on it and he admitted it."

"I don't remember reading that."

"That's because I never wrote it. Want to know why?"

Jack leaned back in his chair. This looked to be a lengthy conversation.

"Okay, why?"

"Because when I was looking through a press release Stanford put out, it said that he spent an afternoon a week reading to blind children. Bullshit, I thought. So I called the blind center and checked it out. Like clockwork, Sally showed up every Wednesday afternoon before football practice to read to the kids. They loved him."

"Nice guy."

"Yeah, nice guy. If the kids could have seen him, they'd probably have been too scared to listen. He's

6-6 and a yard or two wide. Sally's a nice guy, but he didn't get a name like 'Cracker'—that's short for bone cracker by the way—by being a wuss. Anyhow, I couldn't blow the whistle on him. I figured he'd have enough trouble in the pros with a girl's name without me adding to it. He still sends me a card at Christmas."

"Nobody else ever blew the whistle on him? Not even your caller?"

"No. I never figured out why. Maybe whoever called me found out about the center for the blind, too."

"But I don't even know the guy," protested Jack. "Why should he do a favor for me?"

Maggie sounded impatient. "He won't be doing a favor for you, sport. He'll be doing a favor for me. I told him you'd call."

"Thanks, Mags. I owe you one."

"So what else is new?" She hung up.

Not surprisingly, "Cracker" Marion Sally signed on, more for the chance to do Maggie a favor than for the $5,000. So did Patricia Rossi, whose hesitation vanished quickly when the money was mentioned. Soon Marion and Pat (he asked her not to call him "Cracker") were exchanging e-mail messages and telephone calls, arranging the practical skills competition. They learned the apartments to be painted would be similar, that the same model of car would be used for the timed test at tire changing, and that same sized dogs would get baths 3,000 miles apart. Each contestant would receive $100 to purchase painting and dog bathing supplies. A national auto manufacturer agreed to provide the cars for the publicity. (Jack had suggested Hummers, but Laura had insisted on intermediate-size models.) Local dog clubs would provide the dogs. The contest was set for Saturday.

Friday afternoon. Students had largely deserted the campus, drawn to Fort Myer's sun-splashed beaches or other activities not involved with sitting on hard chairs in classrooms. Laura sat at her desk, savoring the solitude. Her computer screen displayed yellow and green fish swimming lazily in a watery blue world. Occasionally, one opened its mouth and bubbles rose languidly to the top of the screen. She studied a copy of the instruction manual for the car whose tire she would change, noting where the jack was stored and how it would be placed. Tonight, she would visit a home improvement store and get some painting tips. That was fair, wasn't it?

After class the previous evening, her newest student, Toby Linderman, had wished her well and asked a number of questions, some bordering on the personal, about how she felt and if she had any tricks planned in the Challenge of the Sexes competition. The questions had made her a little uncomfortable.

She heard a throat being cleared and looked up. Morris Evander stood in the doorway.

"Hi, Morris," she said, perking up.

"I just wanted to wish you well tomorrow, Laura."

"Thanks," Laura said warmly. She gestured for him to sit down, but he continued standing. Evander rarely dropped by her office and she wanted to make the most of it. She ran her fingers through her hair nervously. "Got time for a cup of coffee in the faculty lounge?"

He glanced at his watch. "I wish I could, but I'm running late."

"Of course," she said, hiding her disappointment.

"We're rooting for you, Laura. Just wanted you to know."

She got the impression this was a staff morale-building stop, not a personal visit. She was convinced of it after he commented on how many people had mentioned her initial success to him. And then he left.

Laura shook her head, suddenly depressed. That was the problem. They all *were* rooting for her—students, colleagues, administrators, and secretaries, even the groundskeepers. Who needed that kind of pressure?

Jack was preparing, too, out in the carport behind his apartment building, where he had practiced changing a tire on his Toyota. He had gotten his time down by almost two minutes. If he hadn't been so occupied with tightening lug nuts, he might have noticed nosey Mrs. Dumbrowski, the recently retired school cafeteria aide on the third floor, who was playing with the birthday gift from her son—a new video camera.

In Las Vegas, the "Be a Winner!" show with Bernie and Max had started. Bernie Morgan and Max Rimsky were ex-gamblers who had parlayed a long shot into a million-dollar TV payoff. Once a week, from a glamorous casino on the Las Vegas strip, through the marvel of satellite television, they were beamed into thousands of homes in states where their topic of discussion—gambling—was illegal. As if that discouraged bettors. Even small communities usually have bookies; other states permit off-track horse race wagering if the state gets a rake-off in its own gambling dens. In California, card rooms and Indian casinos are legal. And lotteries? Let's not get into lotteries with mega million payoffs. Even if you were stuck living in a bluenose state that prohibited gambling, you could play poker and black jack on the Internet.

Tonight, Bernie and Max had finished the baseball portion of the program by debating whether or not the Oakland Athletics' pitching was capable of defeating the New York Yankees' hitting in tomorrow's game in Oakland. Bernie thought it unlikely and went with the betting line, which favored the Athletics. He said he'd put his money on Oakland. Baseball out of the way, they turned their attention to one of the most popular segments of the broadcast: Weird Wagers. Every week, they handicapped some oddity not normally a subject for betting. It might be the Boston Marathon or a segment of the Tour de France. Tonight, it was the Challenge of the Sexes.

Bernie wore a plaid sport coat, open-neck blue shirt and gold chain. He flashed cufflinks. "I don't know, Max, I'm not as high on this San Francisco guy as I was before. He got snookered in St. Louis."

"He went for the fences," responded Max. He wore a cashmere sport jacket and coffee brown shirt. A large diamond ring flashed on the little finger of his left hand. "You gotta respect someone who takes a chance to win big. He coulda played it safe and stayed on the Cross-Town."

"Still," Bernie persisted, "he's down 75 points at the start. What'll that do to his self-confidence? Can he shake it off and come back? I'm asking myself."

"So he was thrown off a little by getting there late. Who wouldn't be? You can't blame him for the weather! He picked himself up and went on. The guy's a gamer."

Max swiveled in his chair. Behind him, through a glass window, viewers could see the main floor of the Matterhorn Casino. Tourists in loud shorts, urban cowboys in Stetson hats, and little old ladies with canes fed coins and poked pre-paid cards nonstop into bell-ringing poker and blackjack machines. All the better to whet the appetites of viewers.

What TV viewers couldn't see, of course, was the garish, white-capped steel and foam mountain outside, complete with snowmobile tram, which soared 132 feet in the stultifying desert air. It took up a good part of the RV section of the 1,000-vehicle casino parking lot.

"This practical test thing has to be right up the guy's alley," suggested Max. "Even a guy from California should be able to paint a room and change a tire. I dunno about washing a dog. I see that as a toss-up." He swiveled back toward the camera, having titillated the audience with a glimpse of real gambling.

Bernie shook his head. "No way. I give the Florida lady a slim 'stacks up' in the event." He pushed a stack of blue chips forward for a close-up by the camera. "Sure, the tire change will go to the guy; but the room painting? Do you know how many women paint apartments and houses? Lots." He paused, seemingly deep in thought. "And I give the dog thing to her, too. Every time I see a picture of a dog being groomed in the papers, it's always a woman doing the job. Guys aren't into that. My view: This is a 150-point event. I say 100 for the lady, 50 for the guy."

"What did you have for lunch?" Max asked, "a cannabis salad? This is going to be a slam-dunk for the guy. I say he takes all 150 points." He pushed *his* stack of chips forward. Bernie snorted.

The camera drew back for a close-up of Max. "And that's it from this week's 'Be a Winner! Show'" he said. "You can see all of our picks on Bernie & Max.com. And our new book, 'Play Poker Like a Pro!' is available for only $19.95. See you next week and remember: If you don't play, you can't win!"

In the control room, the director watched the clock and spoke. "Cut to commercial." A beautiful woman slept soundly. On the table next to her bed was a bottle of WakeNoMore, the revolutionary, non-addictive, gentle sleeping aid.

"Bring up theme," the director said. The sound track from "Rocky" blared in the background. "Cut to close-up of Max."

"I can't believe that you aren't picking Tiger Woods to win the Tampa Open after..."

"Cut to Bernie for reaction"

"The Tiger is off his game a little and...

"Roll credits."

The director took off his headset. "We're out of here. Last one in the bar gets the first round."

Chpter 15

*Men are like a deck of cards. You'll find the
occasional king, but most are jacks.*

LAURA SWENSON

That same night, Jack sat watching bowling on
ESPN. The phone rang. He ignored it until the answering machine reverberated with a vaguely familiar and
impatient voice. "Pick up, Kileen. It's Laura Sanders.
This is important." Groaning, Jack put down his second
frosty bottle of Anchor Steam Ale and picked up the
phone. "Dr. Sanders, how pleasant to hear from you,
especially when it's so unexpected. But isn't it a little
late in mosquito land?"

Laura glanced at the computer screen and the
speech she had been writing for the Fort Myers Business Women's Club and the empty wine glass next to
it. She needed a refill.

"Of course, it's late," she snapped. "But I can't get
in touch with you any other time! Don't you read your
e-mail! I've sent three messages."

E-mail. Jack looked guiltily at the computer in the corner of the room. "Actually, I don't check messages much," he admitted, "too much spam."

He became defensive. "I get lots of e-mail at work—editors with nothing better to do trying to justify their salaries. And then there are the readers who want to tear my head off or have great ideas for stories about things like cats that roller-skate."

"Well check it now," she said, irritated. "Oh, and it's not mosquito season. Is it earthquake season there yet?" A click sounded at the end of the line.

Sighing, Jack logged on to AOL and heard a depressingly cheery voice say "you've got mail!" He braced for his daily dose of communications overload. There were 27 messages. He began by deleting, unread, the ones he suspected offered ways to say goodbye forever to fat, make $75 an hour at home, and extend "Mr. Happy" by up to three inches. As he scanned the list for personal messages, a communication popped up in the upper left corner of the screen. It was an instant message from Tiffany Hot Lips, who inquired if he'd like to have a little fun with randy college girls. He declined,

Hit the spam button, and AOL promised Tiffany would never bother him again. Now his list had shrunken to 19 messages. He dumped more messages from addresses he didn't recognize and got down to 5. A Laura 37 had sent one.

He opened it. A brief message informed him her designated monitor, Patricia Rossi, would be calling to arrange the next contest and that she had been in contact with Marion Sally. That was it. No "good luck." Not even a "looking forward to cleaning your clock again." He logged off and mused. I wonder what this Pat Rossi is like?

He found out the next day. Patricia Rossi's telephone call caught him between stories at work.

"Hello," Jack responded curtly, not because he was busy, stressed out, or unintentionally abrupt. He was intentionally abrupt. As a cub reporter, Jack had been taken in hand by a veteran assistant city editor that had been cursed with having to take frequent calls from the public because the city editor, his boss, avoided them. "Be sharp," the editor had counseled. "Not rude, mind you; there'll be complaints—but curt, as if your valuable time is being wasted. That'll put callers on the defensive. You'll be in a better position to deal with dumb complaints or silly ass suggestions for stories."

Jack took his advice. Of course, he had other telephone personas. Most good reporters did. His other personas exuded sympathy, skepticism, warmth, agreement, and, in severe cases of assholes-who-were-eating-up-his-time-and-wouldn't-take-no-for-an-answer—barely restrained anger.

He immediately discarded all of them upon hearing her voice.

"Hello? Mr. Kileen? My name is Patricia Rossi. I'm Laura Sanders' designated monitor."

Her voice resonated in his mind: low (but not *too* low); slightly sexy (but not *too* sexy), and melodious (*very* melodious) with just a hint of hesitancy he found charming. He leaned back in his chair and closed his eyes. He liked to listen to the voices of women he had

met for the first time on the telephone and try to visual-
ize them.

"Mr. Kileen? Are you there?" She sounded worried,
the way people get when they fear the telephone system may dump them into the endless loop of voice
mail from hell. "This is Pat Rossi, Dr. Sanders' designated
monitor."

"Yes, this is Jack Kileen," he replied.

An image began to form in his mind. She was youthful, probably in her 30s. College educated. She had
used the term "designated monitor" without hesita-
tion. Confident. Someone experienced in dealing with
people. A saleswoman? Smooth. A woman comfortable with herself, used to being accepted. Whether
she was a blonde, brunette or redhead he couldn't
tell, of course. Imagination had its limits.

"Go ahead," he said encouragingly, switching into
his warm, puppy dog persona.

"Have you gotten a telegram with instructions for
Saturday's contest?"

Jack let her voice wash through his mind.

"Yes."

"Good. Then I'll meet you at (she rattled off an
address) at about 8 a.m. Do you know where it is?"

He recognized the street as being in the Richmond
District, not one of the pricier sections of San Francisco.

"Yes, I'm familiar with the area."

"Good." She sounded relieved. "I'll have $100 for
you. I'll accompany you to the store and then we'll

return to the apartment complex. It's being renovated. There will be other painters there, but they'll save a room for you to paint."

"Oh, goody."

"Oh, one other thing. I'll have my son with me. Jimmy is 12. You don't mind, do you? I'd rather not leave him alone. I promise he won't be in the way."

Jack opened his eyes and blinked. "Oh, no. That's okay. See you then."

His image of her went from color to black and white. He saw a slightly overweight hausfrau who would spend the morning berating her juvey hall-bound son.

The next morning he discovered how misleading first impressions can be, especially over the telephone. Patricia Rossi turned out to be a slender, dark-haired woman on the short side of 30. She had hazel eyes and a dusting of tiny freckles on her nose. She filled a long-sleeved blue blouse nicely (he always noticed that first), and he suspected her close-fitting jeans concealed shapely legs.

She waited in a used and abused station wagon and got out of the vehicle quickly as he approached. A boy followed, but not as quickly. He seemed to be limping.

"Hi. I'm Pat Rossi. You must be Mr. Kileen. She extended a slender hand. "This is Jimmy." She stood behind the boy, wrapping both hands about his shoulders protectively.

"Yes, I'm Jack. Hi, Jimmy."

Jimmy nodded gravely, studying him with the quiet reservation of a child encountering an adult for the first time.

"Well, you've got a busy day ahead," she said, "changing a tire, painting a bedroom, and washing a dog. What order do you want to do them in?"

"The tire, the painting, and the doggie bath, but let's get the painting supplies before stores get crowded."

"I can follow you to wherever you want to get painting supplies," she said. "They gave me cash to pay for them."

"Let's take my car." He gestured to a nearby Toyota 4Runner. "You don't want to lose your parking place," he said. "This is San Francisco. Parking is a challenge even on weekends."

"Don't I know it," she said, fishing in her purse. "I didn't bring lots of change."

He scooped a handful of quarters from a pocket. "My treat. Lunch, too."

She accepted eight of the quarters, handed him two one-dollar bills, and looked at him coolly. "We'll see."

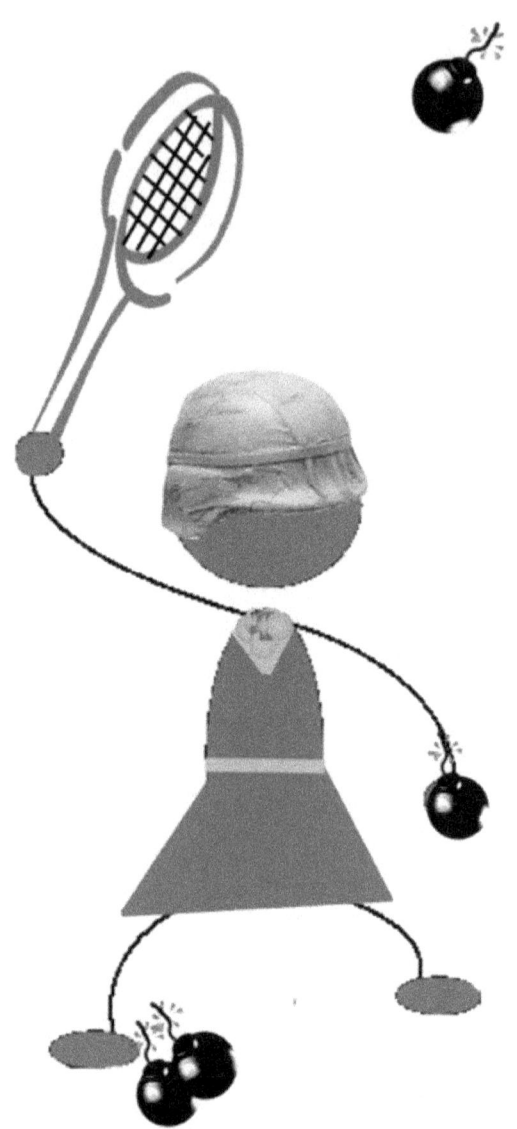

Chapter 16

*Win any way as long as you can get
away with it. Nice guys finish last.*

LEO DUROCHER

The Do-It-Yourself Emporium parking lot was jammed with the vehicles of would-be handymen and a handful of women determined to be their own plumbers, electricians, and carpenters. Outside, at the edge of the parking lot, day laborers chatted in Spanish, hoping to pick up cash jobs and earn a few non-taxable dollars.

Jack stopped first in the auto department, where he bought a four-sided lug wrench, which got him a puzzled look from Pat.

"We'll be going to the auto dealer's first," she said. "I'm pretty sure a wrench comes with the car."

"Not like this one," he replied. She hesitated, started to speak, and stopped.

In the paint department, he bought a cap, several small brushes, and plastic buckets in which to stir paint. The paint would be provided on site.

"That's all you need?? Pat asked.

"For now," he said, smiling cryptically.

Back in the car, she said, "Okay. If you're set, we can go to the auto dealer now."

"Not yet. I've got one more stop to make." After the engine started, he shifted into drive and pulled out of the now-congested parking lot and headed up Geary Boulevard.

"How do you like the wheels, Jimmy?"

The boy patted the seat. "Leather. Way cool, Jack. Why don't we have leather, mom?"

She made a face.

He pulled into a rental supply store.

"Why are we stopping here?" she asked suspiciously. "You've got the paint supplies."

He grinned. "You'll see. I still have to get my secret weapon. Wait here."

He bounced out of the car and went inside. Ten minutes later, he returned, carrying a large box, which he shoved into the back of the 4Runner.

"What's that?" she asked.

"A power paint roller. It's quicker."

"Wait a minute! No one said that you could use power equipment," Pat protested. "I'm pretty sure Laura isn't using any."

He looked smug. "Nobody said I couldn't, either. Let's head to the auto dealer."

In Fort Myers, Laura had decided to tackle the painting first. Appraising the room in a newly reconditioned Homes for Humanity project, she relaxed a little. No one was likely to complain about the quality of work being done free. Still, she knew that a more skilled volunteer painter would be around later to touch up any mistakes.

Laura rolled plastic sheeting over the floor, carefully poured the paint into a pan and adjusted the telescoping roller. She'd tackle the ceiling first. But before beginning, she walked over to the tape deck and speaker she'd brought and slipped in a CD. Stravinsky would be nice to start with, she thought, perhaps "The Rite of Spring." After that, she'd switch to Tchaikovsky's "1812 Overture." She loved the ringing chimes and cannon fire at the end.

Like most homeowners, she had painted before. Now, dressed in worn sneakers, torn blue shorts, and a faded shirt, she was ready. Show time! Squaring the cap on her head, pigtail pushed through the hole in back, she turned. "Start the countdown."

Marion Sally, who chauffeured her around getting supplies, glanced at his watch and made a notation in a small pad almost lost in a large black hand. "The clock is ticking," he said.

Laura had gotten a telephone call from him the night before. Sally identified himself and arranged to meet her in the morning. She had looked up to him from the first. He towered over her by more than a head.

His voice, quiet and assured, didn't fit such a big man. He blocked the doorway, wearing pressed jeans, western shirt, desert boots, and a quizzical expression. He carried a Thermos and a copy of the how-to-get-rich book currently at the top of the nonfiction list. He had also brought a folding chair.

"Please call me Laura," she said.

"Marion," he responded. "Are you ready?"

"What was my time?" Jack wheezed, dropping the lug wrench. It clattered on the concrete floor of the auto dealer's repair shop.

Pat looked at her watch. "Four minutes and 52 seconds."

"My best yet," he crowed.

She looked at him curiously. "Have you done this before?"

"Sort of," replied Jack.

The morning raced by for Laura. She had decided to do the painting first, even though it took longer, to get the toughest test out of the way. She assembled an extension pole and roller and started to work. Soon the ceiling and three walls glistened with fresh paint. Only one wall and the trim remained to paint. She paused to catch her breath. Sally moved his chair periodically, keeping out of her way. The music had stopped, and he looked up, suddenly aware of the silence. "Say," he said, "you didn't happen to bring any Elvis, did you?"

Jack sized up the room. He examined his equipment and supplies. Paint... *check*. Plastic floor cover... check. Masking tape for the moldings and windows... check. Brushes for touch-up... check. Power roller...check. Extension cord... Uncheck! He had forgotten to bring an extension cord!

"Where are you going?" Pat asked.

"I'll be right back," he blurted and dashed out of the room, almost knocking over an opened gallon of paint.

"That's it, I'm done." Laura rotated her head several times, working stiff neck muscles. Afternoon sun bathed the room, and the bedroom's walls now gleamed with a fresh coat of off-white paint just like millions of other bedrooms in America.

"I think that you did well," Sally said encouragingly. "I've never painted a room in only a few hours." He noted the time carefully in his notebook.

Laura collapsed in his chair. 'What's next?"

"The dog. It's right around the corner in the bathroom. I think you'll like him."

She did. The dog was a male golden lab, bored at being shut up in a 6x6-foot bathroom. He hurled himself at Laura, giving her a lavish wet tongue greeting.

"This is Duke," said Sally, smiling. "I think that you'll get along fine."

And they did.

"Where's the manager?" The panic in Jack's voice got the attention of two painters, who were sprawled on the floor taking a break in one of the apartments. "Downstairs. First floor," one offered. Jack flew down the stairs and stopped at the door with the sign that read "Manager." He knocked loudly. The door opened and an unshaven, gray-haired man in worn khakis and a white T-shirt looked at him quizzically.

"I'm painting upstairs. Have you got an extension cord I can borrow?" Jack said breathlessly. The manager considered the question, and Jack braced for the worst. This could cost him the contest!

"How long?" the manager asked.

"What a good dog!" Laura dried Duke's last paw and tried, with limited success, to dodge his slobbery tongue. Duke wagged his tail and panted in delight. Laura attached the leash and opened the bathroom door. "Done," she said. "That's an affirmative," Sally replied, noting the time in his little book. "Ready to change a tire?" Laura leaned wearily against the bathroom wall. "I guess so," she said without enthusiasm.

Pat stuck her head through the open door. Jack was power rolling the walls. The paint flowed off the roller smoothly and evenly. The extension cord was a nuisance, but the time and slopped paint saved by not having to soak the roller repeatedly were worth it. In the background, the Beatles wailed about a hard day's night. Like they knew, Jack thought.

"Hey, got a minute?" she asked. Jack shut off the power roller.

"Take a break and meet your next challenge."

Jack took off his paint shoes and stepped out into the hall. Jimmy restrained—barely—a large dog tugging on a leash.

It was black and white, with short, stocky legs and a deep chest. A large black patch surrounded one eye, and its head looked as if someone had clamped it in a vise and taken a few too many turns. Eyes, narrow and small, disappeared into a tapered skull. It didn't look like man's best friend.

"That's a ..." Jack began.

"Bulldog," finished Pat.

"No, I've seen pictures of dogs like that on TV," he said hesitantly. "Wait! That's a pit bull! They're vicious."

She stretched out a hand and patted the dog's head. "Phooey. Watch. Roll over, Rambo." The dog licked her hand and then obediently turned belly up to be rubbed. She rubbed its tummy vigorously. "See, he's really friendly."

Jack looked doubtful. "Nice doggie," he said and reached out a hand tentatively. Rambo jerked back and sprang to his feet, baring his teeth in a snarl. He gave a guttural, threatening growl.

Jack pulled back the hand hastily. "That's it! I'm not giving a bath to a pit bull. Get another dog!"

Pat shook her head. Jimmy looked at him questioningly.

"This is the dog they dropped off," she said. "I don't know if I can get another one."

"Try," Jack said, picking up his paint cap. He handed her his car keys. "I've got another hour or so of painting." He left the room. Down the hall, Pat could hear Billy Joel lamenting about the tribulations of a piano man on Saturday night. She wished it were Saturday night and she was somewhere else.

"Let's go get another one, mom," said Jimmy. "Bad dog, Rambo!" Rambo panted and wagged his tail but didn't appear contrite.

They returned within an hour, just as Jack was touching up spots with a small brush. He worked quickly and deftly, careful to wipe excess paint off the brush on the rim of the paint can, whistling now and then. At last he stopped. "Time," he said with satisfaction, stepping back to admire his work. Pat noted the time on her notepad.

"What do you think?" he asked.

"It's okay."

"Okay! Rembrandt would be proud of this! Did I ever tell you what I did one summer in college?" He didn't wait for an answer. "Painted houses. Inside and out."

"It looks nice," she said grudgingly. And it did. The yellow coat gleamed in the light from the bay window, and she couldn't see any spots on the window or door-frame. Although she didn't say it, she doubted if Laura could do as good a job. She knew that she couldn't.

"Did you get another dog?"

She nodded. "It's outside in the hall." She turned and preceded him out the door, the fumes of fresh paint following them.

Jimmy had a new dog on leash, but this one sat docilely at his feet.

"What is it?" Jack said suspiciously. He didn't know where the hair ended and the dog began.

"It's an old English sheep dog," Pat replied. "Isn't it adorable! I told the woman at the kennel that you had a phobia about dogs and needed an absolute pussy cat to bathe. Look what they provided!"

"I don't have a phobia. I'm just cautious," he said.

"Oh, is that what you call it? Well, here's Lady Eleanor Randall IV, ready for a bath."

Lady Eleanor Randall IV's tongue hung out as if she constantly tasted the wind. She sat obediently, paws together, black nose twitching slightly. Her eyes disappeared in a tangle of white and gray hair that flowed from the top of her head to her nose. Lost in patches of white, her paws looked five inches wide. Lady Eleanor appeared to be more powder puff than dog.

"Couldn't you get something with less hair?" he grumbled. "No Chihuahuas available?"

Pat felt a twinge of guilt. Actually, there *had* been a Chihuahua available, but she had no intention of making his life easier—not after the lug wrench and the power paint roller.

He reached out tentatively and patted the dog on the head. Lady Eleanor Randall IV looked bored.

"I guess it'll do," Jack said.

Laura leaned on the wrench handle and bore down. The car quivered on the jack and the salesman looked worried. The sticker price was $34,500, not including sales tax, destination, and preparation charges.

Sally couldn't restrain himself. Someone (likely Laura) could get hurt here.

"You've never changed a tire, have you?"

"No," she said, "I always called AAA."

"It usually works better if you loosen the lug nuts while all four wheels are still on the ground."

She looked up. "Really? I must have missed that in the manual."

Sally shrugged. "Safer."

"I usually call AAA if I have a problem," she said. She sighed, lowered the car, loosened the lug nuts, and began to raise it one click at a time, frowning. Gee...this will take a while.

Jack led Lady Eleanor Randall IV into the bathroom and shut the door. He filled the tub with warm water.

"Okay, dog," he said, "into the tub."

Lady Eleanor looked at him through the shock of hair covering her eyes. She didn't move.

Jack sighed, picked her up and placed her in the tub. Whistling, he began soaking and lathering the dog, which panted softly.

He expected to win both the painting and tire-changing contests. He scrubbed Lady Eleanor with vigor. A sweep lay in sight!

Sally shook his head as Laura tried for the third time to lift the spare tire, place it on the wheel, and get the lug nuts started. He looked at his watch... nine minutes and counting.

Finally, she succeeded, tightening the nuts quickly and then ratcheting the jack down rapidly. Too rapidly. The car bounced. The salesman swallowed.

"How did I do?" she said, slumping against a wheel.

"Not bad, not bad," he lied. "About 13 minutes."

Rinsed but still soaking wet, Lady Eleanor shook herself vigorously, spraying Jack thoroughly. He stood up, swearing to himself, and opened the door wide.

"Jimmy, throw me another tow..." He never got to finish the sentence. A bolt of gray and white flashed past him, barreling down the hallway. "Stop!"

Lady Eleanor had no intention of stopping. Pat, who had gone out for coffee and come back, turned a corner, blocking the dog's flight. Lady Eleanor swerved into an open doorway. Shouts followed, then a string of curses. The dog ran past him and Jack dove to the floor in an attempt to catch her. Lady Eleanor eluded him and darted past Pat, startling her into spilling a cup of coffee over her blouse. From his position on the floor, Jack watched the dog disappear around a corner. White paw prints marked her path along the green carpet. Jack looked up into the faces of two angry painters.

"Was that your dog knocked over the paint, asshole?" one inquired.

At Action Central for the *Mari O'Reilly Show* (that's how Cliff Hansen liked to think about his office), Hansen took calls from Pat Rossi, who wanted the show to pay for a new blouse, and Marion Sally. He picked up the phone and dialed Mari's extension. She waited impatiently for the call.

"Well? she asked without preliminaries.

"Kileen," Hansen said. "He went two for three with better times in the painting and tire replacement. If he hadn't lost the dog, he might have won all three."

"But Dr. Sanders is still ahead, right?"

"Right. But it's turning into a race, isn't it."

Mari said nothing. A race wasn't what she had had in mind.

An hour later an intern pursuing a master's degree in theater arts adjusted both of the tiny figures on the V for Victory scoreboard. Laura bobbed slightly above Jack.

Laura 125, Jack 100.

Cpter 17

"The son-of-a-bitch!" Mari hurled the newspaper to the floor. "Did you SEE it?"

"*It*" was a two-picture photo spread in the *Daily News* that showed Jack kneeling beside his SUV in the carport behind his apartment as he practiced changing a tire—and then doing it with a smile at an auto dealer. The slightly fuzzy carport photo had come from the video shot by Jack's neighbor, Mrs. Dumbrowski, who had rushed to a TV station with the tape and then reveled in her moment of fame.

"He p-r-a-c-t-i-c-e-d," sputtered Mari, dragging the word out as if it were obscene. "And that's in addition to renting a power roller and using that, that...whatchamacallit on the car!"

"Four-handled lug wrench," Cliff Hansen offered helpfully.

"Men are such bastards!" Cindy Martinez agreed. She had just broken up with her latest boyfriend, a used car salesman she had met at a singles bar who had gone back to his wife and two children.

Mari and Cindy looked at Hansen.

He smiled weakly.

Jack muttered at the fickleness of the weather god as his Toyota 4Runner splashed through muddy potholes in the flooded parking lot of the Sun and stopped. Rain pummeled the car with staccato blows like the pounding of tiny hammers wielded by midgets. He cut the engine and watched the windshield wipers carve a final arc across rain-dimpled glass.

Welcome to the other San Francisco, he thought, the one the Chamber of Commerce never brags about. This wasn't the image of The City by the Bay most non-Californians got from television. Instead, they were treated to a magical playground in harmony with nature—rust-red filigree of the Golden Gate Bridge stretching to the Marin Headlands...a majestic blue-green bay speckled with tiny white sails...quaint wooden cable cars, climbing steep hills like the Little Engine That Could. Not solar panel-gray skies disgorging torrents of liquid punishment.

As he sprinted to the employee entrance, Rasheed "Downtown" Jones acknowledged Jack's arrival with an airy wave of the hand from a warm, dry wooden shack.

After shucking his raincoat, Jack sat back at his desk, attacking the daily crossword puzzle, his only pretense at intellectual accomplishment. What was a four-letter word for imperial Russian ruler? Ah...czar!

"And this is our Challenge of the Sexes star!"

Jack looked up. Sherril Baines, the paper's managing editor, Features and Lifestyle, stood by his desk. With her was a short man dressed in a dark business suit, white shirt, and red-and-blue striped tie.

"Jack, this is Tom McKeon. He's down from our corporate office in Chicago to see how we're running things here." She smiled a too-bright smile and her words had a slight edge.

If McKeon picked up on the tone of his introduction, he didn't show it. "Nice to meet you, Jack. You've really upped traffic on the Sun's website. Scored a lot of hits."

"Really? said Jack. Ahhh…the bean counter! He'd heard rumors another round of staff reductions was in the works. This was the guy who'd wield the knife, sparing the newspaper's executives from getting blamed about blood on their hands.

"Oh, yes," McKeon continued. "I didn't see your blog, though. You'll be starting one, of course."

Jack blinked. "Sure." Me? A blogger? R…i…g…h…t.

"Are you on Facebook? Twitter?"

'Well…"

"Look into it," McKeon said. "Embrace the technology." He turned to Sherril Baines. "The paper is covering the story, of course."

"Absolutely," she said. "Bob Yee, one of our best reporters, has been interviewing Jack."

Jack squirmed in his chair. Yee was a nuisance and an asshole. But he'd had to talk to him. Being interviewed was more fun in the taking than in the giving.

"This could be a real shot in the arm for circulation. And," McKeon paused, "circulation boosters like this justify keeping specialists on board."

"Specialists?"

"You know, feature writers like yourself, columnists, graphic artists. People who really aren't critical to getting the paper out—value-added personnel is the term I like to use."

Jack nodded. "And if the nonessential staffers become too expensive, what with union contracts and all, the Sun could save money by outsourcing what they do, maybe to China."

McKeon ignored the sarcasm. "Well, actually, India is more likely. More English speakers. Some papers are outsourcing routine reporting of government and police right now. Anybody can read a meeting agenda or a police report and write a formula story, right?"

Jack looked at him closely. Was he serious? He suspected McKeon wasn't a journalist and had never been one. He was a suit from the corporate accounting department. "I suppose," he said, keeping his voice level even though his pulse wasn't. "But don't you think reporters can do it better and more accurately if they actually know the people they're getting information from?"

"Well, yes," McKeon conceded, "but again, that's value added. People will buy the product even if they don't get that, and they're certainly not willing to pay extra for it. They'll still buy the paper for the comics, TV listings, obituaries, and the state, national and international news. We can get that from the Associated Press and other syndicates. Of course, if advertising should recover and classified ad revenue comes back..."

They shared a moment of silence, contemplating the loss of what had been before the dawning of the Internet.

"Craig's List is the anti-Christ," Jack said with passion.

McKeon turned to Sherrill and beamed. "I like him! He's got the right idea. Good luck in your race. Sherrill will be looking into a promotional tie-in."

She nodded and forced a smile.

"Gee, nothing would please me more," Jack replied.

She shot him a warning look, and the guided tour moved on through the newsroom.

Across the aisle, he could see Stan Morrison, the Sun's King of the Road writer, working on another column that answered readers' complaints about the nightmare of commuting on the Bay Area's busy thoroughfares. Road rage, pot holes, oblivious cell phone users, intersections with cameras...there was no end to the pressures facing drivers daily. Never mind the lack of parking.

Jack studied Morrison and felt a sense of foreboding for both of them, like Winston Smith's premonition of stepping into a grave in "Nineteen Eighty-Four."

In Florida, legs thrust under the table, slumped in a chair, Ashford Sloan (a.k.a. Toby Linderman) tried to (a) stay awake and (b) get comfortable. In the darkened room, Dr. Laura Sanders illustrated different types of managerial hierarchies, the red dot from her infrared pointer darting across the screen from chart to chart. Occasionally, she bent over the film projector and removed a transparency, a ghostly white glow bathing her face.

Sloan endured being in a classroom again but just barely. The class ran for two hours and fifty minutes, one night a week, with a 20-minute break thrown in; but sitting on a hard wooden seat and having to pretend interest was draining. Still, after two weeks of class, he was on a first-name basis with most of the other students.

At Ohio State, Sloan had majored in girls, keggers, and sports, squeezing in the odd class here and there. When he did work hard, it usually occurred in a writing class. He had a gift for vivid prose and discovered journalism let you stick your nose into other people's lives and get paid to poke around in them.

He didn't intend to hang around until the end of the semester living one night a week in a motel. But for now, he played the dutiful student, quiet and attentive, taking notes industriously in a spiral notebook on whose cover he had written in bold, black letters, Toby Linderman, Ed. 554. A nice touch, he thought.

His note taking wouldn't have passed scrutiny. When Alice, the scrawny, dishwater blonde with the whiny voice, had observed male managers who denied promotional opportunities to qualified women like herself were chauvinistic sons of bitches, Laura appeared sympathetic, and Sloan had written "agrees male bosses are s.o.b.s."

Graduate seminars tend to be informal, and Laura typically wore slacks and a long-sleeved blouse. Slim and attractive, she looked younger when she let her hair down. But Sloan had his eye on other game. He joked during breaks with Jody, a talkative redhead who flashed an engagement ring but still glanced at him occasionally as if he were a roast she was considering buying at the supermarket. And he decided not to ignore Sarah, a quiet, pretty brunette, who exuded an innocent sexuality he found intriguing. He decided to try and get some telephone numbers during the class break.

His eyes closed briefly and he jerked awake. Laura noticed Sloan's head snap back.

"Okay," she said. "I think it's break time. Twenty minutes. Make a quick coffee run to the cafeteria if you need to do it."

When the break ended, Sloan had batted .500. He had gotten Sarah's telephone number but not Jody's. Damn tease!

But Laura found her students had little interest in discussing managerial hierarchies. They wanted to talk about her experiences in he competition.

"What's next?" the scrawny blonde asked.

"I believe it's the cultural literacy competition," Laura said, trying to shut off the discussion. "But the subject is so broad that I don't know how to begin preparing."

Restrained chuckles. Finally, a professor had to do some studying, too.

"Why don't we help you?" one student volunteered.

Laura shook her head. "How..."

"We could each take a subject area, history, geography, government, or something, and ask questions in class."

Laura considered the suggestion.

Sloan sat upright. Ah, that had possibilities. He scrawled "malfeasance?" in his notes. Using public facilities for individual gain might play.

Laura shook her head. "No. It would take too much class time. Tell you what, why don't you come out to my place on Sanibel Island Saturday night? I'll whip up some quiche and we can see who's smart."

"I'll bring some wine," Jody volunteered.

"Chips and dips for me," chimed in Linda. Linda, the quiet one with the tiny glasses and braids down the back of her denim coveralls, rarely spoke. She made no attempt to appear attractive (the other women at least wore makeup), and Toby had the feeling a wrong comment from someone could launch a rain of tears. They agreed on 8 p.m.

"Will you be able to join us, Toby?" Laura asked.

"Oh, yes," he replied. "Wouldn't miss it for the world." A boyish smile lit his face. Sloan decided he'd offer to pick up Sarah and work on Jody at the party. Two birds with one stone.

Pat Rossi thumbed the stopwatch as Jack lunged past, face red and contorted, breath rasping loudly in the brisk morning air. She shivered in slacks and an Arroyo College nylon jacket. He sweated heavily in shorts and a worn 49ers sweatshirt, the arms of which had been hacked off at the shoulders. They had the track to themselves. Classes didn't start for another hour.

The thought crossed her mind Jack was cute in shorts and had tight buns as he slowed to a jog and then to a walk, arms flailing the air. "Stop that!" she reprimanded herself. "This is the enemy!"

Right now he didn't look like the enemy, only a middle-aged guy coming to grips with the realization a mile seemed to be longer than it used to be.

"How'd I do?" he wheezed, hands on hips, the words spilling out in short, painful gasps.

"Beats me. But whatever you did, you did it in five minutes and fourteen seconds," she replied, studying the stopwatch.

"Should be enough," he said, flexing his left leg, which had started to cramp. He doubted if Laura Sanders played pick-up basketball at the "Y" or pounded a treadmill at a fitness center. Not that he did either, at least not regularly, but some exercise was better than none, which he fervently hoped was what she got. He needed a solid win big time.

Back in San Francisco only two days, he had faced part of the Challenge of the Sexes physical contest, a one-mile run. Rather than ask Pat Rossi to drive into the city again, he offered to hop an early morning Bay Area Rapid Transit train out of San Francisco and ride to Union City. She had picked him up at the station and driven to the college, where he had changed into running togs, loosened up by doing stretching exercises, and prepared to run a mile on the college's dirt track. Fresh from a good night's sleep, he thought he might be able to knock off a five-minute plus mile as he had been doing at the "Y" in San Francisco.

"Got time for breakfast?" he said. "I'm buying if the student union is open."

The breeze blew a wisp of hair across her eyes, and she brushed it away with a graceful gesture. The snug jacket with the large Gothic letter A on the front hugged her slender figure.

Jack smiled and hid his thoughts. "Too bad she's dragging a kid along in her wake."

She shook her head. "I've got a comp class in 45 minutes. I've got time for coffee and that's all."

He showered quickly in the men's gym, treated her to a hurried bagel and coffee at the college union's snack bar, and caught a taxi back to the train station.

As the seared, yellow Hayward hills rolled by his train, Jack tried, with little success, to concentrate on his reading. But the combination of the rhythmic motion of the train, fatigue, and boring nature of the book he held dulled his concentration.

The train shuttered to a stop at the San Leandro station. He opened his eyes abruptly. The book on his lap, "Dummies Guide to Cultural Literacy," slid to the floor. In desperation, Jack had gone to see Charles Beaumont, the Sun's senior editorial writer. Beaumont had listened without expression as Jack explained he had to beat a college professor with a Ph.D. in a cultural knowledge contest.

Jack had always admired editorial writers. Unlike the wage slaves in the newsroom, editorial writers always occupied glass-walled cubicles lined with shelves of books. When he met one in the men's room or in the lunchroom, the writer usually seemed deep in thought.

Beaumont had a salt and pepper goatee, round shoulders, and always wore a white shirt and tie, apparel Jack reserved for weddings and funerals. From infrequent conversations, Jack credited Beaumont with a logical mind, a finely tuned sense of social injustice, and an almost encyclopedic knowledge of arcane trivia. He settled most of the contested bets in the office, yielding only to the sports editor on baseball, which he found boring.

"What do you read?" Beaumont asked.

"What do I read?" Jack considered the question, searching for a trap. "Well, the paper, of course, Time Magazine, and Sports Illustrated. I get the New York Times on Sunday, and when I'm in the barber shop I like to look over GQ and Yachting Magazine."

"Yachting Magazine?"

"Well, the money people pay for those big boats is out of sight," Jack said. "I like to see how the truly rich stay afloat."

"That's it? No books?" Beaumont looked stunned. "Not even novels?"

"Just the books I need for research when I write," Jack said. "Actually, I'm not even sure what cultural literacy is," he admitted.

"It's anything and everything," the editorial writer explained. "It's the sum of man's experience in Western culture—history, geography, science, literature, religion, economics, music, and technology. And that's just a start."

"Well, I've always been a fan of the West," Jack began, feeling better.

Beaumont sighed. "Not the American West, Kileen, the Western Hemisphere, our roots in European history."

"Oh."

Shaking his head, Beaumont turned to the crowded bookcase in his cubicle and extracted a fat bound volume.

"Browse this to get an idea of the scope of the questions they may ask. Is this like a game show where you can call someone for help?"

Jack shook his head. He should be so lucky. "I don't think so."

"Good luck, then. You'll need it."

Jack had set aside Beaumont's book quickly. The type was too small and the information too dense. Instead, he had turned to "Dummies Guide to Cultural Literacy." It had larger type and fewer dates.

Jack returned to the "Dummies Guide." He had finished—okay, scanned—the chapter on American history, nailing the question on how the Watergate scandal had developed, but failing miserably on questions about the Monroe Doctrine, the Alien & Sedition Acts of 1798, and causes of the Civil War. He turned to the chapter on religion. The first question on religion concerned the importance of the god Baal. Jack closed the book with a sigh as the train pulled into the Powell Street station.

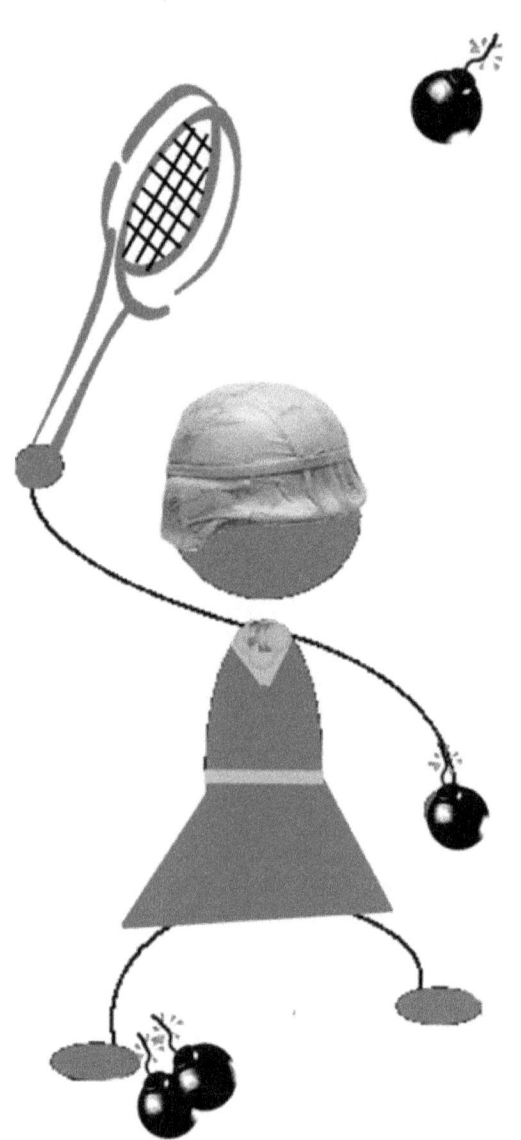

Chpter 18

Hope for the best, but prepare for the worst.

ENGLISH PROVERB

"My man!" Rasheed "Downtown" Jones leaned over and gave Jack a high five through the car window outside the Sun building. "No skinny little girl going to outrun my man Kileen!" He laughed and waved Jack into the parking lot. Jack smiled. Laura had huffed and puffed her way to a time of 7 minutes, 32 seconds, well behind Jack. That added 75 points to Jack's score and he had vaulted ahead of her for the first time, 175 points to 125. The little man in the bubble column bobbed on top.

He sat down at his desk and tried to bury himself in work but co-workers kept dropping by to congratulate him. By mid-afternoon, most of his energy had dissipated, and the letters were starting to run together on the computer screen. The cursor pulsed at him defiantly. He cleared the screen.

That night, a bottle of Anchor Steam ale in hand, Jack relaxed, watching TV. A commercial for an erectile dysfunction product appeared on the screen, and he muted the sound. It was his one admitted self-indulgence, a 50-inch, HDTV, wall-mounted flat screen that dominated the tiny living room. He cringed at the thought of what an earthquake bouncing the Richter Scale at 5.0 or above might do to his television viewing. A hockey game pitting the Rangers and Sharks filled the big-screen television, but he gave it only half his attention. If he missed a score, it would be recreated on instant replay. He turned up the sound. At least it would drown out the rumble of traffic drifting through an open window. The remnants of a partially consumed pepperoni and sausage pizza lay on the coffee table. He returned to the e-mail message printout on the table. It informed him the cultural literacy contest would be telecast live during the Mari O'Reilly show with satellite feeds from Florida and California. Mari would emcee.

"Fat chance," he belched. No way he'd showcase his ignorance on live TV. He had a bad feeling about the outcome of this contest. He couldn't run his way to victory, not against a female Ph.D. who probably spent weekends at the library. The contest pot had been fattened. Initially, the network had pledged a prize of $100,000 to the winner of Challenge of the Sexes. But once public interest soared, one of the program's sponsors, The Road Whacker Tire Co., which faced millions of dollars in lawsuits for manufacturing auto tires that had a distressing tendency to come apart at high speeds, decided to burnish its image. With appropriate fanfare, it pledged a $1 million prize to the winner of the contest. The runner-up would get a "special" prize.

Jack snorted. The only prize he had ever won was in third grade, shooting marbles. He would compete out of pride...and desperation. His only hope was that the runner-up prize wouldn't be a set of tires. He picked up the latest copy of Sports Illustrated Magazine. The copy of "Dummies Guide to Cultural Literacy" sat atop the toilet in the bathroom.

"He chickened out?" Mari chewed her lip, something she seemed to be doing more these days with the rising Nielsen numbers of Jerry Elkins. She glanced at her watch. Almost noon. She hadn't prepared for the afternoon's show, a check for the next payment on her beach house was late, and the manicurist had mangled a cuticle on her left index finger.

"Yes," said Hansen, rubbing it in. "He didn't offer a reason, either."

"Coward!" she grumbled.

Smart, thought Hansen.

"Did he give a reason?"

Hansen shrugged. "He didn't object to a closed-circuit feed. Doing it live spooked him, I guess." Privately, he agreed. Hansen had seen some of the questions suggested. Who could name three novels by Jane Austen? Who would *read* three novels by Jane Austen? Maybe a literature student struggling through a cow college English class.

Mari fingered her damaged cuticle absent-mindedly. "Okay, we'll tape it and run highlights the next day. Don't tell Kileen about the taping." She looked at Hansen thoughtfully. "Too bad we couldn't come up with a way to persuade him to go live." The implied criticism hung in the air like a pregnant fart. He got the message: You screwed up again.

Hansen nodded and thought about the telephone call he had received earlier that day. It had come from Jerry Elkins, Mari's newest competitor on the talk show scene, inviting him for a drink. He'd told Elkins he'd check his schedule and get back to him.

Across town, the ancient air conditioning system at Barnum & Ross publishers labored valiantly, trying to do too much with too little in a sweltering heat wave. At 2:13 p.m., it groaned to a halt. Jessica Longley barely noticed. She couldn't wait to tell her boss that "Alpha Male—Pride of the Pride" had risen to No. 82 on the Amazon book list, only six places below "Saint to Siren to CEO."

On Sanibel Island that night, party time had gotten off to a slow start, with Laura and the women exchanging questions on popular culture. Sloan tried to keep from yawning. He kept up on public affairs—anything likely to land on page one or even the opinion page—but he missed questions about literature, history, music, and science frequently. All those class cuts were catching up.

Dr. Sanders, on the other hand, appeared to be a … what was the term… a Renaissance woman, knowledgeable in a variety of areas. She impressed him. She had known frescos were paintings made on wet plaster and had cited Leonardo da Vinci's "Last Supper" as an example. He grinned. Lots of luck, Kileen.

As parties went, this was a No-Doz special, Sloan decided. He had seen better and livelier ones on week nights at his frat at Ohio State. He settled back on the sofa and took a sip of beer. Still, it had an upside. He was the only guy in a room with seven women at least four of whom were attractive. Plus, there was ample wine and music. Not up to the classic wet dream of knowing a rich, beautiful young nymphomaniac who owned a liquor store, but you couldn't have everything. And the chance—he hoped—to blow a little weed in the professor's house was too much to have hoped for.

"More spinach quiche, Toby?" Laura asked.

He blinked, still not used to being addressed by another name. "Oh, no, thanks. I'm full up. It's delicious, though, really."

She smiled. "I'm glad you could join us. Getting to know people is one of the real advantages of these small seminars." Laura wore loose-fitting jeans, a short-sleeved peasant blouse that Sloan thought wouldn't look as good on a real peasant. Her shoulder-length brown hair hung straight down. Unlike the other women, she wore no makeup. Well, maybe she doesn't care how she looks because I'm the only guy, he thought. His interests lay in seeing the other women let their hair down as the party progressed, figuratively speaking.

"I hope we can help you prepare for the cultural competition, Dr. Sanders," he ventured. "You must be under a lot of pressure. I certainly wouldn't want to match wits on TV." Oh, yeah...Too true! Too true!

Laura shook her head. "No, I'm not under a lot of pressure. This is information you either know or you don't know. Boning up won't really help although I wouldn't tell the other students that."

Sloan uncapped his second Dos Equis, having had the foresight to bring a six-pack. Wine didn't appeal to him, especially when it came from gallon jugs. He'd stick to beer. The women were loosening up now, laughing as they swapped grad school disaster stories, except for Linda, who smiled dutifully now and then but still looked unhappy. An eclectic mix of music, Pearl Jam, Faith Hill, Aerosmith, the Beatles, and Garth Brooks, bounced off the walls. Toby scoped out the professor's CD collection. Beethoven, Mozart, and Bach predominated. He also saw some country and western, jazz, and the Kingston Trio. The Kingston Trio? Golden oldies?

Plus, Sarah had allowed him to bring her to the party. She looked at him across the room and smiled. She hadn't seemed impressed with his rented Lexus, but had been relaxed and talkative as Fort Myers faded behind them in the warm evening. Jody, Toby noticed, hadn't worn her engagement ring. Hmm, what did that mean? He might just get a telephone number after all.

"Toby! Come over here! Take our picture!" Alice waved a digital camera in the air. He took two pictures of the women, arms about each other, wineglasses held high, and then reached into his pocket.

"Wait a minute. It's my turn." He pulled out a palm-sized camera with a short telephoto lens. "Hey, let's show a little life! Wave those glasses around!" Sloan fired off three quick shots from different angles and put the camera away. He chatted briefly with Jody and then wandered about the room, examining old photos of Sanibel Island that hung on the walls. They showed men in dark suits with starched collars sitting on the beach alongside women in full skirts who held parasols. No one looked comfortable or appeared to be having a good time. Not likely with the sand fleas.

Casually, Sloan worked his way around the room, cruising the chips and dips, munching on salted peanuts. With no one paying attention to him, he took a few more photos of the wine bottles on the table and of the women drinking. He managed one shot of Sarah and Jody and Alice with the wine bottles in the foreground.

Sloan slipped the camera back into his pocket. He noticed Dr. Sanders engaged in an intense conversation with Linda, who appeared to be crying. Dr. Sanders led her out of the room.

Intrigued, Sloan slipped out onto the screened porch, which wrapped around two sides of the cottage. He saw a light go on in a room at the end of the porch and walked over. Inside, Dr. Sanders and Linda were sitting on the edge of a bed, their backs to the window. Linda sat convulsed in tears, her hands buried in her lap. Dr. Sanders had an arm about her shoulders. She murmured something and consoled her. Sloan dug out his camera and adjusted the telephoto lens to its maximum reach. He turned off the flash and snapped off several shots. Satisfied, he returned to the party, noting, with little surprise, he hadn't been missed. It was all girl talk, all the time.

The party ended early. He parked the Lexus outside Sarah's apartment. The new moon rode high in the sky, and night air was redolent with sultry, earthy scents.

"Well, have I earned a real date?" He smiled winningly.

Sarah paused, clearly undecided. "I think so," she said at last. "Tonight was fun. I may have misjudged you. You gave me the impression you were just a guy on the make." She looked at him intently. "You almost never say anything in class. You're hard to read."

"I'm an open book," he protested. "Dinner next week?"

"Maybe. Give me a call." She opened the door and slid out. No chance for a goodnight kiss.

"See you in class," he said.

Sloan watched her walk to the door. He felt a momentary twinge of guilt, which he quickly stifled. He took a piece of paper out of a shirt pocket and transferred it to his wallet. It contained Jody's telephone number.

In California, Pat Rossi took a sip of red wine and put down her pencil, tired of marking sentence fragments, comma splices, and subject-verb nonagreements. Some Saturday night. In the game room, Jimmy watched the Dodgers and Astros on television. It had been thoughtful of Jack Kileen to come up to Union City to run, she mused. True, he had put her off with his manipulation of the painting and tire changing, but perhaps he wasn't such a jerk after all.

In Las Vegas, the betting line on Challenge of the Sexes changed to 7-5, with Jack the favorite.

Cpter 19

Caution: Cape does not enable user to fly.

BATMAN COSTUME WARNING LABEL

At 11 a.m. on the day of the cultural literacy test, Jack found himself sitting in a studio at a local TV station, waiting nervously as technicians scurried about setting up the closed circuit TV links. Laura also waited (but not nervously) in a studio in Fort Myers. Back in New York, Mari O'Reilly briefed the panel of experts who would ask the questions. Jack repeated his name several times into the mike as a test and the lights blinked on. The techies were ready, even if he wasn't.

"San Francisco is good to go," he heard.

"Florida is up," another responded.

"New York is on line."

The monitor in front of Jack came to life and a split screen showed Laura, fussing with a pearl necklace, and a panel of four women and three men, who looked even more nervous than he felt.

Mari took charge. "Mr. Kileen, Dr. Sanders, here's the format," she said briskly. "Each panelist will ask the same question of each of you, alternating the order of questioning. There are 14 questions. Neither of you will know the other's response because we'll cut you out. The scoreboard in back of me will register correct and incorrect answers. Ready to go?"

Jack wanted to ask if he could visit the restroom again. Too much coffee. He decided to gut it out.

"No questions?" Mari nodded. "Okay, good luck. The first question is on music."

The Princeton professor started. He beamed, cleared his throat, and the screen went blank.

"What the...?" muttered Jack.

"They cut us out," a young technician wearing earphones and a mike replied. "The lady is getting her question first."

"Oh."

Moments later the screen brightened and the professor appeared again on the monitor. "Mr. Kileen," he said portentously, "what composer wrote The Magic Flute and Don Giovanni?" Jack took a guess. He had hoped for something from the Beatles. "Beethoven?" he offered uncertainly.

The professor pursed his lips. "Mozart," he said, giving the clear impression that any of his students would have known the answer. Dummy!

The camera shifted to the scoreboard. A big goose egg registered by Jack's name. Ah! Laura had one, too! She had missed the question.

He felt a momentary sense of elation. Perhaps this wouldn't be so difficult after all! Bad guess. The next question came from a humorless woman with hair drawn so tightly behind her head Jack wondered why her eyes didn't bulge. She asked him who had remained in the spacecraft when Neil Armstrong had walked on the moon in 1969.

"Uh..." said Jack.

It didn't get any better. After seven questions, the score stood at Laura 4, Jack 1. He identified the line dividing Korea after World War II, the 38th Parallel, as did she. They both missed a question about T.S. Eliot's poetry; but then she knocked off queries on the founder of the Boy Scouts, countries belonging to the Common Market, and the oldest existing English novel while he floundered. She also scored on questions about the Mayan Pyramids, Brown vs. Board of Education, and Keynesian economics, all of which he missed.

The beat went on. Jack tanked. Final score: Laura 10, Jack 2. He had, however, nailed the question about the name of the involuntary muscular movement of the intestines and other tubular organs—peristalsis. Of course, that was a fluke. He recalled sitting in a large zoology lecture session in college while the professor droned on about the process of digestion, mentioning peristalsis. Alert! Alert! Jack's early warning defense system had gone ballistic. The final examination would consist of 200 multiple-choice questions. He had a hunch that peristalsis would be one of them. And it had been. Bull's eye! That provided scant satisfaction, unfortunately, despite the fact that Laura blew the question.

So Laura padded her score, and the little lady in the bubble column bobbed above the little man, 275 points to 175. Jack decided he didn't want to face Reggie "Downtown" Jones in the morning.

The next night, however, things looked up. He scored a date with Pat Rossi. She had had been attending an all-day educational conference at San Francisco State University and had called him to sympathize about his crashing and burning on the cultural literacy test. She didn't use those terms, but he got the message. On impulse, Jack asked her out to dinner. After a long pause, she accepted to his surprise and elation. He wanted help nursing bruised feelings after the disaster on the *Mari O'Reilly Show*.

They had just finished dinner in a small trattoria in North Beach. Half of the tables were empty, which didn't necessarily make the wait staff more attentive. They both passed on dessert but settled for cappuccino.

"Lighten up, Kileen," she advised. "Brooding won't help. It's history. How was the veal?"

"Good," he conceded, cradling a warm cup of coffee in his hands. "How was the pasta?"

"Okay," Pat replied.

He had picked her up on the San Francisco State campus and driven downtown. She wore slacks and a green turtleneck sweater, which contrasted nicely with her dark hair; he wore Dockers, a blue work shirt, and a leather jacket.

"Just okay?"

"Just okay. A little undercooked."

"I always have trouble with pasta," Jack admitted. "I can barely tell the noodles apart at Safeway. Thin, flat, round. It's confusing. How can you tell when it's undercooked?"

"I'm Italian. It's in the blood. My mother had me cooking pasta standing on a chair when I was 8."

She took a sip of coffee. "When it's undercooked, it's tougher, more stringy. Pasta is an art."

Jack nodded. He decided to change the subject. "Are you tied up this weekend?" he asked casually. "The weather looks promising. We could take a run up to Mendocino."

She looked at him intently before responding.

He took that as a good sign. Wrong.

"Let's not rush the relationship, all right?" She left the question hanging in the air.

Ah...relationship. Jack read that as a code word. Relationships meant different things to women than they did to men. To women, relationships had a capital "R." A man could have a relationship with a landlord if they discussed the 49ers' quarterback woes, with a barber whose tech stocks were in the toilet, or with a health club attendant who also suffered from tennis elbow. But not with women. Women saw a Relationship as the first step toward a Commitment.

The existence of a large gay male population in San Francisco meant women outnumbered straight men and had to work harder with a smaller pool of prospects to achieve the most desirable type of Relationship, the continuing kind, the one serving as a potential avenue to the Ultimate Relationship, wedded bliss. It placed greater pressure on dating expectations.

Long ago, Jack had taken to heart the advice of George Washington. In his farewell address as president, Washington had warned against "entangling alliances." Jack picked up on that, even though the Father of His Country had been referring to international affairs, not love. If recovering alcoholics had a 12-step plan to stay sober, he had developed a 9-step plan to stay single. So far, it had worked.

On the first date, Jack usually took women to the theater, followed by a quick drink at a popular bistro. He said good night with a smile and shook hands. The first date might well lead to a second date, so he displayed his sense of humor, knowledge of the theater (he brushed up on the play or show beforehand), and ability to be seen in public without causing undue embarrassment. That meant showing up with a fresh haircut, pressed pants, and polished shoes.

The second date always began at a trendy restaurant to show that he was no cheapskate. The evening usually ended with a light, fleeting kiss, more comrade-like than carnal.

The third date remained open, depending on mutual interests, but he used it to test the "whether." On the third date, he indicated clear sexual interest and read the reaction as to whether or not his date did. If she happened to be a skier, he might mention the current state of the snow pack at Heavenly Valley and feel her out about spending a weekend at Lake Tahoe; if she liked the arts, he might suggest the merits of an arts and crafts show in the wine country, followed by a Sunday brunch. In any event, the good night kiss wouldn't be brotherly.

The fourth date was make or break with sex at the top of the agenda. If the fourth date turned out to be unproductive, there wouldn't be a fifth. But if the fourth date *did* turn out to be productive in both a convivial and sexual sense, Jack would continue the relationship until the ninth date. About that time most women discovered the capital "R" in relationship and began to drop hints they weren't dating anyone else, or perhaps they should keep a toothbrush at his apartment, or that their parents in Orinda were having a family barbecue that weekend and wouldn't it be nice if they could drop in for a few minutes.

"We'll miss the movie if we don't hurry," Pat said, breaking the awkward silence.

Jack snapped out of his daydreaming. It was time to switch to Plan B for Date No. 2. Plan B was reserved for situations in which Plan A didn't fly, but in which he really wanted to get a date.

"Wait. How about bringing Jimmy down on Sunday, and we'll go to a Giants game. I'll get some good seats."

She hesitated, trying to read his expression. "You're sure?" she asked mischievously. "That's not like a weekend in Mendocino."

"Tell him to bring his glove. We can meet at the statue of Willie Mays. I'll call and confirm the time."

They finished the evening seeing a French film that had gotten three stars several years earlier. Apparently subtitles didn't bother critics the way they did Jack. He liked to let his mind wander during movies. But if you did that in a movie with subtitles, you invariably missed a line like, "Mon Dieu! That means Pierre is the killer and Monique is the one who betrayed the Resistance and can doom the Allied invasion!"

He drove Pat back to campus to pick up her car. They said good night with a firm handshake.

Later that night, unable to sleep, he wandered into the tiny kitchen of his apartment and heated water in the teakettle until it shrilled in protest. He ground some frozen Kenyan beans, got out his Bodum coffee maker, and prepared a cup of coffee. While the hot water and coffee granules achieved oneness, he brooded, debating whether or not to get out his little gray book. He mentally evaluated the dwindling list of female prospects. Cathy? Perhaps, but she flew the friendly skies of United Airlines and often overnighted in places like Waterloo, Iowa. Janice? No, she hadn't recovered from the arm she had broken while mountain biking on Mt. Tam. Catlin? No, definitely not Catlin. She hovered at Step 8 and had been looking at him more calculatingly of late as if he were a dress marked down 50 per cent at Bloomingdale's. He put the book away and brooded, surprised that he actually looked forward to a baseball game with a woman who had a 12-year-old chaperone.

Chapter 20

The unexamined life is not worth living.

SOCRATES

Coarse sand clotted between Laura's toes and frothy patches of foam bubbled and dissolved as she walked along the beach. The sky had lost its pink early morning glow as the sun began to assert itself. It would be a hot one. Even as a child, mornings, fresh and untainted, had been her favorite time of day. They presented a tabula rasa, ripe with possibility. For her, mornings constituted the best perk of living on Sanibel Island.

She nodded to an elderly couple walking hand in hand along the advancing and retreating water line. As she strolled Sanibel's beaches, she recognized familiar faces. The beach rat season had ended, the time when winter storms deposited their annual treasure of shells, luring collectors who prowled the ocean's edge at low tide, buckets in hand. Ponce De Leon, upon visiting the island, had named it "Costa de Caro-cles," coast of shells. Laura had her own collection of delicate sand dollars, ribbed horse conchs, and fan-like lions paws, some of which had been in the family for decades. They lined the mantel above the fire-place, served as ashtrays on end tables, and had been stuffed, carelessly, into various nooks and crannies of the bungalow. She inhaled salt air and stopped to watch two gulls squabble noisily over a piece of crab.

Before this crazy contest, her life had been like a placid pool of water, occasionally ruffled by breezes but never really disturbed. No more. She had been forced to get an unlisted telephone number and another e-mail address. Still, that hadn't stopped the flow of snail mail or the people who tried to track her down at work. Fortunately, her co-workers had become protective, referring strangers, usually reporters, to the dean's office. Once there, they encountered Morris Evander, who had proven a surprisingly effective bulwark, deflecting visitors with the curt promise they could "leave a note" in Laura's mailbox. She tore up most without a glance.

But she found herself having conversations with people she had hardly spoken to before, instructors in other disciplines, secretaries, and gardeners. She had been playing bridge on the computer one day when a custodian dropped in to empty the wastepaper basket. He stopped to chat.

"Say, professor, could I get an autograph for my daughter?" he asked, peering over her shoulder at the screen. His name was Julio, she learned. He had parents living in Havana. He had a low opinion of Fidel Castro and enjoyed playing duplicate bridge. Laura and Julio were now on a first-name basis and her office was cleaner.

Her life had changed in other ways. Normally, she resisted outside commitments and activities as a drain on time and energy. She dodged committee assignments whenever possible and steered clear of joining organizations, rationalizing the time was better spent in research and writing. She kept office hours for students as a professional responsibility. But all of a sudden, students who had never made appointments to talk to her outside of class lined up waiting to see her. Most wanted to discuss the Challenge of the Sexes, rather than grades, classroom assignments, and term papers. When Morris Evander asked her to play a prominent role in a fund-raising project for the university, Laura surprised herself by agreeing. The monograph she had been writing lay unfinished by the computer, and a stack of promising books remained unread by her bed.

And she had apparently gained a friend, albeit an unlikely one—Marion Sally. At first, the hulking, soft-spoken ex-football player had intimidated her. But after her depressing failure in the tire-changing contest (Laura feared she'd have to pay for damage to the car after it bounced off the showroom floor), he had bought her dinner, calmed her down, and offered encouragement. Sally had called last night to congratulate her on winning the cultural literacy competition.

"You may not be able to change a tire," he laughed, "but I won't play 'Trivial Pursuit' with you unless you're on my team."

She shaded her eyes from the glare and gazed out over The Gulf of Mexico. The green water near the shore faded to metallic blue, flecked by lazy cream-colored waves. The breeze had died. The sand under her bare feet grew warmer. Her eyes drifted to the horizon and back. She sighed. Time to return to the real world.

While Laura enjoyed an early morning stroll on the beach, her *Glimpse Magazine* student/spy Ashford Sloan stared at the unmoving cursor on his computer screen. With mechanical patience, the cursor had blinked at him from the same spot for several minutes, waiting for a command from the keyboard to continue its passage across the screen. Not likely. Unable to sleep, Sloan had risen in the darkness, showered, jumped in his car, stopped for a bagel and orange juice at an all-night drive-in, and driven to *Glimpse*'s editorial offices. But now, several hours later, he faced a serious writer's block. He stared at the sentence on the screen.

"Worried residents of Benton Harbor, Michigan, have swamped local authorities with reports of a giant alligator sighted swimming off crowded Lake Michigan beaches, terrifying vacationers." Actually, it had been a report to police, probably by a drunk, Sloan decided. But it had the potential for a story if...

Nada.... Zip.... Idly, he typed the word running through his mind: Sarah. How had he come to this? Sarah Ellen Morrison. He saved the alligator file, which had been going nowhere fast, and closed it out. Probably it had been a bad idea to stay over two more days in Fort Myers after Sarah had finally agreed to have dinner with him. He had sold the front office on the delay by claiming he was doing research, which, in a way, happened to be true.

Dinner, at a small restaurant with checkered table-cloths and candles that he had scouted out, had gone well. Wary at first, she began to unwind after a glass of Merlot. Smart and funny, she had a cute little mole near the left corner of her mouth that twitched slightly when she smiled. They began the delicate dating ritual of The First Serious Conversation.

"Why did you finally agree to go out with me?" Sloan asked in his Toby persona.

"Well…" Sarah traced an invisible design on the outside of her wine glass "… you were persistent and handled the 'chicks plus one' party well. Most men would have been driven out of their minds and left early. You stuck it out."

I wanted to see if you if you were just jerking our chains, trying to score she thought.

They both laughed.

"I enjoyed it. I've never been the only male with so many attractive females," he lied.

Well, two out of six isn't bad. Jody is a knockout, too.

"All of us?"

That's baloney sliced thin.

"Well, most. Present company included."

You stand out like a 100-watt bulb among the 25-watters, babe.

Sarah eyed him appraisingly. "You're not what I expected."

Of course, my expectations weren't that high after that sob story about a sister who died.

"What did you expect?"

Here's where I get points for a willingness to accept criticism.

"Honestly?"

What's that line from Disney's "Mulan"—Reflect before you act?

"Honestly. I'm a big boy. Beautiful women have hurt me before."

How's that for combining a compliment and "give me your best shot" at the same time?

She hesitated. "I thought you were a manipulative jerk trying to score.

Let's see how you handle that, sport.

His smile faded.

"You didn't look like a student or act like a student," Sarah continued, toying with a paper napkin. "I'm not sure you do now." Her voice held a question.

Well, that's out in the open at least.

"Appearances can be deceiving," he countered, with a sincere and but slightly wounded expression.

Ouch! She goes for the jugular. But I asked for it.

She nodded. "Yes, they can. And I'm glad they have been."

Maybe I've been unfair. I'm not cutting him any slack.

Over the course of the evening, he found out she was 26, a certified public accountant (surprise there!), and enjoyed soft rock, crab cakes, and "American Idol." She also had parents, long divorced, living in Miami.

Sloan told her he was between jobs, had graduated from Ohio State with a business degree, liked hockey, enjoyed Broadway theater music, and avoided TV as much as possible. He didn't mention he really earned a living writing wildly sensationalistic stories for a lurid tabloid, especially after she mentioned reading the *New York Times* regularly.

When they had closed the restaurant hours later, Sloan drove Sarah home, politely shaking her hand at the door to her apartment. She surprised him by agreeing to take in a film fest with him the next night to see "Vertigo." They were both Alfred Hitchcock fans.

The next night, when he dropped her off after the movie, Toby read "yes" in her eyes and kissed her. The kiss rated an 8 on a scale of 10, and the hug accompanying it hadn't been lightweight, either, he reflected.

Sloan stared at the blank screen and groaned. Then why did he feel as if he'd used a phony placard to park in a handicapped parking space?

A flashing light, followed by a ringing telephone, interrupted his thoughts. He picked up the receiver and heard the voice of Larry Clayton.

"In early, aren't you, boss?" he said to the managing editor.

"I'm always in early. You just aren't here to see it usually. Where are you on the Laura Sanders story? I'm seeing lots of ink on Challenge of the Sexes features; unfortunately, none of it's ours."

"Working on my piece as we speak."

"Good, because class time is over. There are only a few more events left. She's ahead on points, and we'll go with the story while it's still hot. Booze with students, a lesbian angle, and marijuana marathons, right?"

Sloan cursed under his breath. In justifying his soaring expenses (he had put the dinner and filmfest on his expense account, too), Sloan had also padded his description of the party as well. "Booze, yes," he said, "but the lesbian angle is iffy, and what I smelled might not have been weed."

There was silence over the phone. "Spare me the 'maybes.' We do innuendo, remember, just like politicians? Crank it out and forward me a copy of the file. Then the lawyers can agonize over it. I'll pass the croc story on to someone else."

"Alligator," corrected Sloan absent-mindedly.

"Whatever." Clayton broke the connection.

Sloan decided to get another caffeine recharge. He had some hard thinking to do.

Chapter 21

Rasheed "Downtown" Jones looked up briefly as Jack pulled up at the entrance to the parking lot. He shook his head sadly and returned to reading the financial pages of The Sun.

Jack winced. I've let the side down again.

Once inside, he buried himself in work, returning calls, setting up interviews, and doing research. Maggie stopped by his desk to commiserate and offered to buy lunch. Jack declined. He didn't feel like eating. Coworkers turned away quickly when he detected them eyeing him furtively. The next shoe to fall would be the technology test. He had better ace that one.

Meanwhile, in New York, the Committee of Seven met in the conference room of the Eugene P. Doyle Theater, home of the *Mari O'Reilly Show*. The professor from Princeton was in a snit. First, he had been out-voted 4-3, along straight gender lines, to determine who would serve as chair and get to sit at the head of the table. That dubious honor had gone to the nonprofit executive. The rabbi had been the swing vote, and the professor had lost her, despite making a number of pointedly pro-Israeli comments. Worse, the guy from Michigan State University (largely unpublished, definitely second tier) had a summer cold and filled the chilled air with sneezes and wheezes, decimating the box of facial tissues on the table in front of him.

"Can we please get started?" the doctor asked. A urologist, he had tickets to that afternoon's matinee of the latest smash Broadway hit imported from London. No way he intended to miss that.

The nonprofit exec, who hadn't wanted to chair the committee in the first place, put down her orange juice and took charge. "This is the technology contest. It requires computer research, digging out the answers to a variety of questions, and sending an e-mail message with the results to the committee." She looked puzzled for a moment and then brightened. "That would be me, I guess, as chair."

"So what, precisely, do we have to do?" queried the educator from MIT. A professor of engineering, he took a straight-line approach to life's problems.

"Just decide on some questions, I guess," she suggested.

A spirited discussion ensued lasting about 20 minutes, during which the doctor kept sneaking peeks at his watch. Eventually, they came up with five questions they felt could be reasonably researched on the Internet in a limited amount of time. They decided the contest would be held simultaneously in San Francisco and Fort Myers, under monitored conditions as usual.

"Well, that wraps it up, I guess," wheezed the Michigan State guy, starting to rise.

"What about the platform?" asked the MIT professor.

The chair looked puzzled. "What do you mean, 'the platform'?"

"Do they do this on a PC platform or on an Apple platform? Or can they choose the one they prefer?"

Silence filled the room. "Whichever platform is used, they both should use the same one," suggested the rabbi. "No unfair advantages."

"You can't expect someone used to PC to deal with a Mac or the other way around," protested the still-irked Princeton prof.

That led to an even more spirited 30-minute discussion, sometimes barely civil, of the merits of PC vs. Mac computer technology. The urologist had given up taking concealed glances at his watch and stared at the clock on the wall with obvious irritation.

Finally, the nonprofit exec had had enough. "We're not getting anywhere," she said. "Let's let them use whatever computer they have at home. The guy works on a newspaper so he's probably used to using a PC. The professor could be using either a PC or a Mac."

Agreeable murmurs rose about the table. Its work done, the committee adjourned. The urologist led the rush to the elevator.

That Saturday, bright sunlight streamed into the bedroom converted into a den on Sanibel Island. Laura cleared off space around her iMac and looked at Sally. "When can we start?"

He looked at his watch. "Soon," he said. "Soon."

In San Francisco, Pat glanced about Jack's apartment. With the windows open, the sounds of traffic made conversation with normal tones a losing proposition. He had cleared a corner, largely by shoving furniture to one side of the small living room. Magazines overflowed a metal rack, spilling out onto the floor. Some were months old.

A second-floor walkup with high ceilings, the apartment had been built in the 1920s or earlier. Light streamed in through unblocked windows and reflected off shiny hardwood floors. A dining room, or what had once passed for a dining room, led to the tiny living room, which held a battered wooden table with cigarette burns and two chairs, one a comfortable leather lounger, the other a worn armchair. A baseball glove, videotapes, and a sweatshirt formed a pile in one corner. Unopened cardboard boxes lined a wall. In the center of the ceiling, a scalloped round plate hung like a giant nipple, covering where a chandelier had once hung. A hot water radiator, rust visible through chipped white paint, projected from a wall, relic of another heating era.

Student book shelves—pine boards resting on cement blocks—rested against a wall. Like many writers, Jack was a pack rat when it came to books. He had never met a book he didn't think there would be a future use for. That's why he still had a Boy Scout's Handbook, a college biology text, and the 1989 World

Almanac. The oddest book in his collection was "Everything You Never Wanted to Know About Scat!" The latter, an autographed copy, had been given to him by an outdoor writer on a Stockton newspaper, where he had once worked. The writer had become enamored with identifying the droppings of animals in the woods. He had spent a year taking color photographs and getting expert opinions on dried and desiccated leavings of deer, bear, squirrels, mice, owls, and raccoons. Unfortunately, the world hadn't been ready for a book demystifying animal defecation. It had sold 13 copies. Like many people, Jack's serious reading had ended in college.

Pat sipped from the last unopened bottle of water in the refrigerator, which, she noted, contained yogurt with expired dates, carelessly wrapped cheese, apple juice, and a half-filled takeout container of something or other that had contained peppers now coagulating in fuzzy fashion on the top and sides. Amber bottles of Anchor Steam beer lined the bottom shelf of the door.

"I had forgotten how bachelors live," she marveled under her breath.

For this event, Jack had dressed California comfortable: worn hiking shorts, a frayed gray T-shirt, and Teva sandals. He itched to get started.

His Dell computer waited by a window.

"Can we go?" he asked plaintively, looking at his watch again.

"Not for seven minutes," Pat said. "I have an obligation to Laura Sanders to make sure that you don't cheat this time."

"You don't even *know* Laura Sanders," he protested.

"I know her at least as well as you know Marion Sally," she responded sweetly.

They waited.

On Sanibel Island, the big hand reached 12 and the little hand pointed at 2 on Laura's grandfather clock. Unlike most grandfather clocks, this one actually had belonged to her grandfather. Chimes rang twice.

"Okay, we can start," she said.

"Whoa! Whoa! Not by my watch," Sally interrupted. "We're going by Marion Andrew Sally standard time." Laura's fingers drummed an impatient tattoo on the tabletop.

In San Francisco, Pat counted the seconds down: "Ten, nine, eight, seven, six, five, four, three, two, one... Go for the gold!"

Since each already had an Internet connection, they were up and running in no time. Jack made his connection at 11:02 a.m., Pacific Daylight Time. Laura made hers at 2:01, Eastern Daylight Time. The race began.

Laura turned in her chair. "Okay, I'm on line. Where are the questions?"

Sally handed her a sealed envelope, which she hastily ripped open. He retreated to a corner and pulled out his cell phone.

"What do you mean, you don't have the questions?" Jack demanded. His voice rose several decibels above the volume of street noise.

"I have it! I have it! Just wait a minute!" Pat fished through her purse. It had to be in there somewhere! She had pasted a yellow sticky to her bathroom mirror to remind her to bring the questions, which had arrived by courier the day before.

Laura scanned the sheet of paper and read: *Answer the following questions. Both speed and accuracy count. E-mail the answers to: nferlman@comweb. org.*

1. What's a googol?

2. Who first said, "When I hear the word 'culture' I reach for my gun."

3. When was the senior senator from Rhode Island born?

4. What's the current temperature in Anchorage, Alaska?

5. How much does it cost to take Amtrak from Chicago to Philadelphia?

She decided to follow her test-taking strategy from college and attack the questions from easiest to hardest. She'd start with the weather.

Pat dumped the contents of her purse on the couch and began to rummage through them frantically. Where was the envelope!

"I can't find it," she admitted at last, waiting for the explosion.

Jimmy looked up from his Game Boy. He had been sitting quietly by the window, punching keys.

"It's in my book bag with the lunches, mom. You asked me to hold it when we got in the car, remember?" He extracted the envelope and handed it to Jack, who frantically ripped it open and scanned the contents.

Laura looked under AOL's Channels but couldn't find a weather listing. She typed "weather" in the web address bar, which took her to AOL weather, where she typed in "Anchorage" under Search." Bingo! Forty-eight degrees and cloudy.

Pat shut off her cell phone. "You really didn't lose any time," she said, trying to placate Jack.

"What...?" he said distractedly. He swung around. "How would you know..."? He saw the cell phone disappear in her purse. "You and Sally are exchanging information," he accused.

"Knowledge is power," she replied.

Jack returned to the computer. He had heard the word "googol" before. He started to try his favorite search engine, Google, to see if he could find googol. "Googol" in "Google?" Then he stopped. Wikipedia was in his menu bar. The Wikipedia listing explained a googol was the digit 1 followed by 100 zeros in decimal form.

Laura decided to attack the political question next and logged on to Yahoo! In the search window, she typed: "Rhode island senators." Wikipedia was an option and she went there. The names of Jack Reed and Sheldon Whitehouse popped up. She accessed their biographies. Reed's Senate service dated to 1997 and Whitehouse's to 2007. Reed was senior. Two questions down.

The hum of cars, trucks, and an occasional motorcycle grew. Pat walked to the window and shut it. Jimmy gave up the Game Boy for one of Jack's magazines, on which a smiling, scantily clad woman in a revealing bathing suit pouted on the cover.

Pat took one look and grabbed it. "Playboy? Find another magazine."

"Oh, mom!" he protested.

Meanwhile, Jack had become oblivious to everything but the task at hand. He had gotten the weather in Anchorage and knocked off the political question, using a different search engine. The Amtrak question looked tougher.

Laura, on a roll, decided to stick with Yahoo!. She typed "amtrak chicago schedule" into the search window. It gave her several choices, but she selected the official Amtrak website. When that came up, she typed in information for a theoretical trip by an adult. It cost $195 to ride from Chicago to Philadelphia.

Amtrak had turned out to be easier than he had expected. Jack went to the last question, the quote. He typed the words, in quotation marks, into Google's search function and waited. Damn... The first listing attributed the quote to Hermann Goering, Hitler's air force commander. But the second linked it to Joseph Goebbels, Hitler's chief propagandist. Aaaarrggghhh!

He went on the second page of references. He scanned an article titled "Eternal Fascism" by Umberto Eco and read: Thinking is a form of emasculation. Therefore culture is suspect insofar as it is identified with critical attitudes. Distrust of the intellectual world has always been a symptom of Ur-Fascism, from Hermann

Goering's fondness for a phrase from a Hanns Johst play ("When I hear the word 'culture' I reach for my gun") to..."

He sat back thoughtfully. Perhaps Goering and Goebbels had only repeated the quote. Suppose it had originated with an obscure German playwright....

Laura glanced at the time at the top of the computer screen. It made her nervous. Goebbels or Goering? Gobbels or Goering? She decided to count the name credited with the quote most and go with that. Goering by a nose. She filled in the last answer in her e-mail and sent it off.

Jack recalled the results of a study about how long it took for frustrated Internet researchers who couldn't find the answers to their questions to explode into "search rage." It had been 12 minutes, and he neared that now. Goering or Gobbels or Johst? He made his choice and fired off the e-mail message with the answers.

Pat put down the cell phone. "Dr. Sanders beat you by two minutes, 40 seconds," she said quietly. Jack turned off the computer. "Care to join me in a beer?"

But, he would discover the next day, the race isn't always to the swift. Laura had won on time, but the panel had, after more research, invalidated her Goering answer and accepted Jack's.

In New York, the little man bobbed higher in his column of water, edging past the little woman. Jack 325, Laura 275.

In Las Vegas, the odds changed accordingly.

The next day, Jacked nursed a cup of coffee in the newspaper's lunchroom and checked his cell phone messages. He found one he couldn't decipher. It seemed to be in code. He called over one of the interns, a pert, leggy, blonde from Berkeley who was given to saying "wow" whenever someone told her something she hadn't learned in her past 23 years on earth.

"Kari," Jack said, "can you figure this out?"

She took the phone and read the message: LOL... A/S/L/P...BTWITIW/U!

"Oh yeah," she said. "It's a text message. Someone thinks you're hot. It means, "Laughing Out Loud...Age/ Sex/Location/Phone... and by the way, I think I'm in love with you."

She handed back the cell phone. "Someone wants to hook up with you."

Jack shook his head. "I don't have time for flakey women callers."

"Could be a guy," Kari pointed out.

Jack blinked. He deleted the message. He opened another message. It began: WTF! He deleted that one, too.

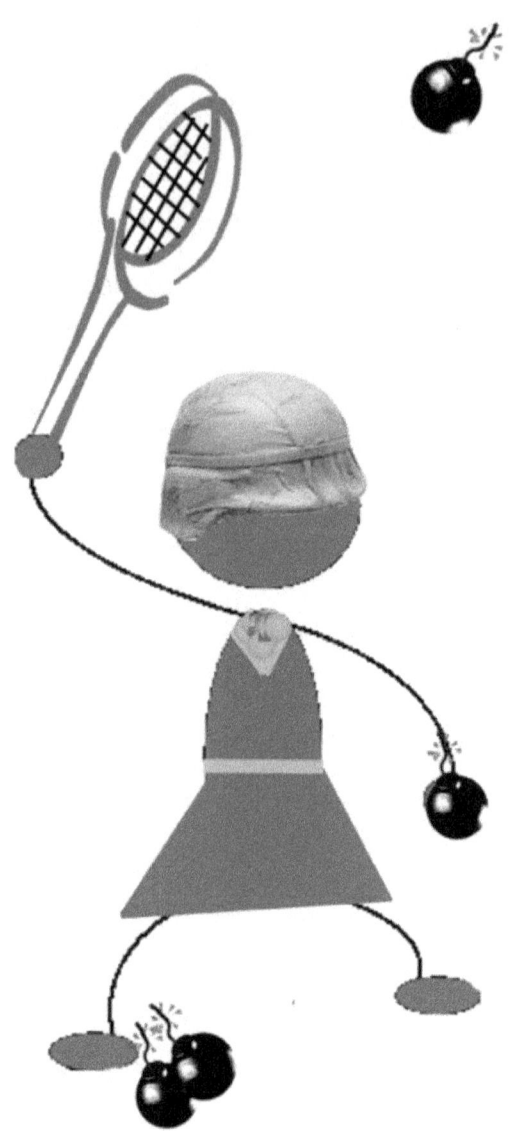

Chpter 22

You've got to take the sour with the bitter.

SAMUEL GOLDWYN

Ashford Sloan sensed trouble as soon as he walked, whistling, into the office. A note on his desk read *"See him __immediately.__"* The initials belonged to the managing editor's secretary. The whistling stopped in midnote. Sloan hurried over to Clayton's office. Clayton gripped the telephone, chewing out a freelancer late with an assignment. He continued the conversation without gesturing for Sloan to sit down. Clayton put down the phone and eyed Sloan wordlessly. He reached into an overflowing basket, retrieved a printout, and looked at it.

Sloan saw that it had been marked up heavily.

"What is this crap?" Clayton said at last. Sloan saw he held a copy of his story on Laura Sanders.

"Is there something wrong with it?"

"You bet there is," Clayton said sarcastically. "Who did you think you were writing for, the *Ladies Home Journal*? Where's the wild drinking party with minors? Where's the marijuana? Where's the illicit sexual relationship between a professor and one of her students, the betrayal of a sacred trust? He stopped, red in the face. "Where's the Ashford Sloan touch that has given our readers so much pleasure?" He threw the manuscript back. "Fix it."

Sloan slunk out of the office without saying another word.

In San Francisco, Jack pulled into the parking lot at the Sun. He looked for "Downtown" but didn't see him. After taking the elevator, he wandered over to the sports department. Maggie sat at her computer, eyeing the screen speculatively. She grunted when she saw him and waved him to a seat.

"With you in a minute, sport. Got to update something." Her fingers flew over the keys. She looked back at the changes and forwarded the file.

He yawned. "Where's 'Downtown.' I didn't see him in his shack. Vacation time? I thought that job was always a vacation."

Her mouth twisted. "He's been laid off, along with the night shift copy boy and two ad salesmen. Cramer in real estate went, too."

Jack slumped. Damn... The cost-cutters were sharpening their knives.

"What's up?" she said, changing the subject.

"I could use some good Giants tickets, three of them," Jack said. "Is the store still open?"

"Maybe... if you make nice-nice. You already owe me for getting Marion Sally to keep an eye on that too-bright lady instructor, remember?"

"Like you let me forget."

She smiled, the smile of a banker about to sign off on a high-interest loan.

"Play chauffeur for four Sharks games in San Jose when the season starts up."

"Two," he countered. "That's my limit. The Shark Tank is too chilly and the noise hurts my ears."

"Three. Last offer." She flicked ashes into a tarnished bowl inscribed "Golden Bears Rugby 1987."

"Two and I'll buy the beer," he said grudgingly.

"Done. You alpha males are always taking advantage of us weak gals."

He laughed. "Right. You and the other female barracudas."

"Why do you need three tickets? You don't have three friends."

"I want to take Pat Rossi, the woman who's monitoring me in the contest, and her 12-year-old son to a game."

"Aha," she chortled. "Bribery. I knew it. Or you're trying to score with mom through the kid."

"No," he retorted, "Jimmy, her son, has never been to AT&T Park." He thought for a second. "Come to think of it, she may not have, either."

Maggie nodded. "Then they should go. I'll see what I can do. Your account is getting overdrawn, you know, sport."

Impulsively, Jack said, "why don't you come along?"

She raised an eyebrow. "I don't think so. I don't know much about 12-year-olds. I'd be a drag."

"No. I'd like you to come."

"Really?" She stubbed out her cigarette and considered the offer.

"You could be the grandmother type he's probably never had."

Maggie coughed, and Jack stepped back from the cloud of smoke that hovered over the desk. "Not in this lifetime."

In the end, though, she agreed to come. Secretly, she was flattered—and curious. This Patricia Rossi might be interesting.

That Saturday afternoon, a cool breeze blew off the emerald waters of San Francisco Bay. Jack adjusted his sunglasses and offered more garlic fries to Jimmy, who declined. Pat and Maggie chatted like old friends, probably about him, he thought glumly. The Giants were beating up on the Reds, 4-1, so he relaxed and enjoyed the view.

AT&T Park had been built for more than $300 million in privately raised money. It seated 40,800, offered gourmet-quality food (the garlic fries notwithstanding), and had 457 toilets and urinals, which he found reassuring by the 7th inning stretch. Their seats in Section 209 offered a good look at action at first base, as well as a fine view of the bay, where cruise boats, bulk cargo carriers, and pleasure boats jockeyed back and forth. Closer, in McCovey Cove, a few kayaks and Zodiacs bobbed, their hopeful operators ready to pluck from the water any balls hit over the right field fence for home runs.

AT&T was among the sponsors that put its corporate stamp on the park, thereby forcing television sports announcers to intone reverently "we're at AT&T Park...." If the trend continued, Jack decided, every ballpark, football stadium, and Little League field would eventually shill for big-bucks advertisers. He could see it now. Yankee Stadium, the house that Ruth built, as Yankee Nissan Stadium. Or would it be Nissan Yankee Stadium?

They had met at the bronze Willie Mays statue outside the entrance to the park, the sky an azure canvas. Jimmy's glove, unfortunately, turned out to be a catcher's mitt.

Maggie, vivid in white slacks, purple blouse, and Giants jacket, looked nervous. She spotted them and walked over, smiling broadly. "Hi, I'm Maggie, Jack's main squeeze at the office."

Jack choked and Jimmy looked puzzled. "What's a main squeeze, mom?" he asked. "Is that like a squeeze bunt?"

Pat never batted an eye. "I'm Pat, and I'm not Jack's squeeze, outside the office or anywhere else."

"A squeeze is just a good friend," Maggie explained. "You must be Jimmy." She extended her right hand, which he shook hesitantly.

"Yes, mam."

"Oh, don't call me 'mam,' just Maggie."

"Yes, Maggie mam," he replied dutifully.

She nodded approvingly to Pat. "Polite kid. You don't see that much these days."

"Let's go inside," said Jack. He had already explained to Pat that Maggie had provided the tickets. "Nice glove, Jimmy, way cool," he said. Jimmy looked pained. "What's the matter?" asked Jack, baffled.

"I think that 'way cool' is out, Jack," offered Pat sympathetically.

He accepted the rebuke and scrutinized Jimmy. The kid wore a Stanford t-shirt, jeans, and sneakers. A nondescript cap, worn backwards, shaded a tanned neck nicely but left his face exposed to the sun.

"I can live with the shirt," commented Jack. (He had never forgiven Stanford University for dropping 'Indians' as its mascot and replacing it with 'Cardinal'; nor did the loopy green tree that danced around center court at Maples Pavilion during basketball games impress him.) "But we need to do something about the cap. You need a Giants cap. It's on me."

Pat started to say something and stopped.

"Wow, thanks, Jack," Jimmy exclaimed.

After Jack bought Jimmy a hat, they continued to their seats, which offered great sight lines of the field and boat traffic in the bay. The day wore on, a feast of warm sun, blue sky, and good company.

"All's well that ends well," Shakespeare had written, but he hadn't anticipated the Reds scoring six runs in the eighth Inning and winning 7-4. Jimmy didn't seem to mind. He waved his new Giants cap excitedly and cheered for every Giants batter. Maggie had left before the end of the eighth inning to return to the paper, and when Jack walked Pat and Jimmy back to their car, she gave him a quick peck on the cheek and whispered, "thanks."

All in all, a pretty fair day, he decided.

"Where's Cliff?"

Cindy looked up at Mari. She continued typing rapidly, engrossed in transferring Mari's scrawled handwriting from her brain to her fingers to the keyboard of the computer. She hated it when anyone interrupted her often too-rapid typing. Fortunately, the days of liquid paper correction had ended.

"Where's Cliff?" Mari repeated impatiently. Today's show in the can, she wanted to check on the new viewer ratings.

"He left early," Cindy said, shifting her gum. "He said something about a dental appointment, but there's nothing on his calendar."

Mari frowned. She didn't like the hired help leaving early, especially without telling her. "If he comes back, tell him I'm in my office and I want to see him."

Cindy returned to her typing. Where had she stopped? She got up to speed and then paused, torn between "it's" and "its." Oh well, the spellchecker would catch a mistake.

Cliff Hansen, however, hadn't gone to the dentist. He sipped a brandy Manhattan cocktail, seated in a booth in the rear of Hanigan's, a blue-collar bar on 40th Street, waiting for the one, the only, Jerry Elkins, star of the Jerry Elkins Show. The bartender, engrossed in "Wheel of Fortune" on a TV above the bar, ignored him. A sign over the bar bragged of offering the "Best Irish Coffee in Town!" That was clearly suspect since the bartender appeared to be Vietnamese. Elkins had suggested meeting at a more upscale drinking establishment on East 60th St., but Hansen had nixed that. It was too close to CBS and ABC headquarters, and he didn't want any word filtering back to Mari that he had been sleeping—oops—drinking with the enemy.

Elkins slid into the booth and loosened his tie. "Sorry I'm late. I had a last-minute production meeting. You know how those go."

Oh yeah, thought Hansen. "No problem. What's on your mind?" He was still nervous about sneaking out to meet Elkins. He wanted to get right to the point and get out of there.

A grandmotherly waitress, who apparently had been in hiding, came to the table and Elkins ordered a beer.

He flashed the all-masculine, full-toothed yet inviting, high-voltage smile that made the hearts of millions of women go pitter-patter from 3-4 p.m. every weekday.

"Okay, let's skip the foreplay," he said. "My producer's husband has been transferred to Seattle, and she's packing her bags, too. I need a new producer pronto, and the name that keeps coming up is yours."

That probably wasn't true, Cliff decided, but he guessed he'd probably made the short list of candidates.

"You've kept that show afloat for three years," Elkins continued. "I hear that the Challenge of the Sexes setup was your idea."

Hansen, impressed with his knowledge, felt flattered, despite himself. "Well...I contributed to it, of course," he replied modestly, "but Mari's the go-to-gal." He tried, and failed, to interject a tone of loyalty into his voice.

"Of course, of course..." murmured Elkins. "But perhaps you might want to consider moving on to new challenges, more responsibilities and more money."

"Oh, I couldn't leave Mari," Hansen said, joining the dance. "At least not now." Aha...the door had opened.

Elkins drew a gold pen from a shirt pocket, picked up a napkin, and wrote a figure on it. He shoved it across the table. "Not even for this?"

Hansen glanced about the empty room. "Why are you writing on a napkin? There's no one here but us."

Elkins sat back. "Don't you watch people do deals on TV? They always write on napkins. We're in television, right?"

Hansen nodded. Either that or at an electronic funny farm. He picked up the napkin and glanced at the figure. It amounted to $10,000 a year more than his salary. That equaled a year's private school tuition for his daughter. "I'm afraid that we're not on the same page," he said regretfully, sliding the napkin back.

Elkins' lips tightened. He studied Hansen's face, looking for an involuntary twitch of the mouth or a blink of the eye to indicate he was bluffing. He didn't find any. "Perhaps I can sweeten that." He crossed out the original figure, wrote a new one, and pushed the napkin back.

The napkin, smeared with purple ink now, didn't prevent Hansen from seeing the new amount, a figure $20,000 higher.

"What about vacation?" he temporized. "And I don't do fill-in stuff on other shows when Mari's off the air." (That wasn't exactly true. He *usually* didn't do fill-in stuff.)

"Not a problem. When I'm off, you're off," Elkins replied.

Hansen kicked it around. He didn't know squat about Elkins and didn't dare put out feelers as to his reliability, honesty, or track record in screwing his fellow man. Mari would find out. "You'll match the other perks?"

"What other perks?" asked Elkins. His face tightened in suspicion.

"These." Hansen pulled out a copy of his contract and handed it over. He had learned in the Boy Scouts to be prepared. Elkins scanned it rapidly. It provided for full medical, dental, vision, and psychiatric care, 401K payments, transportation and parking allowance, (excluding limos), state-of-the-art big screen TV and digital satellite service, subscriptions to the *New York Times, TV Guide, and Time Magazine*, and health club membership.

"Psychiatric care?"

"You never know. Producer on "45 Minutes" came to work with a bullwhip one day. Said he wanted more output from the writers." Hansen shrugged. "Stress."

"Yeah," Elkins said finally. "It's a deal." He squinted at the salary line on Hansen's contract again, but Hansen had blacked it out.

Encouraged, Hansen decided to push a little more. "I'll need to give six weeks' notice."

"No can do," Elkins said flatly. "That's a deal-breaker. I can give you two." They settled on three weeks' notice, less if Hansen could get away earlier. Hansen knew that even three weeks would drive Mari up the wall.

Then they shook hands and ordered another drink. Elkins admitted that some of his recent guests had been pretty weak, and Hansen told him not to worry. Where he went, his Rolodex followed.

Chapter 23

The most decisive actions of our life ...
are most often unconsidered actions.

ANDRE GIDE

At 1 p.m. Wednesday, Laura enjoyed just such a respite in the university's faculty club with her best friend, Gina Sabbatini. Gina munched the chef's salad with a Pepsi while Laura had succumbed to a piece of vegetarian pizza and bottled water.

As she looked about the room, Laura thought how misleading the term club could be. Mention the words faculty club and most people conjure up images of a London men's salon: members sunk in stuffed leather chairs perusing *The Times*, sherry in hand, as cigar smoke wafts upward and sunlight seeps in around drawn velvet drapes. Reality, of course, is often different—at least at a non-Ivy League, taxpayer-supported, southern state college. The faculty club at Florida Southwestern University consisted of two remodeled trailers linked together next to the campus cafeteria.

Venetian blinds substituted for velvet drapes, filtering glaring sunlight.

The décor was 1950s American kitchen with chrome-edged tables and aluminum chairs with plastic seats. A sofa and pole lamp stood against one wall scarred with torn tape from signs and posters. The faded sofa had broken springs. In an obvious attempt at fostering the spirit of collegiality, the administration had installed a faux fireplace, whose electric flames could be kindled at the touch of a button. Given that the temperature usually hung in the high 70s or 80s, this feature received little use. Utilitarian like the college it served, the room provided employees with a place to drink a hurried cup of coffee, enjoy the cafeteria's $3.98 cuisine de jour, or brown bag it.

What faculty and staff (no social barriers existed at the university) enjoyed most about the Faculty Club wasn't the ambiance but the fact it was the only student-free zone on campus. Harried instructors, stressed-out administrators, and overworked, underpaid support staff could escape, however briefly, the queries, requests, pleas, and complaints of those they were paid to serve. More than one college employee had been heard to remark, "This would be the ideal place to work if it we didn't have to deal with students."

"A dollar fifty for your thoughts" interrupted Gina.

"What...?" said Laura.

"Inflation. No more penny thoughts."

Laura smiled at her friend, a bubbly, chunky red-head with freckles, and unfailing good spirits. She reigned as the Molly Brown of the campus, unsinkable and upbeat. Of course, being a phys ed teacher who didn't give homework assignments, ask for term papers, and required only quizzes, not tests, improved her disposition. It also didn't hurt that she taught archery and social dancing. The students liked her because she let them boogie as well as waltz, and the administration liked her because she collected all of the arrows after class and had never had a student make like Robin Hood and skewer another student who resembled the Sheriff of Nottingham. Laura liked her because they had an understanding: Gina Sabbatini was gay but didn't push it. When they had met, Gina had taken in Laura's slim, compact figure, shoulder-length brown hair, and hazel eyes, and struck up an immediate friendship. It took Laura only a little while to realize that soulful glances, light touches, and offers to watch some "interesting videos" could lead to full contact sport in the horizontal mode. She had put an end to that quickly, but they had remained friends.

"My bio rhythms are off," complained Laura. "The intellectual line is ascending, but the emotional line has plateaued, and the physical one is headed down. I could probably balance my checkbook tonight, but I'd likely get depressed and eat a box of chocolates."

"Never trust a computer program," laughed Gina. "They'll break your heart every time. How *are* you doing?" she asked seriously.

Laura considered her response. "Okay, I guess. But I'll be glad when this thing is over, win or lose. A million dollars would be nice, I suppose, but I wouldn't know what to spend it on anyway."

Gina rolled her eyes. "Let me help. I've got lots of ideas."

They both laughed.

"Anyway, I'm ducking reporters, falling behind on my writing and paperwork, and losing patience with students who cut corners all the time.

Gina nodded in sympathy. "You're under a lot of pressure, kid, but hang in there."

"And I've got the income tax thing coming up next." Laura's shoulders slumped. "I don't even do *my* income tax. How am I going to figure out someone else's?" She brushed back some errant tendrils of hair from her eyes. They flopped back. Irritated, she pushed them away more vigorously.

Gina stood up. "Come on. I know what you need."

"What do I need?"

"A make-over," said Gina impatiently. "New hairdo, manicure, eyebrow pluck."

"I don't think..."

"That's the problem," she lectured, "you don't think of yourself, only others. Take the appointment I have with my hairstylist this afternoon. I'll make another. Alma loves reconstructions. After all, you're representing the university now. Best foot forward and all that."

Laura sighed and glanced at her watch. After all, she did have the afternoon free. Nothing awaited her at home except cleaning the house and Buffy's constant demands for affection. Perhaps she did think of others too much. Toby Linderman hadn't been in class last night for the first time. She hoped that he wasn't ill.

Jack didn't have a faculty club to go to for lunch. In a busy week of writing assignments, he squeezed in eating time at his desk, reading the first edition of The

Sun. In addition to the usual typographical errors, he found a number of interesting stories. Among them:

The producer of a series of action film megahits confessed on Entertainment Tonight he sometimes felt guilty about making violent, mindless, anti-social movies—but he'd probably continue anyway since they were so profitable.

A *Chicago Tribune* series about how winning the lottery ruined people's lives turned up one exception: an Illinois man who had quit his mailman's job, deserted his wife and three children, and was living happily on a beach in Tahiti with a 22-year-old exotic dancer named La Donna.

The remorseful president of a giant stock brokerage that had flamed out said he would return his salary and bonuses, repay a company loan, and sell his luxury homes in Aspen and Miami to bolster the company's gutted pension plan. His wife had him committed for psychological evaluation.

The annual *Sports Illustrated* Swim Suit issue was banned in Iran, driving the price of bootleg copies to 29,835 rials, or $15.

Meanwhile, a clerk at the Fort Myers office of the Internal Revenue Service provided Laura with Form 1040, Instr 1040, Package 1040, Instr 1040 (Tax Tables), Instr. 1040 (General Inst.), Form 1040 (Schedule A&B), Instr. 1040 (Schedule A&B), Form 1040 (Schedule C). Laura declined, for the moment, Form 1040, Schedules D and SE.

Ashford Sloan, aka Toby Linderman, completed his rewrite of the Laura Sanders article, forwarded the file to his boss, and went out and got drunk.

Cliff Hansen followed Mari into her office and shut the door. The shouting that ensued upset Cindy and made her make more typing errors.

That night, Jack got a call from Pat and Laura got one from Sally, directing them to be available at 11 a.m. the next day to participate in a conference call with Mari. The subject: adventure racing, the final test.

The next day, when they both had come on the line, she informed them the final contest would be held in October in Costa Rica. They would participate in one of the events of the international Enduro Challenge, a three-day race, pitting a dozen men and women who organized their lives around rigorous training in running, biking, swimming, paddling, and climbing. For that, they got to risk broken bones, heat stroke (or hypothermia), exhaustion, and sleep deprivation to win a prize that barely paid for airfare, meals, and post cards. Unless, of course, you considered it a perk to have friends and relatives see you on television mud-splattered, exhausted, and wigged out.

"Here's the deal," Mari said. "This isn't a team contest, like some of the adventure races. It's solo, every man and woman for himself or herself. They will be doing three events. The contest coordinator has agreed to let you tag along on one of them. You get to pick which one."

"How is it judged?" asked Jack.

"Let me turn you over to Jim Schaeffer," Mari said. "He's the Enduro Challenge coordinator. He'll answer your questions."

Schaeffer's voice sounded upbeat.

"Hi, folks. Glad to have you with us." He chuckled. "Don't worry, we won't expect you to do what the other contestants are doing. They've worked for a year to get in shape for this."

Should that make me feel better? Jack wondered.

Schaeffer went on. "There are no points for style. Fastest time wins."

Laura sounded wary. "What are the events?"

Mari sucked in her breath. In the back of her mind lurked the fear they might flat out refuse to do this thing. Then what would she do?

"Okay," Schaeffer continued. "The first event is a 62-mile bike ride."

"That sounds doable," Jack ventured. He had done 20 and 30 milers on weekends.

"The ride is through the jungle, some of it at night."

"Jungle?" said Laura.

"Oh, I wouldn't worry," Schaeffer reassured her. "The wild pigs aren't active at night and snakes usually avoid the bike path." He paused. "It's the weather that could be a problem. If it rains, the bike path can be a bit difficult in places. You might get stuck in mud and have to spend the night there."

An image flashed through Jack's mind of a river flowing across the bike path while darkness fell and clouds of ravenous mosquitoes arrived for a one-course meal. "Go on."

"The second test is much faster. Contestants will rappel down 107 feet into a cave, pick up a marker, and then climb out. This is essentially a technical and speed challenge. You'll be wearing coveralls, helmets, and gloves, of course, and small oxygen tanks in case of emergency."

Jack didn't like the sound of that. "What kind of emergency?"

Schaeffer laughed. "I'll bet you've never been in an underground limestone cave in the tropics. The temperature is above 110 degrees, usually, and the smells from mildew and bat guano..."

"Bat guano?" Laura broke in. "There are bats?"

"Yes, they nest in the cave during the day. Don't move around much unless they're disturbed."

"And noisy people with lights climbing up and down ropes doesn't disturb them, right?" challenged Jack.

"Well... yes, but don't worry. These aren't the vampire bats that drain blood. Besides, vampire bats usually only bother cows."

"Phew! You had me going there for a moment," Jack said.

Schaeffer ignored the sarcasm. "No, it's the spiders that are a concern," he continued, "because..."

Laura cut him off "Never mind. What's the third test?"

"River run in kayaks," said Schaeffer. "Twenty-seven miles on the Rio Verde, the first 18 in white water. Class 3 and 4 white water. Rocks, whirlpools, cauldrons, and waterfalls."

The telephone line went silent.

"Of course, we wouldn't expect you to do that, the white water section," he said hastily. "Far too dangerous. No, you'd put in below the rapids on a placid stretch of the river that rarely gets above Class 1. My mother could run it in an inner tube." Unless the river rises, Schaeffer thought, but that isn't likely. He decided not to share the possibility with Jack and Pat.

"There's an easy take-out point about eight miles down river, just before the rapids begin again. Miss O'Reilly will have a crew there to help you beach the boats." He decided not to mention that below the take-out point the rapids resumed at Caballito del Diablo, the devil's darning needle, where rock walls funneled the stream into a narrow, angry channel that hissed between jagged boulders. Jack and Laura sounded spooked enough already.

"Well, what do you think, gang?" Mari said heartily.

Jack decided that honesty, if not courage, offered the best chance of living to his next birthday. "I've only been in a kayak once," he admitted. "And that was in a two-person boat where I sat in front and didn't have to steer."

"I've never been in one at all," blurted out Laura.

"Not a problem," Mari broke in reassuringly. "This thing is a month or so away. We'll get you kayaking lessons and you'll be pros by then."

"They tell me that this stretch of the river is like a duck pond," said Schaeffer.

"You've never actually seen it?" asked Jack, doubt in his voice.

"Well…no…not in person, but I've seen photos and video. Really, I don't think that you've got anything to worry about. If conditions turn nasty, we'll just abort the run."

Jack shook his head. You won't need to, pal. I'll be a no-show.

The line was silent again.

Laura thought about snakes and bats and spiders. "Okay, I'm in," she said.

"Okey, dokey," said Jack without enthusiasm. "We get life preservers, right?" Most of his swimming was done at the "Y."

"Absolutely," replied Schaeffer. "Plus cell phones and GPS devices." He thought about adding first aid kits and survival supplies would be available but decided against it.

"Good! exclaimed Mari. "This will be a terrific finale!" She thanked them and hung up, visualizing the video possibilities for her show.

Chapter 24

*Fame is a vapor; popularity an accident;
the only earthly certainty is oblivion.*

MARK TWAIN

Jack threw his jacket over the back of the chair and collapsed into it, screening out the bustle of the newsroom. He had just returned from Capitola, down the coast, and interviewed artists who constructed elaborate sand castles with moats, drawbridges, and towers on the beach. It had been hot, the pungent fragrance of rotting seaweed had filled the air, and he had forgotten to take a hat or water.

The telephone rang. He groaned.

"Kileen."

"Tom Borston from the governor's office, Mr. Kileen. How are you doing today?"

"Fine." A lot better when people stop interrupting my recovery time.

"Good...good," his caller said warmly. "I'm on the campaign staff of Gov. Morris, and I just wanted to say that he's greatly impressed with both your book and your performance on Challenge of the Sexes."

Jack nestled the phone to his left ear. "What can I do for you Mr. Borston?"

"Jack, the governor would like you to join him for a one-day swing through the Central Valley Thursday. We'll fly into Stockton, Modesto, and Fresno for brief rallies at the airport and then hop back on the plane. Maria Morales will be along!"

Jack reached for the name. Maria Morales...Oh, yeah... the hot new Latin singer. He looked at his calendar. "I don't know, Tom, Thursday looks..."

The voice on the other end of the line gushed insistently. "The governor loved the book, Jack. We might be able to work in a few plugs. All you have to do is smile and wave."

"Is he still trailing the 'Destructor' in the polls?" The line fell silent.

Jack clutched the phone tighter. Oops, shouldn't have asked that. The "Destructor" was Johnny "Rambo" McLean, a millionaire former Australian surfer dude turned Hollywood actor. After roles in a few easily forgotten slasher films, he had morphed into a combination Silvester Stallone-Arnold Schwarzenegger-Tom Cruise action-adventure star that dominated the box office. Fans repeated his signature line, which he usually delivered after a fearful heroine warned him to be careful about a) entering a burning building, b) challenging heavily armed terrorists or c) facing a cyborg from the future. Pecs flaring, delts rippling, he guaranteed a triumphant outcome: "You can take it to the bank, ba-by!" In a state dominated by Democrats, Republicans saw him as a potential Moses, leading them to the Promised Land—the state house in Sacramento.

Gov. Eddie Morris, on the other hand, was a bland career politician who elevated no blood pressure. A former mayor and termed-out state senator, he had clawed his way up the political ladder by offending no one, advocating any and all social programs regardless of cost, and soaking up contributions from special interests like a thirsty lawn at the end of a drought.

In most states, his opponent the "Destructor," an actor without any political experience who starred in movies featuring explosions and car smashups, would have been laughed out of the governor's race. But this was California, which had already sent two ex-Hollywood actors to Washington, one as president.

"The governor is more concerned with getting his message across than in reading polls, Jack," Borston said. He injected a suggestion of disappointment in his response.

"You said that he liked the book"

"Well...he's reading it now, actually."

Jack nodded to himself. R...i...g...h...t. "Thursday looks bad," he said. "How about in a week or so?"

It might be a four-hour swing for the governor, but he would have to fly to Sacrament first and then fly home after the rallies. It would cost him a full day and he'd have to change his day off at work.

Borston hemmed and hawed. "Thursday would work out best."

And then it hit Jack. Next week or the week after wouldn't work because he might not be leading the "Battle of the Sexes." He might be losing, and politicians didn't hang out with losers.

Tempting, but... "Thank the governor for me, Tom," Jack said. "I'll have to pass, I'm afraid. I'll be happy to appear with him if he makes a swing back to San Francisco."

Borston, the warm draining from his voice rapidly, made one last appeal. "Jack, I suspect that you're a Democrat. Most working stiffs are. This is your chance to help the party."

Bad guess. "Actually, Tom, I vote independent," Jack replied. He felt a twinge of guilt because he numbered among the millions of people who only went to the polls during presidential elections. Too busy.

Friday wound down. He finished his piece on the fascinating art of sand castle construction and clocked out. The weekend was at hand. People often have exaggerated ideas of how bachelors spend their weekends, he decided. Wine, women, and song? More likely it's beer, laundry, and a video rental. He thought about the baseball game. That had been fun. He hadn't minded the kiss on the cheek, either. On a whim, he picked up the telephone and called Pat. She answered on the first ring.

"I thought you'd be out practicing your kayaking skills," she said after hearing his voice.

"Not funny. I'm still dumping sand out of my shoes after an assignment on the beach in Capitola."

She laughed. "What's up? Are the Giants out of town?"

"Beats me. I wondered if you might like to hop a train into town and have dinner Saturday night. No garlic fries and Coke, I promise."

She was silent for a moment. "Okay."

"Okay? Great!" His spirits soared, just the way they had in 3rd grade when he'd asked freckled Mary Lou Schecter if she wanted to get an ice cream soda and she'd said yes.

"I'll pick you up at the Powell Street station," he said. "Shoot me an e-mail with your arrival time. Say hello to Jimmy for me." He put down the telephone. Gonna be a good weekend after all!

Saturday was cool, so Jack and Pat decided to walk up the hill from the train station to the Mark Hopkins Hotel on Powell Street. After taking the elevator to the Top of the Mark, the 19th floor sky lounge, they relaxed over drinks and enjoyed the 360-degree, knock-your-socks-off, wrap-around view of San Francisco Bay. Tiny boats, sails mere flecks of white, danced on the blue-green waters. Bulk cargo carriers shrunken to the size of dimes inched their way to the docks in Oakland. As dusk settled over the bay, lights winked on in office buildings throughout the city.

For dinner, Jack took Pat to Fleur de Lys, a four-star French restaurant on Sutter, where they enjoyed the pepper-encrusted Hawaiian swordfish.

She looked at him suspiciously. "You certainly know how to impress a girl, Kileen. This beats that North Beach spaghetti place hands down. "

"You deserve the best, milady," he said. "Dessert?"

"No, not for me," she protested. "I'm full."

"Coffee, then." They settled back, savoring the moment.

"What now?" he said at last. "A movie... a show if we get lucky and score some tickets... or a night club?"

Pat sighed and patted her stomach. "Let's just take a walk and work off some of the calories."

They strolled back to Powell Street and walked south, past the tourists waiting for cable cars at Market Street and continued on to Fourth Street. Just down Fourth, they stopped and found a bench in Yerba Buena Gardens, a green oasis in a concrete desert. Traffic noise and people faded.

"This has been fun," he said, "but if you want real excitement, you should come kayaking with me."

"An expert already? How many lessons have you had?"

"Only one," he admitted, "but natural athleticism reveals itself early."

Pat looked doubtful. "I think I'll wait until you get more experience."

He glanced at his watch. "What train are you going to catch?"

"Are you trying to get rid of me already?" she said lightly.

He studied her half smile and dark eyes. Should he be reading more into her words? "No, I just thought that with Jimmy..."

"Jimmy's with his father this weekend."

That got his attention. She had never talked about her ex before.

"We rarely see him," Pat continued, "but yesterday Ralph showed up, new girlfriend in tow, and said he wanted to show Yosemite to 'Glenda.' He invited Jimmy to come along, probably out of guilt."

"Oh..."

"Yes, 'oh.' Jimmy jumped at the offer, so how could I say no? They're gone until tomorrow night."

He picked up on that quickly. "Does that mean we have Sunday, too?"

She looked at him. "If you want it.... and tonight as well."

They caught a cab back to Jack's apartment, which looked much neater than the last time that she had seen it.

"Did you get a maid?"

"Oh, no. I just straightened up a few things." Actually, he had spent the afternoon cleaning—just in case.

He opened a bottle of red and called out from the kitchen. "Put on some music."

Pat investigated his CD library and selected some Big Band music. When he returned with the wine, he put the glasses down and held out his hand.

"Dance?" Her eyes never left his as he took her in his arms, conscious of the warm pressure of her body and the fragrance of her hair against his cheek. Time dissolved as "Sentimental Journey" played in the background. They danced, Jack nuzzling Pat's neck. She drew away and studied him, her face serious. They stopped dancing, ignoring the music, and walked wordlessly to the bedroom.

After removing her blouse, she reached back and unhooked her bra. She let it slip to the floor and stepped out of skirt and panties. Kicking off her shoes, still turned away from him, she threw back the cover on the bed and slid beneath the sheets. Jack hurried to join her.

For a moment, neither spoke, both aware that soon nothing would be the same between them again. He kissed her gently, and then more assertively, the tingling of their bodies pressed together erasing the last distance between them. Tentatively at first, then with growing confidence, they explored the unfamiliar terrain of each other, touching, caressing, and kissing. When arousal changed to urgency, she guided him inside her. She shuddered and gasped, gripping him as tightly as he gripped her. In their lovemaking, they ascended a peak and then descended together. Afterward, heart still pounding and pulse still racing, he touched her cheek gently and kissed her closed eyes, his lips as light as the brush of a butterfly's wing.

She looked up.

"Are you..." he began awkwardly.

"Am I what?"

Jack stopped, unsure.

"I'm fine," Pat said. She ran her nails lightly down his arm and smiled. "I had pretty much given up on sex. I haven't been with a man for two years."

He exhaled sharply. "Two years…"

She looked amused. "This isn't a regular weekend activity for me, Kileen."

"I never thought…" His voice trailed off.

She gave him a look he couldn't decipher. "I know that you didn't." She waited for something.

Jack started to say something and stopped. He had run out of glib patter. He didn't know what to say.

Pat waited a beat and looked away as if making up her mind about something. Then she reached over and gave him a hug. "Thanks." Her voice caught for a moment.

"I've got to go." She threw back the covers and presented him with her slim, bare back. She began dressing.

"Go? Now?" He sat up in surprise. "Why?"

"I can still catch a late train to Union City. I'm sorry, this just doesn't feel right." She softened her tone. "Don't blame yourself, Jack. It's me. I'm just not ready to get involved with anyone." She dressed quickly, wriggling into her skirt and stepping into her shoes. "Besides, what if Jimmy comes home early? I should be there." She had switched to the mommy mode.

He swore to himself. Damn! "I'll drive you to the train station."

"Don't bother. I can catch a cab," she said in a low voice.

"No," he insisted, "I'll drive."

The theaters had just let out, and Market Street teamed with people. Neon signs beckoned at bars and restaurants, and the air hummed with the restless nighttime energy that only a big city generates. When Jack dropped Pat off at the Powell Street train station, she gave him a sad smile.

He watched her walk down the stairs. If he could turn back the clock, what should he have done differently? No answer came to mind, at least none he was willing to think about.

Chapter 25

*The hardest thing in the world to
understand is the income tax.*

ALBERT EINSTEIN (ATTRIBUTED)

It may be, as Supreme Court Justice Oliver Wen-
dell Holmes observed, that taxes are the price we pay
for civilization; but then again, he died in 1935. Before
then, only about ten per cent of Americans even *paid*
income taxes. But by 2010, the 1040 form that began
with two pages of instructions in 1913 had swelled to
101 pages. Of course, that's only *one* tax form. As a
recent Secretary of the Treasury noted, the Internal
Revenue Service (*Infernal* Revenue Service?) now
offers about 700 forms, and tax code provisions run to
about 7 million words. The colonists who dressed up
as Indians and dumped British tea into Boston Harbor
were ahead of their time.

Over the years, members of Congress have railed
against the complexities and inequities of the U.S. tax
code at the same time they larded it with tax breaks
for horse breeders, baseball clubs, oil companies,

broadcasters, and such. The result: most Americans throw up their hands in despair before April 15 and run screaming to a professional tax preparer, an option not available to Laura and Jack.

"It's not that bad," murmured Sally, reassuringly.

"Do you do your own taxes?" Laura said.

Sally looked uncomfortable. "Well, no, but I have some complications with stocks and rental property."

"I don't," she retorted, "and I still turn to 'tax services' in the Yellow Pages."

They waited at a long table in the conference room of Sally's real estate office in Naples. Laura had driven there, unwilling to ask Sally to travel 60 miles to Fort Myers again. It looked to be a long day.

Meanwhile, in Union City, Jack sat in Pat's spartan office at school, also waiting. An awkwardness had arisen between them. Neither mentioned Saturday night in San Francisco.

On the wall above Pat's desk, the big hand of the clock crawled toward 10 a.m. Pacific Time, the hour at which Sally and she would hand over the envelopes delivered to them the day before. The envelopes contained instructions and 1040 tax forms. Jack leafed through a magazine, humming. Pat raised an eyebrow. "How can you do that when you've got only hours to prepare a tax form with information you've never seen before?"

"I don't mind doing taxes," he said, flipping a page.

She looked at him in skeptically.

"No, really, I don't. Never have. I've never used a tax preparer."

Unlike many writers, Jack had always been good at math, beginning with simple algebra in high school and ending with statistics in college. Other reporters at the newspaper, lost in a maze of ratios, percentages, and averages, often came to him for help with financial stories. Jack guided them through the numerical wasteland.

He looked about the tiny office. A desk, two chairs, and a filing cabinet took up most of the floor space. Wall shelves jammed with books and papers contributed to a feeling of claustrophobia despite a window looking out on the blank wall of another building. He realized why she kept the door open.

"I won't be working in here, will I?"

Pat shook her head. "No, I've lined up an empty classroom with a nice, big table so that you can spread out." She wore white shorts, open-toe sandals, and a T-shirt decorated with the image of a snarling cat, symbol of the Arroyo College Cougars. Since real estate development in the foothills kept shrinking cougar habitat, he wondered if the college might have to choose a new mascot in the future. A bulldozer perhaps?

No, she definitely wasn't the cougar type, he decided. Too nice. A boat would be more appropriate. She reminded him of a spanking new yacht: trim, compact, sparkling, with clean lines that commanded attention.

Pat caught him in an admiring glance. "What are you looking at?" she asked suspiciously.

"The cougar. Amazing how realistic an artist can make a cat appear."

Promptly at 1 p.m., Florida time, Laura slashed open the 11x14 envelope and removed a copy of the Form 1040 instructions. The booklet contained 101 pages of general admonitions and tax tables, followed by dozens of other pages of specialized guidance for dealing with itemized deductions, interest and dividend income, capital gains and losses, and earned income credit. At the bottom of the cover she saw a comforting message: *The Internal Revenue Service • Working to put service first.* In addition, she found a two-page individual income tax return form and another two-page form to report deductions, interest, and dividends.

"I think that I'm developing a headache," she said.

Jack ripped open his envelope. He ignored the tax material and began reading the other instructions, the ones from the contest committee. He read:

Prepare an itemized 1040 tax form that could be filed under the following conditions:

Taxpayer:

Married couple, 42 and 40, with two dependent children.

Income: $82,000 in salary, $1,340 in gains from the sale of stock, $2,000 in capital gain distributions, $1,500 ordinary stock dividends, and $732 in bank interest. Current year Federal income taxes withheld, $9,334; Social Security taxes paid, $6,273.

Deductions: state income taxes withheld, $1,113; property taxes, $2,2543; medical expenses, $1,250; charitable contributions, $432.

Time: Unlimited.

"Gee, I wouldn't mind being in this guy's shoes, except for having the wife and two kids," he said, regretting the comment almost before the words left his mouth.

Pat glanced over the income information and her gaze turned frosty. "How do you know it's the husband and not the wife who's the bread-winner?"

"Point taken," Jack conceded. He placed his calculator within reach, got another cup of coffee, and set to work. The clock was not his friend. Of course, neither was the I.R.S.

Nor Laura's. She sighed and began re-reading the instruction booklet. Sally eased out of the room to make some telephone calls. It always made him uncomfortable to watch people in distress, especially women.

In New York, Cindy tensed as the office door opened. She hoped it wouldn't be Mari. On the other hand, Cliff hadn't been a lot of laughs the last few days, either. Since he had given Mari two weeks notice, Cindy hadn't worried about the air-conditioning. The office seemed chilly enough.

Unfortunately, it turned out to be Mari. And she was in a foul mood.

"Has the 39th floor sent down the new ratings yet?"

"No, but I could call."

Mari gave Cindy THE LOOK, which Cindy interpreted as "why am I surrounded by idiots?"

"Don't bother." No way would Mari give the s.o.b.s in suits the satisfaction of knowing her anxiety level.

Instead, she began flipping through the inter-office mail. "Any calls on the temporary producer's opening?"

Cindy knew the answer to that without checking any notes. "No. Not yet."

After Cliff had stabbed her in the back with his departure, Mari had sent a message out on the net-work's e-mail system that a temporary producer's slot had opened on her show. She intended to take her time in selecting a permanent replacement. After all, the Mari O'Reilly Show was a moneymaker for the net-work.

She started to walk back to her office and then stopped. "Oh," she said, as if struck by an afterthought, "when Cliff goes out to lunch, I want you to do some-thing for me."

Cindy looked up.

"I want you to start copying the names and tele-phone numbers in his Rolodex. We may not have him, but we'll have his contacts."

Cindy hesitated. "He locks up the telephone list in his desk when he leaves the office and takes it home with him at night."

Mari's mouth tightened. There was just no trusting some people.

As soon as she left, Cindy picked up the New York Post and looked up at the clock again. Not even 11 a.m. and she had already reached a 5 p.m. level of exhaustion/regret/depression/anger. Why should Mari take those stupid scoreboard standings out on her? It hadn't been her idea. And Cliff leaving? That, too. She turned on her iPod, slipped on earphones, and surfed through the menus until she found her favorite uplifting song: Ethel Merman belting out "There's No Business Like Show Business!"

Chpter 26

Never thrust your own sickle into another's corn.

PUBLICUS SYRUS

The next evening, as Jack prepared to pull a tuna casserole out of the microwave oven, the phone rang. Tuna aside, he was in an upbeat mood. Why not? He had knocked off the tax problem in less than three hours. Pat had compared notes with Sally, who reported Laura had tossed in the towel after five fruitless hours. Sally didn't add she had polished off most of the bottle of Merlot they shared at dinner. And the little man had bubbled his way higher on the Mari meter. True, the cooking competition loomed, and that would undoubtedly result in him being behind again, but you couldn't go through life worrying about everything.

So he was surprised and pleased to pick up the phone and hear Pat's voice. After some meaningless small talk, she got to the point.

"How about coming and joining me at a barbecue Sunday?"

Now barbecues were not high on Jack's list of favorite recreational activities. He had spent too many afternoons with a rapidly warming beer in one hand, looking furtively for shade and wondering when singed meat would be forthcoming.

"Well... Let me check my schedule and..."

"You owe me one, Kileen," she said curtly. "As a matter of fact, you owe me several ones. I gave up last Saturday to baby-sit you filling out tax forms, remember?"

He remembered and felt guilty. "Sure. What's the occasion?"

"The administration is stalling on a pay raise," she said. "They don't want disgruntled instructors showing up for class with picket signs, so the vice-president for academic affairs is giving a barbecue for faculty." The cell phone made her voice sound tinny. "The union wants a good turnout as a show of strength. Since there are no students, at least we can drink."

"You're not inviting me just to bask in the company of a famous author and TV celebrity and hint I'm your off-campus squeeze, are you?"

"In your dreams," she said sharply. "It's at 2 Sunday afternoon. I can pick you up at B.A.R.T. if you decide not to drive."

"Count me in. I'll wear my surf city shorts and 'Grateful Dead' tank top."

"Do that and you'll never leave the train station alive. I have to work with these people."

Her mood encouraged him. Perhaps they could work something out after all. And then he had another thought. What stage in his nine-step plan to avoid entangling alliances was he at now? Maybe it didn't matter.

Life is filled with sunny days and rainy days, hopefully more of the former and fewer of the latter. Sunday was promising. Jack whistled as he walked down Market Street. Life was good—at least for now. He had begun his practice sessions in a kayak with some trepidation. The little boats wallowed alarmingly and wearing a life jacket restricted movement. He had started out with other beginners at a lake and then ventured off into the channel at Jack London Square in Oakland. He couldn't do an Eskimo roll in a kayak, but there probably were some Eskimos who couldn't, either.

Meanwhile, the observation credited to Mark Twain that the coldest winter he had ever spent was a summer in San Francisco didn't apply on a sun-drenched August day. Of course, with San Francisco's weird weather patterns, he knew it could be foggy in the Sunset District and sunny in the Mission District.

A breeze picked up as he walked along Market Street's red brick sidewalk, bound for a B.A.R.T. station. About his feet blew discarded candy wrappers, crumpled cigarette packs, torn newspaper pages, and other urban effluvia. Yellow taxis darted through breaks in the traffic, and orange and white streetcars stood out in the somber stream of autos like dandelions poking up in a green lawn. At Powell Street, tourists queued up for cable cars that would whisk them, bells clanging, to Fisherman's Wharf. Sidewalk vendors at cloth-covered tables hawked silver bracelets, rings, necklaces, leather belts, and paintings. A bearded man coat stood on a plastic crate and warned passers-by they were bound for damnation unless they stopped sinning. Cooing pigeons, heads bobbing, ignored the stream of pedestrians and went about their business of recycling the leftovers of sidewalk lunches.

At Fifth Street, an elderly Chinese man sat before a wooden box and folding chair, waiting for someone to sit down and pay him $1 for a game of speed chess. Back from the curb, against a building, an attractive young woman had set up a shoeshine business, dark rags slapping leather vigorously.

But farther down, Market Street melted into a succession of porny palaces, hole-in-the wall stores with cheap cameras and electronic toys, and small restaurants, the type that offered 2 eggs, 2 strips of bacon, 2 potatoes, and 2 pieces of toast for $4.50. And if tourists ventured on toward the United Nations Plaza, which few did, they would be treated to a more depressing view of San Francisco, a sprawl of the homeless, the confused, the drunk, and the drug-addled, spinning out wasted hours within sight of the gleaming, gold-leafed dome of City Hall.

Jack stood for a moment on the corner of Market and Powell, letting the vibrant life of the city flow over and around him. Then he hurried down the steps into the train station. He waited only a few minutes before the Fremont train arrived, preceded by a blast of air expelled from the tunnel mouth, a cone of light, and a deafening roar.

The train swept out of the transbay tunnel into bright sunlight and made him a brief participant in the lives of his fellow passengers: parents with excited children who streamed out the doors at the Lake Merritt station, bound for the Oakland Museum; baseball fans in green and gold Oakland A's caps, anticipating a game at the Coliseum; night people, men who had driven taxis, worked in factories, cooked in restaurants, guarded docks, and cleaned offices, sleeping slumped against the windows; fit young men and women in shorts and T-shirts who held onto expensive trail bikes, waiting to get off in San Leandro or Bay Fair or Hayward. The Hayward hills, blanketed with stubble of grass bleached brown and seared by the summer sun, unfolded through the train window. On the higher slopes, pockets of green survived in gullies, marking the winter's watercourses. Jack put down his magazine. Union City was the next stop.

Pat waited at the turnstile, ignoring the admiring glances of several young louts on skateboards who were doing wheelies and flipping boards from pavement to hand near a sign reading "No Skateboarding." Jack could understand their interest. Pat wore white shorts, a T-shirt urging the world to "Save the Whales," Nikes, a visor cap, and sunglasses. He felt overdressed in khaki pants and a blue sports shirt. As they drove south along the flank of the eastern hills, signs proclaimed Union City an All-American City. He wondered if, like the children of Lake Woebegone who were all above average, all California cities, indeed all American cities, would eventually become All-American cities.

Soon they were at the party, frosty beers in hand, pretending deep interest as the host, who wore an apron with the picture of a pit bull holding a fork and spatula, demonstrated his barbecuing expertise. The house, built in California mission style, had a red-tile roof, white stucco walls, and intricately carved wooden doors. It snuggled up to the parched, grassy hillside, which must have made for sleepless nights during fire season, Jack decided. At least it wasn't Los Angeles, where coyotes sometimes came down into the canyons at night for a late snack of neighborhood kitty. An overhead trellis of brilliant red bougainvillea shaded the patio, and rounded paving stones surrounded a small fountain that bubbled seductively.

Their host, Bob somebody—Jack promptly forgot his last name—stood before a gleaming aluminum barbecue festooned with a maze of knobs and dials and burners. He flipped up the hood, stepped back from the billowing smoke, and began turning baby back ribs.

"What do you think?"

"It's... impressive," said Jack, unsure how to respond.

"You betcha! Combination rotisserie and smoker," their host beamed. "This baby has almost 700 inches of cooking surface. Look at those grates—steel and porcelain-enameled. Those three burners will crank out 60,000 BTU!"

Pat looked at Jack. She wasn't sure what a BTU was and didn't intend to ask.

"Fires up like a champ!" Bob continued. "It's got multi-spark ignition." The last came out almost reverently.

"I can do it all—ribs, burgers, chicken, ham, roasts. You name it."

Jack tried to look impressed. Man had come a long way from searing meat over open flames inside drafty caves. Now he did it with propane in expensive metal boxes in windy backyards.

"Try one of these." Bob deftly grabbed a sizzling rib using tongs, slathered it with sauce, put it on a paper plate, and handed it to Pat. She took a bite, screwed up her face, and took a gulp of beer.

"My own sauce. I make it a gallon at a time. The secret is in the Tabasco," he confided. "I may try to patent the recipe. You know, like Paul Newman did with salad dressing."

Pat swallowed again. "I'm sure there won't be anything else like it on the market, Bob," she managed to say.

He closed the hood of the grill and the smoke was choked off.

"Cost almost $3,000," the cook said casually, awaiting a reaction.

Pat looked at him in disbelief.

Jack nodded approvingly, guy to guy. "And worth every penny, Bob."

They wandered about, chatting with Pat's co-workers and friends. Even the administrators seemed nice, not stonehearted employers bent on driving overworked instructors to the food bank. An outreach coordinator exclaimed "Are you the Kileen who writes those feature stories in the Sun? I loved the one about people using coffins for coffee tables." Modestly, Jack claimed responsibility for that particular contribution to literature for the masses. When they were alone, Pat admitted, "I don't buy your paper." He gave her no out. "Read it online. Won't cost a cent—for now at least."

They left the party at sunset. Before driving to the train, she invited him in for a drink. Pat and Jimmy lived in a modest, three-bedroom ranch with a close-cropped, patchy front lawn, and a well-shaded back-yard. A bird feeder swung from a low branch of an oak tree, and quarrelsome house finches jockeyed for space at the seed openings.

"That's a nice backyard," said Jack. "This beats living in an apartment. You could even have a dog."

"Sssh...! Don't mention that! Jimmy wants one but I've been ducking it. I've got enough complications in my life as it is."

Jack blinked. Ouch! They went inside. Jimmy had wandered off to his room, guaranteeing them some privacy. They relaxed in the family room. Bookcases and art prints lined the walls, and a TV set and DVD player occupied a corner. He nursed another beer; she had a Diet Coke.

"You've probably wondered about Jimmy and me and have been too polite to ask," began Pat. "I've appreciated that. I met Jimmy's father when we were both student teachers. He was always the life of the party, which should have been a warning sign. We had lots of fun—right up until Jimmy was born with a left leg an inch shorter than the right one."

She paused. "That bothered Ralph a lot. So did missing the parties when we couldn't get a babysitter. Pretty soon we were different people living in the same house. Then he announced one day he had taken a job in Oregon. He said we could join him later." She dropped her eyes to the glass. "He didn't mention the girlfriend, one of his students. I found out about her later. I divorced him two years ago."

"That must have been rough," Jack said.

"He calls Jimmy twice a year," she went on, "at Christmas and on his birthday. Last year he missed his birthday by a week." Her voice held a hint of bitterness.

"That's why I'm concerned about you getting too close to him, Jack. He's been hurt enough." She shook her head sadly. "He gets B's and A's at school and rarely whines at doing chores around the house. He plays catcher in a youth baseball league. They use a pinch runner for him. He can bat and you should see him throw out runners at second base. Not many 12-year-olds with two good legs can do that."

"You have a right to be proud of him," Jack said. "Maggie had him pegged as a good kid when she met him."

Pat looked wistful. "This has been fun, Jack, it really has. Jimmy had a great time at the game. And the other night... well, it was special, too."

She held his gaze and her voice had a slight tremor. "I resisted dating until I met you. You're a nice guy but you're not the type to make commitments. That's okay, but I've got Jimmy to think about. I can't let you into our lives on a part-time basis. It isn't fair to him. Kids get their hopes up." She gave him an unwavering look. "So do adults some times."

"Pat..." he began, ready to marshal counter-arguments.

"No," she replied firmly. "You have your life and we have ours." She put down her glass. "Ready?"

On the ride back to the train station, It struck him that their evenings seemed to be ending in silence.

 Chapter 27

We have to distrust each other.
It is our only defense against betrayal.

TENNESSEE WILLIAMS

"Whoa, pard... you look like you got rode hard and put up wet!" A gravelly voice splintered by a cough broke Jack's concentration.

Maggie stood by his desk, wreathed in a gray cloud as usual. A vision in a flame-red blouse and purple slacks, she wore gold earrings to complete her personal vision of femininity.

"Go away," he growled. "I'm busy."

She plopped down in the chair by his desk. "Sure you are. I've been watching you stare at that computer screen for 15 minutes. Did you plan on using that funny-looking board with the letters and numbers sometime soon or keep trying to avoid carpal tunnel?"

Lunchtime. The Sun newsroom was largely deserted except for a few reporters who hunched over computer keyboards or read the first edition of the Sun for errors in their stories that copy editors had missed or made themselves. One woman had a bandage on her right wrist. Ah, yes, Jack thought, carpal tunnel syndrome, the journalist's version of miner's black lung disease, except it isn't fatal, just painful.

He pretended to re-arrange papers on his desk.

"Where's your ashtray?" she coughed. The cigarette glowed dully between yellowed fingers.

"Next to your knee," he said, indicating the wastebasket. "Try not to set the place on fire. I thought you were at the ballpark."

She stubbed the butt out hastily. "No more than I can help it right now. It's a jungle out there, sport. Urine testing time again. The mood isn't mellow."

Jack didn't smile.

Maggie looked at him more closely. "So what is it… money? The crackdown on overtime by our blood-sucking owners? Or work… they're sticking you with obits to write again?" She looked at him more closely. "No? Then it must be a woman. Tell Auntie Maggie."

"There's nothing to tell."

Her face lit up. "It *is* a woman. Not that nice Italian girl with the kid who was at the Giants game, I hope. Paula… Priscilla…?" She pretended to be ransacking her memory. "Oh, I remember, Pat, isn't it?"

Jack shot Maggie an irritated look. Wasted. Maggie thrived on other people's irritation. When you can make a living dredging quotes from losing pitchers with earned run averages above 6 and batters who are caressing the ball at under .200, the irritation of co-workers doesn't register as a blip on the radar screen.

"I'll bet it's the old commitment thing," she continued. "That's it, isn't it? I'll bet she told you she's got a kid and responsibilities, and you don't look like someone worth taking out long-term insurance on."

"Kiss off, Maggie," said Jack, losing patience. "If I want advice, I'll read Dear Abby."

Maggie looked at him sadly. "Let me give you some anyway, from an old hand at affairs of the heart. Like the song goes, 'You've got to know when to hold and know when to fold'; but you've also got to know when to bet."

"Is that from Maggie's advice to the lovelorn?"

She looked at him for a long moment without answering. "Yes, I guess it is, as a matter of fact. I haven't always been a funny dressing, hard-nosed, bitchy old broad." He started to speak but she cut him off. "In my salad days, I was engaged to a bright young engineer for IBM who got transferred to Poughkeepsie, N.Y. Poughkeepsie, N.Y.! They had a double A ball club there, and I happened to be next in line to cover the Giants in San Francisco! The first woman!"

"So you passed on Poughkeepsie."

"I passed on Poughkeepsie. And I passed on the nice young engineer." She gave him a look difficult to read. "He still sends me Christmas cards with pictures of the kids." She looked away.

"Your business is your business, sport, but let old Maggie give you a final piece of advice based on going home alone too many nights and spending too many years in too many ballparks watching too many men play a kids' game. Sometimes it gets to the last inning, and you don't get another chance at bat."

She shook her head and left, leaving Jack with the same thought, one that he had been trying to avoid.

"Mari O'Reilly calling for Nancy Ferlman," Cindy said in her this-is-a-priority-call voice. She loved placing calls for Mari because it made her feel important.

"Just a sec," came the reply.

"Nancy Ferlman."

Cindy's finger hovered over the transfer button. "Please hold for Mari O'Reilly." She pushed the button. Mission completed.

Mari came on the line as important people always do—last.

"Good morning, Nancy."

"Good morning, Mari," came the wary reply. "What can I do for you?" Ferlman served as executive director of an agency that found affordable housing for people who found most housing unaffordable. She had reluctantly accepted the chairmanship of the contest coordinating committee. It didn't take long for her to discover Mari took a close and personal interest in the committee's work.

"I just wanted to see how you were coming along. We're almost in the home stretch now." And losing.

"Have you worked out plans for the cooking contest yet?"

Ferlman sighed. "No. We're meeting tomorrow. I suspect this will be pretty much up to the women on the committee. The men are no help."

Mari kept her voice light. "Well, what do men know about cooking anyway? After all, this is where we get to show who's boss in the kitchen, right?" That didn't apply to her, of course. Mari had never been married and usually nuked dinner in the microwave oven at home. On the rare occasions when she entertained, she took guests to a restaurant, thereby increasing both her return dinner invitations and frequent flyer miles.

Ferlman didn't argue the point. Her husband prepared dinner two nights a week for her and their two teenagers. He alternated between hotdogs or hamburgers and frozen pizza.

"I just wanted to make sure the menu you decide on will be a true test of cooking skills," Mari rattled on. "After all, a dinner for four should be memorable, shouldn't it?"

Actually, Ferlman had discovered early in marriage the most memorial meals she had prepared for guests were the ones she'd like to do over.

"We're working on it," she said noncommittally.

"Well, I wouldn't make it too easy." Mari's voice held an edge. "No ice cream for dessert or anything like that."

Ferlman had had enough. "We'll select a menu that is tasteful, economical, and demonstrates cooking ability," she said, "but no one here is playing Martha Stewart."

"Oh, I'm sure it will be just fine. I intend to use your menu myself when the contest is over," Mari lied sweetly. "Well, I won't keep you any longer. Let me know if you need anything."

"You can count on it," Ferlman said curtly and hung up.

A rapid "peck-peck-peck" sounded on Mari's closed door, and Cindy stuck her head in. "The new guy's here." Mari frowned. What new guy? She hadn't made a decision yet on replacing Cliff. The door opened wider. A silver-haired man in blue Armani stepped in confidently. He smiled, revealing perfectly capped white teeth. "Hello. I'm Chip Wilson. And your secretary is correct, I'm your new producer."

Laura picked up a sand dollar. Broken. She tossed it back and shielded her eyes from the sun. She couldn't imagine living somewhere other than Sanibel Island. But did it count as a real island, linked to the mainland by a ribbon of concrete? As long as men have sailed ships and written books about the sea, she knew, living on islands had been idealized. Images of waving palm trees, tangy salt air, azure waters, and virginal beaches beckoned irresistibly. Reality, of course, was somewhat different. A steady diet of coconuts and fish, hot, sticky temperatures, and the company of mosquitoes and sand fleas can quickly degrade the experience. The other element that added to the allure of islands is the possibility of solitude, withdrawal from the hectic work-a-day world of horns honking, boom boxes blaring, cell phones ringing, and helicopters "whup, whup, whupping."

One of the attractions of island life was predictability, absence of the unexpected. But now she had a new challenge, kayaking. She had started in the calm waters of a cove under the watchful eyes of an instructor. The one-person boats proved to be surprisingly agile, and she started to feel more comfortable paddling and steering. But she didn't kid herself she was ready to tackle fast waters.

Laura's life on Sanibel Island amounted to a compromise. She had the palm trees, beaches, and salty air. Air conditioning offered a refuge from the humidity, and fine-mesh screens kept the mosquitoes at bay. What she didn't have was the isolation. Not in the age of the telephone, cell phone, fax machine, and e-mail. Tuesday afternoon rolled around, and she had been hard at work refilling the bird feeders, fertilizing the wilting cherry tomato plants, and fighting the unending battle against the weeds that threatened to overwhelm her backyard. She had tried to push the memory of the income tax failure out of her mind. Unable to do that, she vowed Jack Kileen wouldn't be smiling that overbearing smile after she cleaned his clock in the kitchen. She had entered the Challenge of the Sexes grudgingly, without emotional investment. But to her surprise, that had changed the first time she saw the little man bobbing at the top on Mari's meter. Now she was committed and determined to win. The red light flashed on her answering machine when she entered the house, hot, sweaty, and thirsty. After pouring a glass of ice tea, she picked up the phone. Morris Evander had left a message and he sounded... what...? Irritated? Flustered? Concerned? Probably all three, she decided.

"Laura! Pick up if you're there! This is Morris. I need to talk to you. It's important."

His urgency puzzled her. Unlike some administrators, Evander never bothered her at home. She glanced at the clock. 5:30 p.m. He had probably left for the day, but she tried anyway and got his answering machine.

Oh, well, she had to go to school anyway to teach her leadership class.

She finished her ice tea, took a shower, and collected her lecture notes for the class that night. She wondered if Toby Linderman would be there.

When Laura arrived on campus, Evander's office was locked. She unstuffed her mail box. She tossed: junk mail—business circulars, notices about meetings and events long passed, and administrative memos about parking lot closures for resurfacing, a new lecture series, and the Labor Day pay schedule. She kept: letters and telephone messages from students, congratulatory and commiserating notes from faculty members (she found more of them these days), and, in an envelope marked IMPORTANT, a request from Evander to call him at the first opportunity.

Humidity enveloped her like a damp blanket. The building's air-conditioning system labored on, unable to cope with the frequent opening and closing of doors as students arrived for evening classes. Inside her classroom, the women huddled at one end of the large table. She didn't see Toby.

"Good evening, what's the big attract..." she began. Laura stopped in mid-sentence. Sarah stood rigidly, arms crossed tightly across her chest, staring out the window. Linda sobbed uncontrollably, tears and mascara merging into thin black rivulets dripping down her face. The others shook their heads and pored over a magazine on the table. Laura stepped closer. She saw that it was a copy of *Glimpse*, one of those sleazy tabloids that she bypassed at the supermarket after reading the headlines. The bold headline at the top of the front page screamed:

Secret Life of the Challenge of the Sexes Prof—Booze, Pot, and Sex."

Under the headline she saw pictures from the party: bottles of wine, students holding glasses in the air and laughing, and Laura, sitting in a darkened room with her arm around Linda's shoulders. Next to the article was a photo of Toby Linderman. Except the name under the photo identified him as Ashford Sloan.

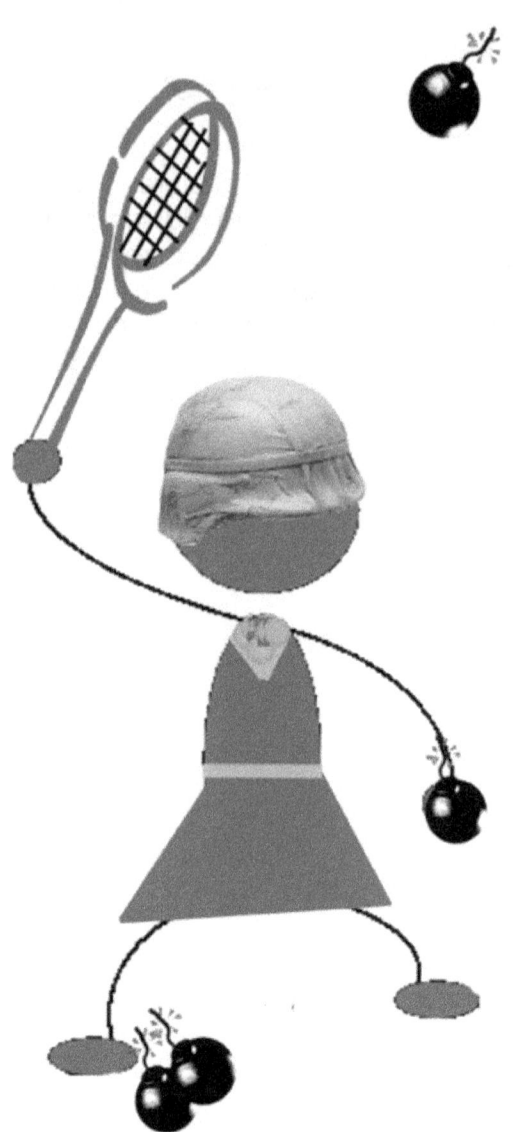

Chapter 28

*Never Explain—your Friends do not need it
and your Enemies will not believe you anyway.*

ELBERT HUBBARD

Laura thought she had stumbled into a wake. Sarah looked dazed, adrift in another world not of her choosing. Linda still sniveled, mascara dripping down both cheeks. She resembled an Indian warrior who had tried to put on war paint after guzzling too much firewater. The others clustered together, nudging one another indignantly after discovering yet another distortion of the truth about the party. Laura, too, had trouble concentrating, so she gave up, assigned a reading, and dismissed the class.

Now, the next morning, she forced herself to re-read what Ashford Sloan, aka Toby Linderman, had written. He had created a clever concoction of innuendo, fabrication, half-truths, and downright lies. But, she guessed, it might not be libelous, otherwise *Glimpse* and other publications of its ilk couldn't stay in business. The picture of the women holding up their wine glasses had a caption that read: "Students enjoy liberal amounts of wine and beer. *Only Toby had been drinking beer, Laura recalled.* "One student, apparently drunk, stumbled and sent a glass crashing to the floor, giggling afterward." *Rita had been washing a glass at the end of the party. It had slipped from her wet, soapy hand and broken.* Next, she read "a familiar smell, not unlike marijuana, wafted through the smoky room." *The smell had been cedar incense, as Toby well knew, and no one had been smoking, let alone smoking marijuana.*

Finally, worst of all, was the thinly veiled suggestion that Laura and Linda had withdrawn furtively to a bedroom for lovemaking. "The professor and a student slipped out at the height of the merry-making. With the door shut, but visible from an outside window, they could be seen. The party-loving professor embraced the younger woman passionately." *Damn! Now she had been labeled a lesbian as well as a seducer of innocent students!*

Laura flung the magazine to the floor. It landed near a startled Buffy, who half-opened yellow eyes and then closed them slowly. Dogs may have an innate ability to sense their owner's discomfort and offer unconditional support. Not cats. Cats are concerned only with potential disruptions in the chain from food source to can opener to dish, and assume that most problems will go away if ignored. The emotional state of the opener of the can doesn't concern them.

And then the telephone began ringing. Her first call came from an agitated aunt in Iowa. After calming *her* down, Laura fielded calls from Morris Evander, who expressed disbelief and offered support; the university's vice-president of public affairs, clearly shaken, who began by suggesting she say nothing to the press and finished by urging a limited, modified, partial hang-out—whatever *that* was; Marion Sally, mad as hell and thundering about "character assassination," and, big surprise, Jack Kileen, who had gotten her number from Patricia Rossi. "Ignore the bastards," he had counseled, "nobody believes what's written in that rag, anyway." Easier said than done, she thought; but the call from Kileen had depressed her even more because it had made her realize the *Glimpse* article might lead to more than just embarrassment. Somehow or other, the campus newspaper and the Associated Press had also gotten her telephone number. (The squeaky-voiced young man from the student newspaper had stammered, clearly not used to asking professors embarrassing questions.) Both he and the A.P. guy had inquired if she had any reaction to a statement by the university's legal affairs office that "allegations contained in the *Glimpse* article will be investigated." She unplugged the phone.

In Chicago, Ashford Sloan arrived at the office to high fives, bounteous praise, and ill-concealed envy. The story had been picked up (and was already being picked apart) by major newspapers, press associations, radio, and television. His telephone call slips listed *Time Magazine*, *CNN*, *Educator Today*, *Celebrity TV*, and *Audubon Magazine*. He frowned. *Audubon Magazine?* He swept the slips into the wastepaper basket. He wasn't in a mood to pump up other publications or television programs. It worked the other way around at *Glimpse*.

"Hey, chiller, you scored big time!" Sloan turned to see Sonny Nevasconi (Sonny Nevers in print). His mood worsened. Nevasconi reminded Sloan of himself only months before—bright, brash, bumptious, and absolutely without scruple in pursuit of a byline. Somehow, he had never figured out why, the kid thought of him as a mentor.

"Booze, broads, wicked weed...how do you get all of the killer stories?" Nevasconi continued enviously. "What do you do, plough Clayton's wife as a favor?"

"Cream rises," Sloan replied. He wasn't sure what the phrase actually meant since the only cream he came in contact with was in tiny plastic containers in restaurants. "And stop calling me 'Chiller.'"

"You chill them, dude," Nevasconi said admiringly. "I'll bet that broad iced up like an orange grove in a freeze." Like many new Floridians who watched TV news, Nevasconi tended to think of winter in terms of its effect on citrus crops.

Sloan dismissed Nevasconi and began running through his telephone messages. He stopped when he heard a familiar voice, Sarah's, sobbing and angry. "You're a slime ball, Toby. I trusted you....We all trusted you. Dr. Sanders is a fine teacher and a fine person. There was nothing sexual between her and Linda and you know it." Sarah's voice broke. "You lied to her and you lied to me. And I thought that you were someone special." She hissed with rage. "I never want to hear from you or see you again." He heard a click. Sloan put down the phone, ignoring the rest of the messages. He sat there, alone with his thoughts in the busy newsroom. No one noticed.

A few yards away behind a closed door, Larry Clayton sat at his desk, the morning sun warming his shoulders. He had increased the printing run of the current issue by 200,000 copies and wished he had increased it even more. Sloan's exposé (he liked to think of *Glimpse's* semi-fictional reporting in those terms) had been a natural, and he had planned it from the git-go. He took pride in his deft handling of the suggestion of a lesbian relationship, carefully enhanced by darkening of the photo to make it appear as if the women had been in a room with the lights turned off. Sure the story would probably deflate like a punctured balloon in 48 hours. Most of them did. But a lot of readers standing in checkout lines at supermarkets across the United States would have bought it by then. And more would buy it after the bubble burst, just to see what the fuss had all been about or to see if *Glimpse* would apologize and express regret for being wrong. It wouldn't. William Randolph Hearst been known to lurk near newsstands to see if one of the sensationalistic headlines in the *San Francisco Examiner* would prompt a potential reader to exclaim "Gee Whiz!" Well, this was a "Gee Whiz!" story. Clayton would take the successes where and when they came.

It wasn't easy being managing editor of "The Magazine That Reports What Others Are *Afraid* to Report." First, that morning, he had gotten an angry telephone call from a guy in the Nevada Fish and Game Department, who had scoffed at the story that a 12-foot alligator had been sighted swimming in Lake Tahoe, near the North Shore casinos. Then a lawyer had written a letter threatening to sue *Glimpse* over the picture of the alien baby his client claimed to have had. He said the second head had been added in the *Glimpse* photo lab, which, of course, it had. Finally, Clayton had read the Associated Press story that Dr. Laura Sanders would be investigated by the university for allegedly providing alcohol to students "and other misconduct." He felt a sudden tinge of discomfort. Could it be conscience? No, probably just acid reflux. He opened a drawer and pulled out his bottle of antacid.

Mari O'Reilly bit her lip in frustration. That stupid scoreboard Cliff Hansen had dreamed up continued to be a nagging reminder that the guy from San Francisco led in the Challenge of the Sexes, which, by the way, hadn't jacked up her ratings as expected. Then Hansen had decamped to the opposition, leaving her with a new producer to break in. Now this. She expected the *Glimpse* hit piece had been blown out of all proportion, but some of her viewers didn't shine as the brightest bulbs on the Christmas tree. They'd probably believe it, and Mari wanted this thing to end with a clean, clear, FEMALE victory! Now what?

She still considered her latest setback when Chip Wilson, the smooth, slick, silver fox in Armani, walked in without knocking. Over drinks with him (and by pumping her sources), she had learned he was a refugee of the news wars at a cable TV network, loser in a bitter battle to take the place of the retiring news division VP. The winner had cleaned house, re-assigning his majesty's disloyal opposition to supervising the network's 6 a.m. morning program. Wilson, a veteran of corporate wars, had taken the hint and jumped at the opening as Mari's producer. He claimed he hoped to broaden his experience on the entertainment side of the business, but Mari figured he was in a holding pattern until another network news job opened up. As if she had a choice. She needed a producer, and he happened to be the most qualified candidate available.

"I've got the guest list for tomorrow," Wilson said, "and it looks good. We nailed Rory Catalano, the star of that new gangster show, 'The Altos.' Also, the doctor who wrote "Transfats Are Good for You."

"Okay," Mari said listlessly.

He raised his eyebrows. "You sound as if someone dinged your Porsche."

"It's nothing." Her eyes returned to the copy of *Glimpse*.

Wilson made the connection. "Ah, the knife job on the Florida professor. That's got you upset?" He looked puzzled. "Why?"

"Why? Because I've been building her up for weeks!" Mari exploded. "She's going to win the cooking test hands down. Now her image is shot to hell. What if the university cans her ass before we finish?"

Wilson shrugged, and she noticed pectorals rippling under a taut white dress shirt. Not like that round-shouldered, balding, treacherous bastard Cliff Hansen. Unfortunately, Wilson wore a wedding ring.

"Five will get you ten a little legwork shows this thing as just another tabloid science fiction piece," he said. "But what if it isn't? This has pumped new life into the contest." Wilson cocked his head. "How are you going to play it on the show today?"

She threw up her hands. "What can I do? I'll be shocked, I guess."

He leaned forward, both hands on her desk, and his aftershave, which hinted of a piney forest after a fresh spring rain, enveloped her. It smelled expensive. "Don't just be shocked. Be angry! Be outraged that a sleazy rag would make a gutter-level attack on a fine educator! Denounce *Glimpse* and its cheap hacks posing as journalists." He pounded the desk in righteous indignation, knocking over a pen set and scattering papers. Mari recoiled and then realized Wilson wasn't angry at all. He was smiling.

She drew in a breath. That might fly. Yes, that just might fly. But then she had an unsettling thought.

"What if our professor really did have a booze, drugs, and sex party with her students?"

"Then that's the time to be dismayed and betrayed. But not now." He paused, brows furled, appearing to give the whole scenario deeper thought. "If you handle it right, this could be your finest hour."

Mari replayed the words in her mind. My finest hour... My finest hour...What's to lose?

Chapter 29

Truth is generally the best vindication against slander.

ABRAHAM LINCOLN

They had been waiting outside the president's office for almost 20 minutes, a clear sign to both Laura and Morris Evander that THIS WAS SERIOUS! If she had been surprised at seeing Evander after being summoned tersely by the president's secretary, he had been more surprised at seeing her. Evander had done a double take. Laura's long brown hair had been cut short and tapered. It fell just short of her shoulders, the ends curling inward and framing her face. Heeding a suggestion from Gina's hair stylist, she had changed her lipstick to better complement her natural coloring and had begun using mascara lightly.

"Laura... you look different...." Evander began, his voice trailing off.

She forced a smile. "Lack of sleep does that, Morris."

"No, I meant..."

"Thank you," she said simply, accepting his compliment.

Unfortunately, the president didn't have compliments in mind when they entered his office. The now infamous issue of *Glimpse* lay on his desk.

"Sit down," he said curtly. Laura didn't detect a "please."

He looked surprised at seeing Evander. "I didn't expect you, Morris."

Ah, thought Laura, Morris isn't part of the Inquisition. She glanced at Evander and half smiled. He didn't smile back.

The president, whose background had been in physics where immutable laws of nature governed a predictable universe, wasted no time. Normally, he dealt with budget overruns, hiring and firing, faculty squabbles, downsizing, and technological change—but not public relations catastrophes. In fact, he sweated once a year when humbly presenting the university's budget request to a legislative education committee. He survived by speaking hurriedly and sprinkling his remarks with the names of the university's prominent graduates in the legislature. Already that morning, the president had taken calls from two regents and a state senator who wanted to know "just what the hell is going on over there!"

"This regrettable situation..." he began abruptly.

"What regrettable situation?" Laura asked.

That set him back. His voice hardened. "Well, Dr. Sanders, I mean the party you had for your students, the one with alcohol and drugs and God knows what else."

"Didn't happen," responded Laura promptly. "No drugs, only wine and beer, and there was no 'anything else.'"

"This... magazine... describes things differently," he sputtered.

"This... magazine..."—she mimicked his words and phrasing—"is distorting what happened." She almost said "full of shit" but restrained herself in time.

The president's face grew red. "That's *your* version of events."

"It's the only accurate one," she countered, no longer cowed, just plain angry. She had met the president once before at a faculty lunch, but clearly he didn't remember her. He would after this meeting.

"A reporter for that scandal sheet enrolled in my class under a false name and attended a party at my home under false pretenses. Everything else is untrue. Nobody got drunk or used drugs. And I didn't have sexual relations with a student. I consoled her because her boyfriend had just dumped her. End of story."

The president leaned back in his chair and glared. Goddamned faculty! Give them tenure and they lose all respect. He really meant deference, but didn't realize it. "I hope for your sake that you're right," he said, "Because tenure won't protect you from an act of moral turpitude. In any event, I'm going to suspend you until an investigation is completed."

"Don't!" said Morris Evander.

"What?" the president asked in surprise. Department heads were to be seen and not heard, except at budget time or graduation. Otherwise, they weren't team players.

"Don't suspend her," Evander said firmly. "The article is hogwash. First, all the women are graduate students and at least 21; no minors are involved. Secondly, I've talked to several of them, including the young woman in the picture with Dr. Sanders. They all maintain the party was innocuous. No drugs, no excessive drinking, and no sex. And," he leaned forward, "they are willing to sign statements to that effect."

Taken off guard, the president tried to rally. "But..."

"There are no 'buts,'" Laura said firmly. "I've been on the faculty here for six years without complaint. My student evaluations are outstanding." She glared back at him. "Suspend me, and I'll hold a press conference and say I'm being railroaded to protect the university's reputation."

THAT got the president's attention.

"Let's face it," continued Evander, "it's common practice for faculty to entertain graduate students, alcohol included. I've done it and I expect you have, too."

That brought the president up short. In fact, he had been lucky at another college when a Ph.D. candidate in astrophysics had wrapped his car around a tree after having had several beers too many at a party at the home of the president, then a lowly associate professor.

And that's how it ended. Evander, trying to smooth things over (as an administrator, he didn't have tenure), suggested the president issue a statement saying the university found the article false and unfounded. The president, unsmiling, said that he'd reappraise the situation now that he had additional information. Later, after personally talking to two of the students, he issued a terse statement calling *Glimpse's* charges unfounded and reprehensible. He made a mental note to examine Evander's budget requests more closely.

Only the cooking competition remained before the contest finale. The e-mail message laying out the details arrived at the computers of Marion Sally, Pat Rossi, and Cindy Martinez within seconds of each other, coursing through the electronic universe of the Internet. Sally and Pat, who were working at their desks, were alerted to new messages and glanced at their screens. They opened the files immediately. The message on Cindy Martinez's computer went unread for 32 minutes while she shopped during an extended lunch break. But when she saw it, she opened it, printed it, and rushed it to Mari. Reactions varied.

"Good, good..." murmured Mari.

"Oh, boy!" exclaimed Pat.

"Thank God for 'Hearty Guy' microwave dinners," mumbled Sally. His second thought was "*the poor bastard.*"

When the messages eventually filtered down to Jack and Laura, they discovered they would be expected to prepare a dinner for four with a prescribed menu. They could choose the wine, but that was about all. Jack could select two guests; but the fourth guest would be the director of the San Francisco Culinary College (in Jack's case) and the food editor of the Fort Myers Blade (in Laura's case). They were to be the judges.

The menu listed four courses:

French onion soup

Caesar salad

Veal scaloppini

Raspberry soufflé

Dinner would be Saturday night, only three days away, so they got busy. Laura networked. She called friends, colleagues, and relatives, soliciting recipes.

Jack went to the bookstore and buttonholed an owlish-looking young man wearing a maroon apron. "Where are the cookbooks?" he asked. The young man pointed. "Aisle 12, Sections G&H."

"Two sections?" Jack asked.

The clerk considered the question. "Well, you've got your general cookbooks, then the more specialized ones for meat, fish, vegetables, soups, and desserts. Then there are the pasta, vegetarian and ethnic...."

"Thanks. I get the idea." What Jack found surprised him. Books on cuisine, high and low, fancy and plain, quick and dirty, microwave and wok, filled the shelves. He wondered how his mother had gotten by with just Betty Crocker as a guide. Of course, they *had* eaten hot dogs a lot.

He settled for three books: "Even You Can Cook!", the "Klutz's Guide to Preparing Dinner," and "Why Eat Out?" After studying some of the recipes in the more sophisticated books, he could see eating out had its advantages. But when he got home, Jack found veal scaloppini and raspberry soufflé weren't listed in *any* of the books. He swore. Should have checked the indexes, I guess.

In desperation, he turned to Reginald Quimby, the Sun's restaurant critic and food editor. Quimby occupied a cubicle next to the dollhouse or the women's department or, on more politically correct newspapers, the lifestyle section. Quimby visited new restaurants to sample the cuisine before the health department received complaints. In addition, he filled three columns of space twice a week with tantalizing recipes, few of which he'd ever prepared himself. He harkened back to the television days of the "Galloping Gourmet," claimed to have been an acquaintance of Julia Childs, and disdained Rachael Ray as "nouveau." Despite working on the same floor in the same building for years, Jack had never met the man. They lived in different worlds.

He stood uncertainly outside Quimby's cubicle. Quimby looked up. "Come in dear boy," he said. "Do come in. I was just deciding how unkind to be to "Le Continental," that dreary little Eurocuisine bistro that just opened on Geary near Union Square." He sighed. "Mixed review, I'm afraid. The Chinese long beans were flaccid, the Caesar salad too acidy. But the coq au vin had a pleasant bacon and wine-flavored broth with onions, and the chocolate truffle cake with vanilla gelato is superb." He licked his lips in recollection.

Quimby was a Brit. He had been hired in a burst of Anglo-American fellowship by a retired editor of the Sun who had been downing pints of room temperature

Guinness at the time at a London pub while on a journalistic junket.

Today, Quimby wore a monogrammed purple dress shirt with ivory studs and a pink tie. They went well with his charcoal gray pants. Jack wondered if he and Maggie would hit it off. They could always discuss fashion.

"What can I do for you?" Quimby inquired. "You're involved in that silly thing on the telly, aren't you?"

Jack admitted that he was indeed involved in that silly thing on the telly and got to the point. He handed Quimby the menu for his four-course dinner. "I've got to cook this," he said.

Quimby perused the list. "Um...onion soup, a Caesar, scaloppini..."He pursed his lips reflectively. "Oh, and a raspberry soufflé. Tricky, that. They can collapse quite easily, you know."

"That's the problem," responded Jack. "I don't know. I do hamburgers and scrambled eggs real well. I can cook spaghetti and meatballs when pushed. The rest of the time I eat out or sacrifice a TV dinner in the microwave."

"There's nothing here terribly complicated," Quimby said encouragingly. "Pressing some garlic, separating egg whites, reducing liquids...I can give you some recipes if you like."

"Separating egg whites?"

Quimby nodded. "Right. From the yolks. That's not hard. Your real problem, I think will be coordinating all of these courses. That takes a bit of timing and experience."

"I'll bet," said Jack. "Could you at least give me a suggestion for wine to serve?"

Quimby's face brightened. "Of course, dear boy. I recommend a red, but not a heavy one. Try a Pinot Noir. That goes well with veal."

"Any one in particular?"

Quimby thought for a minute. "I prefer a L'Ecosse, a '96 if possible. Not as pricey as some, and it has a beguiling cherry flavor with just a hint of oak."

"That sounds like my kind of wine," Jack agreed. "Did you say 'press' garlic?"

"Yes. Of course, you can mince the garlic if you prefer for the scaloppini. Shall I research some recipes?

"Thanks anyway," said Jack. "I've got some thinking to do." He went back to his apartment and cracked an Anchor Steam. He led in the race by 50 points, but if he tanked on the cooking test, which seemed increasingly likely, he'd be down by 25 points with only one event left. Perhaps he could find some easier recipes on line. He logged onto AOL and went into Google. There were recipes available, but they didn't look easy. He groaned over one with directions for preparing raspberry soufflé: "whisk the egg whites to soft peaks." What the hell did that mean? Also, how could he prepare four courses of *anything* in his antiquated kitchen? Only the microwave was post-Vietnam. He rarely used the oven.

All of this research into food had set Jack's dinner bell to ringing, so he went to the freezer and examined the larder. It felt like a Mexican night, so he selected the Hearty El Grande Supreme with two tamales, a beef enchilada, and refried beans washed down with a bottle of beer to be followed by a liberal helping of Ben and Jerry's Phish Food ice cream. Afterward, he turned on the television and searched the cable menu until he found a cooking show. Watching the chefs slice and dice without adding fingers to the salad while talking to the camera usually held his attention. But not tonight.

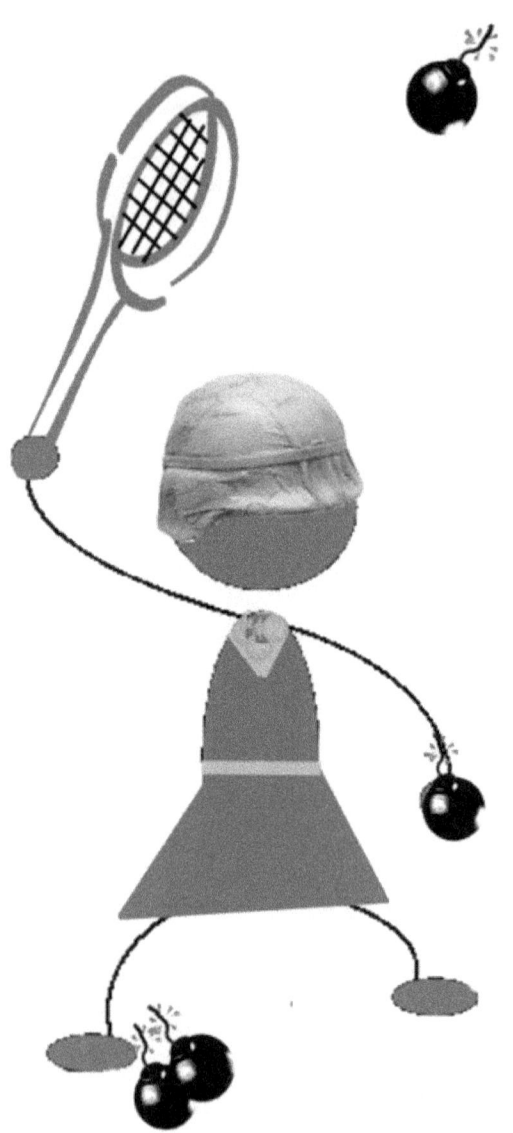

Chapter 30

Preach not to others what they should eat,
but eat as becomes you, and be silent.

EPICTETUS

Jack twists in bed, the sheets enfolding him like a shroud. He groans and a whimper escapes. Images flit through his mind. He sees himself imprisoned in a sand castle as the tide surges in...plunging over a waterfall in a kayak while Mari O'Reilly stands on a bank laughing. And then he is standing in a kitchen, naked except for a stained white apron and a San Francisco Giants cap turned sideways. He wears heavy mitts embroidered with pink and red roses.

Blinking from the glare of floodlights, he realizes this is the set of the *Mari O'Reilly Show*. The studio lights have been turned off, but he can hear the audience murmuring behind a wall of darkness. Gleaming copper pans, large and small, hang from hooks above a stainless steel table behind him. A buzzer sounds.

"Open the door and take it out," a flat, mechanical voice commands.

He turns to find an oven. He opens the door. A dense cloud of smoke and an acrid burning smell assail him. There is a round metal mold inside, which he grasps carefully, eyes watering.

"Put it on the counter," directs the voice.

Jack lifts the mold and its hot, smoking contents onto the wet stainless steel counter. For an instant, the only sound is the hiss of hot metal and drops of water in conflict. He looks up, bewildered.

"The soufflé has fallen," the voice sneers. "It is fallen and burned."

He sees who is speaking now. It is Laura Sanders. She steps from the shadows, wearing a towering white chef's hat and spotless, full-length coat and trousers. She brandishes a soup ladle and gestures at the shriveled and burned mess on the counter. Grouped behind her are female acolytes, midgets in similar spotless chef's attire. They begin keening.

"His soufflé has fallen. Fallen... Fallen..." They begin circling Jack ominously, intoning the same sad dirge: "Fallen... Fallen..."

"No," protests Jack, "it's not my fault, the oven..."

"Yes," says Laura dismissively, "you have failed. Not only do real men eat quiche but they cook raspberry soufflés. Real men cook soufflés."

"Fallen... Fallen..." The words cut like tiny lashes. Faster, faster... the tiny acolytes spin about him in a macabre dance until they become a blur. Boos and hisses rain from behind the wall of darkness. Jack is helpless, shriveling inside his apron until the Giants cap covers him completely. He is trapped in darkness and terrified. "No...o...o...o...!"

Heart pounding, dripping sweat, he sits up. The digital clock beside the bed reads 2:12 a.m. He has been asleep for about four hours. The readout flips to 2:13. But that is all that changes.

Laura studied her list: for the soup, onions, French bread, and Gruyere cheese; for the salad, Romaine lettuce, croutons, Parmesan cheese, and (yuck!) anchovy fillets; for the scaloppini, veal, of course, dry white wine, garlic salt (better check on that) and lemons; finally, for the soufflé, soufflé mold with collar (got to buy one), raspberries, eggs, and powdered sugar. She had the other ingredients. Now, who should be the guests? The food critic, of course—no choice there—and she decided to invite Sally. How about Morris Evander? The furor over the *Glimpse* article had subsided quickly as the students who attended the party came forward to tell their stories. Plus, there had been letters to the editor in the Blade from former students defending her. Finally, Linda and her boyfriend had made up and she had publicly credited Laura with helping her. Laura grabbed her car keys and purse and dumped a protesting Buffy from the kitchen counter. Time to go shopping.

Jack awoke, grumpy and tired. He brewed some coffee, rejected eggs for two pieces of toast, and considered his options. Then he went to the telephone, called Reginald Quimby and explained what he had in mind.

Quimby, surprised and pleased that someone who actually worked in the business of real news would ask his help, agreed readily.

"Of course, dear lad, I know just the place. It's the "Purple Pelican" on the Embarcadero. I gave it a glowing review just last week. Diverse menu and superb wine cellar." He lowered his voice. "You know when I praise a restaurant, I usually get a call offering me a free dinner for two. Why don't I see if I can trade that for part of what you have in mind?"

"You're at the top of today's 'good guy' list, Reg," Jack responded. "Can I get you some decent Sharks tickets?" It would mean putting the arm on Maggie again, but he could add another game to his obligation to drive her to see the team play in San Jose.

"Sharks? Thank you, no, I never watch hockey. Too violent." Quimby paused. "You don't happen to have access to wrestling tickets?" Images of muscular, sweating men grunting and straining filled his mind.

"See what I can do," Jack promised.

"D Day" came. The Challenge of the Sexes great dinner cook-off had arrived.

On Sanibel Island, Sally helped Laura carry dirty dishes into the kitchen in preparation for dessert.

"Have another glass of wine," he counseled. "It'll relax you."

"I shouldn't..."

He laughed. "Why not, it's going well. You've got enough vino for two parties."

True enough. She had decided on a California wine despite the irony. It was a 1996 Iron Horse Sonoma Chardonnay and everyone, including the food editor of the Blade, seemed to like it. In fact, the food editor,

Louise Rawls, had surprised her. Laura had expected a frumpy, middle-aged, super critical critic. Rawls turned out to be an attractive blonde in her late 20s, who flashed an engagement ring, laughed at Evander's jokes, and complimented Laura on the dinner—so far. Once out of the office and lubricated with a few glasses of wine, Morris Evander had shown a new, and pleasing, side of his personality. Jokes? That was a side of him she had never seen. So far it had gone without a hitch. The soup had been oniony, the bread browned but not singed, and the cheese malleable. The salad had been fresh with just the right touch of garlic she admitted to herself, and surprisingly, the pasta served with the scaloppini had been cooked to perfection. Only the raspberry soufflé remained as a challenge.

In San Francisco, Jack patiently manipulated the cork in the champagne bottle. Gently... gently... It eased out of the bottle softly as a lover's kiss, rather than careening off the ceiling as usual.

"The French say removal of the cork should sound like a contented woman's sigh," he explained, pouring the Krug Clos de Mesnil for his guests. Pat didn't know whether to laugh or be impressed. Another observer, the director of the culinary college, wondered if he could remember the line. Writing it down now would be tacky.

"Pour the bubbly, Jack, and spare us the fortune cookie philosophy," said Maggie.

The small living room had been cleaned up for the occasion. A dozen or so trips to the basement with boxes of books, sports paraphernalia, empty bottles in cartons, old softball trophies, months' old TV Guides and Playboy Magazines made the room appear larger.

Scrounging under the couch, he had even turned up a missing DVD rental and a white sock. Unfortunately, he had thrown its counterpart away. Oh, well, I'll lose another one soon and have a pair again, he thought. The door to the dining room opened invitingly. Jack's battle-scarred table had been covered with a white cloth. Two gleaming candleholders and settings for four, complete with matched china and polished silverware, all rented, awaited.

Pat sipped her champagne and sniffed the air. Then she did it again. Nothing. No beguiling odors wafted from the kitchen. Jack glanced at his watch and poured the last of the champagne. After the downstairs buzzer sounded, he released the lock and opened the door, ushering in two men in white jackets who were carrying bulky insulated plastic cases. They placed them on the floor and unzipped the covers, removing Styrofoam tray after Styrofoam tray.

"Ah, dinner has arrived," said Jack.

The culinary college director looked at him in disbelief.

"You ordered takeout?" he said.

"The best the Blue Pelican can provide," Jack said, signing a slip for the two men and ushering them out. "Why should we suffer from my atrocious cooking when we can enjoy a really good meal? If I cooked, the meal would be memorable—but maybe not the way we might like it."

"I like your thinking, sport," agreed Maggie. She reached into her purse and held up a bottle of Pepto Bismol. "Now I won't need this."

Jack began scooping up the Styrofoam trays and ladling out the food. "Let's eat before it gets cold. We've got it all. French onion soup, Caesar salad, veal scaloppini, and raspberry soufflé."

Pat looked troubled. "You'll get no points for this in the contest," she pointed out.

"Who needs points?" Jack said, pulling back a chair and sitting down.

He reached for a bottle of wine. "We'll be drinking a '96 L'ecosse pinot noir. I think that you'll find it precocious but not presumptuous with just a taste of cherry. Bon appétit."

"Bummer," said Sally sympathetically. Laura felt more like screaming. They were looking at the sunken remnants of the raspberry soufflé. She scraped it into the garbage disposal, straightened her shoulders and marched back into the dining room. "Any one for vanilla ice cream with the chocolate cookies?"

Nancy Ferlman sighed and picked up the telephone. Her secretary had just interrupted her to announce, "that woman is on the line again. You know, the one from the TV show."

"Hi, Nancy," Mari began without delay. "I'm sure that you got the results of Kileen's cooking fiasco. He ordered take-out!" She tried to sound mystified.

"Yes, I got them. I understand that Dr. Sanders had some problem with the dessert."

"Yeah, the soufflé went south," Mari conceded. "But she should still get full credit because everything else turned out okay."

There was silence on the other end of the line, and then, wearily, "Okay. I'll check with the others on the panel; but my guess is that they'll give all 75 points to Dr. Sanders."

Mari hung up with a smile. Hours later, the little woman bobbed above the little man again, Laura 350, Jack 325.

 Chapter 31

*Help your brother's boat across
and your own will reach the shore.*

HINDU PROVERB

The Continental Airlines jet banked for its final approach to Juan Santamaria International Airport in San Jose, Costa Rica. Mari gazed out the window. A lush green canvas rose in checkerboard fashion. She stretched out in the plush, wide seat in the first-class compartment and debated whether to have another glass of wine. Fly coach? She'd made that mistake only once since becoming a television personality. Too many people recognized her. At best, they'd point and whisper; at worst, they'd ask for autographs or want to chat. Who needed that? She had been lucky enough to catch a direct flight from New York City that took only five hours. Much of that time she had spent planning her next move and brushing up on Costa Rica, a country she had never visited before. She had hoped Laura's win in the cooking contest would put her over the top for good, but it hadn't. Whoever won the adventure-racing test would win the Challenge of the Sexes. And she didn't intend for it to be Jack Kileen.

So she was bound for Utilo, Costa Rica, on the banks of the Rio Verde, the stream on which the kayaking test would take place. Unwilling to plough through thick guidebooks offering detailed information, Mari had turned to the U.S. government agency that provided the most succinct report about Costa Rica on the Internet: The CIA. Well, why not? That's what Americans pay taxes for. The Cold War was history, and the spooks couldn't spend all of their time trying to infiltrate a shadowy world of international terrorists when almost none of their agents spoke Arabic. So why not offer The CIA World Fact Book on the Internet?

Mari's view of the world happened to be as egocentric as that of other Americans. She had a mental map in which North America, with the United States center stage, floated in a sea of blue. Other continents drifted about it at a respectful distance as lesser satellites. She had known Costa Rica existed somewhere *down there* with the other banana republics, but not much more. Now she knew it lacked an army, navy, and air force, and was smaller than West Virginia. With Nicaragua on the north and Panama on the south, it nestled between the Caribbean Sea on the east and the Pacific Ocean on the west. The climate was tropical, which meant warm. The most important import was tourists, and the most important exports were coffee and bananas. The population was 95 per cent literate, mostly Catholic, and spoke Spanish. There were four volcanoes, but fortunately none had erupted recently. Too bad. Images of burning lava would have added a nice sense of danger to background video footage of the kayak race. Oh, well. You couldn't have everything.

After retrieving her overnight bag, Mari walked into the crowded terminal. Taxi drivers swarmed outside customs and one accosted her, trying to wrest her bag from her. Thin, tanned, and determined, he wore gray pants and a colorful sport shirt. She resisted. "How much to the Estrada Hotel?"

"$20," responded the man, trying for the bag again.

"Demasiado!"—Too much—she responded, thereby using up 20 per cent of the phrases in Spanish she had jotted down. If they didn't hurry, she would have to use the one that inquired as to the whereabouts of the ladies room.

They settled on $15. He led her out of the turmoil of the airport terminal to his taxi.

The Estrada Hotel appeared to be upscale. At least it had a concierge. After checking in, Mari arranged for a car with driver for the morning and went into the restaurant, where she ordered a bottle of Imperial beer and arroz con pollo. The beer went well with the chicken and rice. She went upstairs, checked her e-mail and telephone messages, and crawled into bed.

Utilo, where the kayaking race would start, turned out to be more a scattering of buildings than a village. It consisted of small houses half-hidden in thick foliage behind wooden fences, a few bleached-front stores, a metal-roofed church with an overgrown graveyard, and a restaurant whose sign had faded and cracked. The marina on the Rio Verde River boasted the community's newest acquisition, a shiny wooden dock on creosote-soaked pilings thrust iinto placid, rippling brown waters. Small boats, some with electric motors, bobbed beside it, tethered to narrow walkways that projected out from the dock like arms on a cross. On the shore, a rusted rack of iron pipes supported about a dozen canoes and kayaks.

A small office of weathered gray boards, much older than the dock itself, stood beside rock steps that ran down the bank to the water's edge. Mari hadn't recovered from the ride from San Jose. They had taken the Pan-American Highway briefly before swinging northwest on rural roads. Although he had been hired for the entire day, the driver had driven rapidly, even in the city, using his horn frequently. Once on the highway, he had passed slower cars and trucks with abandon under conditions that frightened her—and she was used to New York City taxi drivers. She ordered him to slow down. He had shrugged, changed the station on the radio, and done so grudgingly. She recalled another statistic about Costa Rica: It had one of the highest auto fatality rates in the world.

The door to the marina office was open so she stepped inside. Behind a counter, a man sat trying to open a jammed desk drawer. "Excuse me," she said, ""I'm looking for the manager."

He turned. "And you have found him." He looked her over. Mari was still in her big city clothes, a maroon skirt and white blouse. She had shucked the jacket in the cab, which lacked air conditioning. She didn't look as if she wanted to rent a boat to go fishing.

"Are you Mr. Castillo?" That was the name of the person she had been told would provide the kayaks for Laura and Jack Kileen.

He was middle-aged with a neatly trimmed, pencil thin mustache and dark eyes. He wore a blue work shirt, the collar of which had begun to wilt in the morning heat. Above a clean T-shirt, damp gray hair curled.

"I'm Mari O'Reilly. I called two days ago about renting two kayaks on the day the Enduro Challenge competitors come down the river. Also, I wanted to arrange for our two people, a man and a woman, to be picked up after they paddle down the river and driven back to San Jose."

He gestured for her to come around the counter and sit down on a metal folding chair. "Yes, yes, I remember now. That is not a problem." He mentioned a figure for the rental of the boats and the pickup and transportation.

Mari took out a credit card and passed it over. He ran the card through and had her sign. "That is taken care of," he said. "I will reserve two of the kayaks, our best, new ones, for your people. They will only be going a short distance down the river, and I will have people and a truck waiting where they come ashore."

"There is one other thing," Mari began carefully. This was going to be the hard part, conveying what she wanted to convey without spelling it out. "Neither of them is experienced in using kayaks."

"Don't worry. There is no need," he assured her. "The river is tame this time of year. They will be wearing lifejackets and can carry cell phones in case there is trouble."

She pretended to be thinking. "Even so, the man is much stronger than the woman. It wouldn't be a fair race."

He looked at her, puzzled, wondering how that concerned him. "But that is..."

"Avoidable," she said, finishing his sentence. "They'll be on the river separately and timed individually. But in fairness, I think the man should have some type of handicap. Not officially, of course," she said hurriedly. "And I realize something like that would require a special service from you, for which I'm prepared to pay generously in cash."

Castillo looked thoughtful. Although English was his second language, he had no trouble translating what she had said. He decided "officially" really meant "publicly." But what did "generously" mean?

He shifted in his chair. "You realize, of course, that the Enduro Challenge paddlers must pass before your people can get on the river. The racers will be taken out farther down the river. The tourism department has instructed us to help the Enduro people wherever possible. It is the international publicity on television, I think."

Mari nodded. "But something could be done...."

Castillo leaned back reflectively. "So," he said, "it might be that the man gets on the river late, perhaps with darkness coming on. He might miss the takeout point and have to get off farther down. That would cost him time, no?"

This was going better than she had expected, Mari thought. Castillo was a quick study. "Yes. Of course, or if his boat sprang a leak or something... that would slow him down, wouldn't it? They do leak sometimes, don't they?"

He frowned. "Yes, the old ones do if they hit something and spring part of the frame. But not the new aluminum ones."

Mari looked thoughtful, weighing the merits of old vs. new kayaks. "It would be too bad if you only had two kayaks available, one new one and one older one. Of course, the woman would get the new one, wouldn't she?"

"Yes," Castillo agreed. "Custom would dictate that. It could be," he reflected, smoothing his mustache, "that a late rental reduced my stock of boats so only two were left. You would not hold that against me?"

Mari's eyes widened as if she were shocked, shocked at the very thought. "Of course not. Those things happen. The agreement only specifies that you have two kayaks ready for use. Details are up to you."

He looked at her calculatingly. "This would require special expenses... arranging for trucks... moving boats ... that sort of thing. He didn't mention the risk of being found out, but they both were aware that would be another cost.

And so they got down to it. He wanted to replace his beat-up pickup truck. He suggested that a new truck might be acceptable. It would cost about $17,000. She laughed and offered to replace his ancient wood desk with its scarred sides and broken drawers for $500. Eventually, they settled on $2,500, which would make the down payment on a better grade of beat-up pickup truck. In addition, Mari agreed that if she got an additional bill for damages to the kayaks not exceeding $1,000 after the race, she'd okay it. She reached into her purse and withdrew $2,500 in crisp, new 100-dollar bills. She had been nervous about this all day since visiting the bank and cashing traveler's checks. But cash doesn't leave a trail, paper or otherwise.

While Mari sweltered in Costa Rica, Ashford Sloan could detect an early frost in the air at the offices of *Glimpse*. The door to Larry Clayton's office was open, but Sloan decided it would be better if he knocked rather than just walked in. He had a feeling his relationship with Clayton had taken a hit after the Laura Sanders story. Unlike some of *Glimpse*'s fabrications, this one hadn't developed "legs" as they say in the entertainment business. There had been no new developments, lots of denials, and no follow-up.

"Can I interrupt you for a moment, boss?"

Clayton didn't look up. He had been editing a story about a dog in Maryland that supposedly could predict fires. The dog, a Chesapeake Bay retriever, had awakened its owners by barking when a barn began blazing in the middle of the night. It had done so again the next day when dry grass smoldered but hadn't broken into flame. Probably got a good nose, thought Clayton. He decided to add a third incident, perhaps one with somebody's life being saved. Yes, that should do it.

"What can I do for you, Sloan?" he asked without looking up.

Sloan noticed that he hadn't been invited to sit down. "I just heard about that kidnapping in Hollywood. You know, the movie star's kid."

Clayton nodded absent-mindedly.

"That's one I could do, boss. My kind of story." Sloan calculated it also would mean spending a week or two in California, away from the office, which wouldn't hurt, either.

Clayton looked up. "It's already covered. Nevasconi is on it. Flying out this afternoon."

"Nevasconi..." protested Sloan, "isn't he pretty green for something like this?"

Clayton smiled thinly. "No more than you were when you started here. Besides, the kid did a nice job on the story about the woman in Tennessee with the Elvis Presley doll that warbled "Blue Suede Shoes" when you squeezed it." Well, he reflected, something that might have been "Blue Suede Shoes. They both knew no one had looked into *that* one too deeply, but the pictures had been sensational. A big seller with the Graceland crowd.

"Well, I just thought I'd check...."

"Thoughtful of you," said Clayton dryly. He returned to his editing.

Sloan wandered back to his desk. He sat down and scratched the itch above his upper lip. He had decided a mustache would give him a more mature look after Clayton had starting referring to Nevasconi as 'the kid.' Sloan decided his days at *Glimpse* might be nearing an end. He was no longer the new kid on the block. Maybe he should consider helping out with that weekend news show on the local PBS outlet after all. It had been an off-hand suggestion made by a woman at a party after a few drinks. Sloan had laughed it off. But now... Television might be interesting. And if that didn't work out, he could explore teaching journalism at a junior college or something. He could see himself standing at a lectern, gazing out at fresh, eager students—Prof. Ashford Sloan, role model and mentor, the Mr. Chips of journalism education.

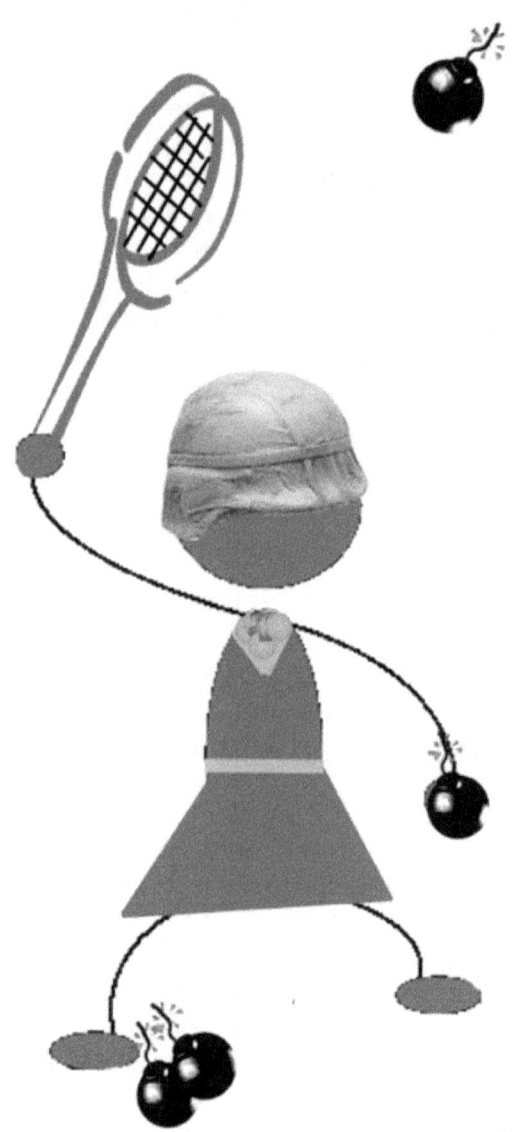

Chapter 32

"Water, water, everywhere,
And all the boards did shrink.
Water, water everywhere,
Nor any drop to drink."

SAMUEL TAYLOR COLERIDGE

In at least one respect, rivers are like people, energetic in youth and measured in maturity. Rolling past the hot, dusty shores of Utilo, the Rio Verde resembled a wide, rippling, dun-colored flood. Only an occasional kingfisher, perched on a branch above its banks, or a few hopeful egrets probing the shallows, paid it much attention. The Rio Verde is less glamorous than other Costa Rican Rivers. It lacks the sweep of the Chirripo, sometimes compared to the Salmon River of Idaho. Nor is it often likened to the General, which creates a six-meter wave at Chachala, or the Pacuare, known for its beauty. An unpretentious stream for most of its length, the Rio Verde ends its life in the Pacific Ocean.

But high in its upper reaches, where the Enduro Race kayakers were about to begin their run west, the river stirred and foamed and frothed in cataracts of Class 3 white water. And that was before it began raining. Costa Rica's wet season ran from May through November, the time of year that renews the low-land fields and encourages new life in the mountains and jungles. Throughout the country, the average rainfall amounts to 100 inches per year, but that varies widely with time and place. Before the race, The Tico Times forecast several days of what the natives called a *veranillo*, or little summer.

Laura and Jack didn't worry about the chance of rain; they worried about whether Carlos would get them to Utilo alive. They had arrived in San Jose on separate flights the day before and taken orange taxis to the Estrada Hotel, where reservations had been made for them. Laura had dined there, but Jack had explored, finally eating at an outdoor restaurant where he had feasted on square tamales made with white corn meal, mashed potatoes, and pork, washed down with sweet ice tea. They didn't meet until 8 a.m. the next morning while waiting outside the hotel for the driver who would transport them to Utilo and the kayaking test.

Laura had been curt in responding to his greeting and then immediately berated herself. *Why do I do that! I got myself into this. It's not his fault, jerk though he is.* But Jack's flip manner irritated her, and her own nervousness didn't help.

Nothing's changed, Jack told himself. *She's still the ice princess.*

But they became closer, at least physically, as they bounced around in the back seat of the car Carlos raced over bumpy country roads. Once they had left the city, the scenery changed to sparsely settled farm-land and meadows afire with lavender morning glories and passion flowers. Cattle grazed in the still-cool morning air. Doves exploded from roadside ditches and brush as they rocketed along, clouds of dust rising in the car's wake. Overhead, turkey vultures, growing more active as the air warmed and created thermals, circled lazily in the sky. Through it all, Carlos kept the pedal to the metal, switching between fading radio stations. Traffic no longer a challenge, he inched the speedometer higher, daring something or someone to wander incautiously into the car's path.

"Say, I took a nice lady out here last week...." He swerved to avoid something small, dark, and fast that scurried across the road. "She said she is on television back in the states. Funny name... Mary... Mori..."

"Mari," said Jack suspiciously. He looked at Laura. "Did you know she flew down here?"

Laura looked guilty. "She might have mentioned it. We talked on the telephone a few days ago. She arranged for the kayaks."

"She didn't call me."

Laura stared out the window and didn't respond.

She looks different somehow, Jack decided, but he couldn't put his finger on it. It might have been her hair, shorter than he remembered. Women were always changing their hair. Men got haircuts every three weeks or so from barbers who could discuss engine displacement and the potential of the Patriots' rebuilt defensive line. Nobody discussed hairstyles.

Laura's right foot banged against the wooden picnic basket Jack had placed on the floor between them. No room in the trunk. The trunk overflowed with hoses and brushes and chemicals for Carlos's other job, cleaning swimming pools.

"What's in the basket?" she asked, after her foot had collided with the basket again.

"Survival supplies."

She wanted to ask more, but his smile (she read it as a smirk) stopped her. No way did she intend to think about survival. Kayaks still scared her, despite the lessons.

At about 11:30, Carlos slowed at a crossroads and turned left. A sign read *Utilo* 2. Kilometers? Miles? It didn't matter. Soon they were traveling through the main street of town. There were few signs of life. The cool morning had yielded to the heat of day. Even the dogs lolled in patches of shade, tongues hanging out. The car pulled to a halt at the marina, where they got out and stretched. Carlos began drinking water from a bottle thirstily. He didn't offer to share it. Jack and Laura walked down the steps to the small wood shack at the head of a new dock. Several men stood next to two kayaks tied to the dock. One turned upon seeing them and hurried over.

"Miss Sanders... Mr. Kileen... I am George Castillo. Welcome to Utilo." He removed a wide straw hat, took a handkerchief from a pocket and wiped his forehead. "Everything is ready for you."

"When can we begin?" asked Laura. The sooner the better. She was growing more nervous by the hour. The hot ride from San Jose had sapped her strength.

She never slept well the first night in strange places any way.

He shrugged. "Not for several hours. There has been rain in the mountains. The river is rising. Not a lot," he hurried to assure them. "Also, one of the kayakers had an accident."

"An accident?" said Jack.

"Yes, he hit a rock and overturned, losing the kayak for a few minutes. But he is back on the water. The others should start passing us within an hour or so." Castillo kept his worries to himself. Of course, that's if there are no more mishaps. He decided not to share this opinion with the two Americans, who were looking uneasily at the water, gauging its strength and power.

"You can go into Utilo for lunch, or if you have brought something to eat, use our picnic area." He gestured to a weathered table under a thatched cover overlooking the river. "I'm keeping in contact with the people running the race by radio. I'll let you know when the first racers are due."

"Thanks," said Jack. "I brought my lunch."

"I guess I can go into Utilo," said Laura unenthusiastically. She had seen the restaurant with peeling paint and faded Coca-Cola sign. Right now, she'd gladly take a McDonald's Happy Meal without the action figures.

"Why not join me?" suggested Jack. "I've got enough for two." He walked to the car and got out the picnic hamper. Soon they were enjoying grilled chicken sandwiches, sliced tomatoes, potato chips, and warm bottled water. On the table, unopened, stood a bottle of red wine, but neither risked drinking. After a while they stopped trying to make polite conversation and contented themselves with swatting the flies.

Toward mid-afternoon, the first racer appeared, a black smudge on the chocolate ribbon of water. Up closer, his white helmet and orange lifejacket contrasted with the maroon kayak he paddled rhythmically, the current pushing at its back. If Laura and Jack expected some recognition, they didn't get it. The paddler never glanced at the shore. Soon another racer followed and then another. By this point, the Rio Verde had widened and smoothed into Class 1 water, a clear, wide channel with occasional small waves flecked in white.

"The current seems faster," Laura said nervously.

Jack nodded. The river seemed to run faster and higher. Stones at the water's edge that had caught the sun's light and reflected it back earlier were under water. Not by much, but definitely submerged.

"Maybe a little faster," he conceded. They waited another hour in the heat. Even in the shade, humid air enveloped them like a suffocating blanket. The water they drank seemed to evaporate from their bodies. To the east, ominous gray clouds had begun forming.

About 4 p.m., Castillo bustled over. "Only one more racer to go and then the senorita can depart. The pickup team is leaving now with the camera crew."

The pickup team, Jack noticed, consisted of two bored-looking young men, lounging by a dirty white truck smoking and talking. The camera crew consisted of another man in jeans, crew-neck sports shirt, and a jungle hat. He sat with his back to the marina shack, fanning himself with a magazine.

"Remember," cautioned Castillo, "watch the right bank of the river about nine miles down. The bank is open for about 100 meters. The current slows there because the river widens. My son Carlos and his friend will wave their hats to signal you. Pull into the shore right away."

How do you judge nine miles? Laura wondered. Dumb question. No odometers on a kayak. Her lips tightened. I'd better spot these guys fast.

"What if we miss the pickup point?" asked Jack.

Castillo looked uneasy. "It would be better not to miss it. There are some small sloughs running off the river that you could take if necessary. But don't go another five miles down the river whatever you do."

"Why not?" asked Laura, thinking that she probably wouldn't like the answer.

"Because there the river drops sharply for several miles into a narrow chute in the canyon. It is called caballito del diablo—the devil's darning needle. Only experts attempt it in a kayak."

Jack and Laura exchanged glances.

"But do not worry. The takeout point is obvious," he said reassuringly. "A red sign precedes it with the words 'Beach kayaks here.' Just stay to the right."

"Did you mention that devil something or other to Mari O'Reilly when she was here last week?" Jack asked, irritated.

"Miss O'Reilly..." Castillo hesitated. "I don't recall. Maybe, maybe not."

Laura looked nervously at the river. "It's running higher and faster, isn't it? Perhaps we should do this tomorrow."

"Oh, no!" said Castillo. "It will be okay." He decided not to mention it had been made clear to him by the Gringo lady that the kayaking event had to be run that day to fit her television schedule or he would have to refund the money—and lose the new pickup.

"Maybe it is a little higher," he conceded, looking thoughtfully at the sky.

Shortly after 5 p.m., the last kayaker swept past. He looked longingly at the people on the bank and gouge marks scarred the bow of his boat.

Castillo bustled up. "We are almost ready," he said. "Miss Sanders can leave soon. We must leave a few minutes for the last of the racers to be picked up at the take-out point."

Laura looked doubtful. "Isn't it getting late?" She also didn't like the looks of the clouds, which were darker.

"No," Castillo said. "We have hours of daylight left. You will be on the water only briefly. You have your cell phone?"

Laura nodded. She sweated in a waterproof paddling jacket, and had been given a too-large helmet that bobbed up and down when she moved her head. She walked down to the water. A bright blue kayak, its shiny exterior unmarked, bobbed beside the dock, held in place by two men. She squeezed into the open cockpit, stuffing the clear plastic dry bag containing the cell phone and a water bottle between her legs. She tightened her life jacket and was handed a paddle.

"I will report your starting time by radio," Castillo said. He almost said "good luck" and then caught himself. No need to add to her nervousness.

Laura swallowed and wet her lips. No turning back now.

Jack gave her a thumbs up as she pushed off from the dock. The current toyed with the tiny boat briefly and dragged it toward the center of the river. Before Jack had taken several breaths, the kayak had become a small blue dot on a brown canvas.

Jack made a last visit to the wooden shed that served as a restroom and donned his life jacket. "How long do we wait?" he asked Castillo.

"About 15 or 20 minutes," the marina manager responded. "We don't want you both arriving at the takeout point at once. You are likely to paddle faster."

That made sense to Jack. He eyed the thick clouds suspiciously and glanced at his watch. It was almost 6 p.m. He paced up and down the dock, sweltering in a life jacket that seemed to keep the moisture in, rather than out, clutching a water bottle, and dry bags, one large, one small. He carried the helmet rather than wore it. Too hot. He felt impatient to begin, the way he usually did before a tough interview. His gray kayak, scarred by previous encounters with rocks and trees, rubbed against worn tires cushioning the dock. Something caught his eye. A glint...a reflection. He looked closer.

"Is this thing leaking," he asked. "I can see some water inside."

Castillo squatted and looked intently. "Oh, yes. There is a little water, but it is nothing to worry about. All of these old boats take on a little water. Once you are moving, it will stop."

That didn't sound terribly logical to Jack, but then again his experience with kayaks was limited. A few of the bigger boats he had been on while day fishing out of San Francisco or Monterey had leaked a little.

Another thought struck him. "Why isn't this a new boat like the other one?"

Castillo spread his hands apologetically. "We ran short because of the race. But this boat is fine. I stand behind it."

Fine, thought Jack, but you don't have to go down the river in it, do you? He straightened abruptly, working out a crick in his neck.

Castillo looked at his watch again. "It is time."

Jack wedged himself into the boat. His weight raised the stern of the kayak and muddy water sloshed along his hips. He squared away his dry bags, tightened his chinstrap, and took the paddle in both hands. He nodded at Castillo and felt himself being pushed away from the dock. He took three quick strokes and became a prisoner of the river.

Chapter 33

That tuft of jungle feathers, That animal eye.

WALLACE STEVENS

For the first minute or two, Laura fought panic. The river's banks flashed by, patches of green and brown appearing and disappearing, farms and pastures giving way to rougher scrub land. Then she became too busy to notice. The current pushed her along, toying with the slim kayak. Her practice sessions in sheltered waters in Florida hadn't prepared her for this. Gradually, she adjusted to the current's pull and asserted control over the tiny boat. She found she could guide it. She began to work her way to the right side of the river. Sneaking a hurried look at her watch, Laura discovered four minutes had gone by. *Got it under control*, she repeated to herself. *Got it under control.* And then the first drops of rain dimpled the water.

Jack faced the same problems as Laura, but he was stronger and soon controlled the sleek little shell that bore him along. Light faded, but that barely dented his consciousness. Nor did the heat or occasional wave that broke over the bow and splashed into the open cockpit. He concentrated on exploring the parameters of the power he possessed over the Rio Verde and those the river possessed over him. Then the water ahead became pock marked, and he became aware of a series of light touches on his helmet. Soon they became blows.

Laura's world shrank to a dense, gray cocoon of mist and water. The left bank of the river vanished from sight. The right bank, visible at times, disappeared at others, blurring into a dim outline in the driving down-pour. She was in an *aguacero*, a torrential rain, the force of which drove people to shelter wherever they could and drivers to pull over to the side of the road. She stopped paddling and put her watch up in front of her face, squinting as rain pummeled the thin skin of the kayak. Seven minutes had passed. Where was the red sign marking the take-out point? If she could have turned around, she might have seen it—behind her.

Jack could see only a few yards in front of the kayak. He pushed aside the thought of what it would be like to hit a log in the river at full speed. Worse, he felt the kayak becoming sluggish. He felt more water sloshing about his hips and suspected the leak had increased. Rain slashing into the open cockpit didn't help, either. Perhaps he should have used a cockpit cover. But then he recalled his lack of aptitude at completing a full roll in a kayak when it overturned. No way. How to unsnap a rubber cover while upside down in a river during a storm wasn't in the instruction manual.

Downstream, at the takeout point, Marcos and his friend (or former friend after today) stood in a clear-ing peering into the heavy rain that punished land and water. They were soaked to the skin. Dense underbrush choked both sides of the clearing. This was the only open place to beach boats for miles. Marcos, in charge because he drove the truck, had assigned his friend Roberto the job of recording the finishing times of the two kayakers. Roberto tried to shelter a note pad under a thin jacket.

"Do you see anything?" Marcos asked. His voice competed with the steady pounding of the rain.

"No. It's too early. Let's wait in the truck."

Marcos took a step forward on the bank. The river sang with a new urgency at his feet. "We wait here." With a new pickup truck at stake, his father would kill him if he failed to bring out the crazy Americans. The man with the camera had retreated to the shelter of the pickup truck.

"There! On the river! Look! It is a boat! Marcos's friend pointed. They waved their hats and shouted frantically, ignoring the downpour.

Laura, concentrating on paddling, looked up in shock as a clearing with two waving boys appeared out of the gray void and slid past. She stared in disbelief as a green wall of jungle closed in again.

Marcos threw up his arms up in frustration. He turned to Roberto and shook his head. Nothing came easily. Water dripped down his arm as he checked his watch. "Record the time," he said. He pulled out his cell phone.

As the rain eased, Jack glimpsed the sign and then the clearing. He scanned the bank and saw two figures almost lost against the dark foliage. But he didn't see what he had been looking for, Laura and her bright blue kayak. Irritated at him as she usually seemed to be, he expected to see her standing on the shore to let him know he'd lost again. But only two figures stood on the bank. Where was she? If she had missed the takeout and continued down the river, a likely possibility, she'd need help. He could see the two boys, who were waving their arms wildly, as he drew abreast of them. Jack lifted his paddle and pointed down the river. He swept past.

"Now what?" asked Roberto, shifting back and forth in water-soaked sandals. He had just jotted down the time of the second American's passing. Marcos stared disconsolately down the river, thoughts of the truck pushed out of his mind. Five miles farther along the Rio Verde awaited a rock-strewn chute of tumbling water—caballito del diablo, the devil's needle.

Cindy Martinez pushed open Mari's door without knocking. She hurried over to the 65-inch television set and switched it on.

"What are you doing?" Mari demanded, looking up from her desk with irritation. She had been waiting for a report from Costa Rica for hours.

Outside the building, night had fallen. Bands of light blinked on and off in the dark towers as cleaning crews, the night people, advanced floor to floor.

"They're missing," Cindy said breathlessly, working the TV control. "A violent storm blew up on the river. Dr. Sanders didn't see where she was supposed to get out and Kileen went on past it, too."

Mari sucked in her breath. Unbelievable! What next, a plague of locusts?

Cindy turned up the sound. A solemn young woman in a raincoat held a microphone up to the face of a man who looked familiar.

Yes! Mari recognized him. It was...what was his name...Castillo, the marina operator. He stood on a dock, dark and roiling water behind him.

"It's been four hours since the two Challenge of the Sexes contestants vanished down this surging, rain-lashed river," the reporter said dramatically, gesturing at the barely illuminated water. "Rescuers won't know until tomorrow if they managed to get off the river before it reaches the deadly falls ahead. All we can do is wait for daylight. This is Maria Ramirez for Channel 4 news in Utilo, Costa Rica."

Cindy switched off the television and looked at Mari. For once, her boss was speechless.

Chapter 34

Truth is the only safe ground to stand on.

ELIZABETH CADY STANTON

As suddenly as it began, the rain slackened and stopped. The sun, low in the west, reappeared. The river narrowed, funneling through shoreline that looked thick and green and dense. Laura looked at her watch. Six more minutes! She must have missed the takeout point. Her shoulders slumped. She rested the paddle across the open canopy, fatigue replacing adrenaline. She had to get off the river—and fast. Ahead, on her left, she could see an opening in the wall of greenery and a muddy channel. Laura dug her paddle into the water hard and swung into the narrow channel.

She worked her way down the slough for several minutes, looking for a clear, dry place on a bank to beach the kayak. Despite aching shoulders and arms, she had more control over the boat in the weaker current. But the jungle seemed to be closing in on her, so she decided to turn around, paddle back to the entrance, and go farther down river. She had never felt so alone, so helpless. *Damn!*

But she wasn't alone. Submerged in the water to eye level, a crocodile raised its head, sensing vibrations from the kayak's approach. It couldn't have articulated possible causes: a large fish blundering into the slough... a monkey missing a branch and tumbling into the water. It only associated the change in its environment with the possibility of food.

A fundamental law of physics states two objects can't occupy the same space at the same time. When Laura's kayak struck the seven-foot crocodile, it thrashed in surprise. The boat shuddered and overturned, dumping her into the water. Alarmed, the crocodile decided the sudden blow and commotion probably meant whatever had struck it had to be too big for dinner. Submerging, it swam off, powered by broad sweeps of an armored tail. Laura found herself swimming, too. She took several desperate strokes. The life jacket had inflated, buoying her, and then her feet sank in soft mud. She lunged forward and dragged herself, hand over hand, up on the bank.

No more wishful thinking for Jack. The waterlogged kayak floated lower. Each stroke took more effort. His arms felt like lead weights. He'd have to land soon, but where? The rain had passed, and the sun dipped beneath the horizon. A stultifying silence descended on the river as if the life had been drained from it. The stream narrowed and openings appeared in the jungle wall. Should he go left or right? Now or later? If he didn't do it now, would there be a later?

Gloom shrouded the water as light faded rapidly. Sweat bathed Jack's face. He stopped paddling to wipe it off. Then he resumed steady strokes, ignoring his burning muscles, the boat wallowing beneath him like a disobedient beast. Decision time. He hoped Laura had taken the first slough leading off the river. He swung the kayak's bow toward it and entered the muddy ribbon of water. Slowing the forward motion of the kayak sharply in the dim light, Jack eyed the overgrown banks slipping by.

"Here! Over here!"

He stopped paddling and drifted with the current. What was that? The mangrove channel had become a dark tunnel of grotesque shapes, choking the water's edges with roots that resembled tentacles. Beyond them, the jungle loomed, an uneven slash of indistinct greenery. Then he heard a weak voice again.

"Help! Help!"

He saw a white face in the gloom and drove the kayak toward it. Laura stood on the bank, holding onto a shrub with one hand and waving frantically with the other. With a quick series of strokes, Jack paddled the sinking kayak toward her and drove it part way up on the bank with the last of his strength. She seized the toggle rope on the bow. He squeezed out of the cockpit, stumbled in the waist-deep water, and then struggled up the bank. He took the toggle rope from her and pulled the kayak higher onto the spongy ground. They both sank to the ground in exhaustion.

"Miss Livingston, I presume?"

Her eyes fluttered, and her lips opened and closed without speaking.

"Are you all right?" he asked. When she didn't answer, he repeated the question. "Are you all right?"

Laura shivered in her thin paddle jacket, bare legs, and once-white sneakers covered with mud. "I...I... guess so. There was something in the water. I hit it and the kayak overturned. The current...." She stopped.

"You can take off the helmet," Jack said wearily, unsnapping his own and shrugging out of the lifejacket.

"Oh..." She did the same.

He reached into the kayak and pulled out a water bottle.

"Here, you must be thirsty." He handed her the plastic bottle and watched as she began to drink feverishly.

"Hey, not so fast. That may have to last us for a while. Lost yours?"

She nodded. "Everything. Water, cell phone, GPS... They're all gone along with the boat."

"Then you didn't call 911?"

She grimaced. Color returned to her face. "Is everything a joke to you? We could have died out there!" she snapped.

Light vanished as if squeezed from a tube, and a low mist rose on the water. Night wrapped them in a warm embrace. On the opposite bank, trees and vines and logs began to lose their shape. Jack could have sworn he saw two ruby red dots appear briefly and then vanish in a quiet swirl of dirty water. He decided not to mention it.

He reached into the boat and rummaged for the two dry bags. Then he flipped the kayak upside down to drain it. As he unzipped the smaller of the bags, he heard a sloshing sound and muddy water poured out.

"Uh-oh." He removed a cell phone, flipped it open, and turned it on.   "Dead," he said regretfully.

"That figures," said Laura. She sounded depressed. "But they should be looking for us since we missed the takeout point."

That wasn't likely and they both knew it. There would be no rescue attempt before morning.

Jack leaned back. "Well, Wonder Woman, what now?"

"Don't call me that!" she fired back. "You missed the takeout point, too."

He started to say something and bit off the comment.

Fetid air, ripe with the odor of decaying vegetation, settled over the mangrove swamp. Flickers of grayish white marked the last herons settling down for the night in trees, and scarlet macaws squawked in protest from somewhere. Behind them, in the black mass of jungle, a branch snapped.

"It could be worse," Jack said. "We might be on that French torture course, the Marathon de Sables—racing 150 miles in the Sahara Desert with scorpions and snakes for company."

"At least we'd be warm." Her teeth chattered, whether from immersion in the water or tension.

"Maybe I can help with that." He reached into the large bag. The interior was dry. He sorted through the contents and pulled out a jacket. "Here...this will help preserve your body heat."

She shrugged into the jacket gratefully and zipped it up tightly. "Thanks."

"How about a fire? People who are lost always build fires," Jack said.

"So build one."

"One roaring bonfire, coming up."

"I'll bet you were an Eagle Scout," she replied, "pushing little old ladies into traffic."

He shook his head. "Nope. Never got that far. Failed the clean living test in Cub Scouts."

"I'm not surprised."

He noticed her shivering had stopped. She was breathing evenly.

"Do you have matches?" Laura asked.

"Yes, and a fire starter stick," he replied. "Never leave home without them. All we need is some semi-dry wood." He pulled a penlight from the bag that was dry and pushed himself to his feet.

"Where are you going?" she asked nervously.

"Not far. I'll be right back," he reassured her.

He foraged quickly, overturning downed branches at the edge of the clearing for dry bits of grass and twigs. Shining the narrow beam of light into the ends of logs to ensure there were no nasty surprises waiting, Jack pulled out chunks of dry bark. Soon he had a struggling fire going whose tendrils of light pushed back the dusk and revealed a small, pie-shaped patch of sand and grass, yielded grudgingly by the jungle.

"Ready for dinner?"

She looked at him in surprise. "Dinner?"

"Granola bars—breakfast, lunch and sometimes dinner on demand."

"No wonder you resorted to getting a takeout dinner for the cooking test."

"When you've got it, flaunt it; when you don't, fake it," he said lightly.

He reached into the dry bag and extracted two oatmeal and raisin granola bars. He handed her one. Laura stripped off the wrapper and fed the flames, which flared briefly. She began eating hungrily. When they finished the bars, he broke a piece of chocolate in two and gave her half.

"This has been my goal all along," said Jack, settling back against the kayak's side. "To lure you to a secret lair, ply you with tepid bottled water, and use a gourmet meal, under a full moon, to lower your resistance to my charms."

She sniffed. "In case you hadn't noticed, there's no moon. And you're short on the charms."

"Ah, but at least the gourmet meal worked out."

A chattering sound emerged from the jungle. Her eyes flicked to him.

"Monkey. Nothing to worry about," he reassured her.

They shared a companionable silence.

"What happens tomorrow?" she asked.

"My guess is they'll search the river first, check below the devil's needle, and then start combing the sloughs. It shouldn't take too long."

He hoped so. If not, one of them would have to paddle out in a leaking kayak and brave the river again. He didn't want to try *that*, paddling upstream against the current.

"You won't leave me here?" she said fearfully.

"No," he said. "You can paddle out. I'll wait here." An unpleasant thought crossed his mind. And if you get lost, this could be the last place I'll ever wait.

That seemed to reassure her. "What now?" she said.

"Well, we could tell ghost stories or sing camp songs."

She shook her head. "I don't know any ghost stories and I'm not in a mood for singing. No, let's do confession time."

"Confession time...?"

"Confession time. When I was in college I belonged to an all-female hiking club. When we were sitting around a campfire, we had 'confession time.' Everyone had to tell something about themself that they'd prefer to keep a secret. We had to promise never to reveal it."

"Ahh...true confessions. I'm listening," Jack said.

"You go first," she challenged. "Do you really believe men are superior to women?"

"You're not wearing a wire, are you?"

Laura hunched forward, knees tucked under her chin, bare legs red in the firelight. She slapped at a mosquito.

"Well, do you?" she persisted.

He thought a moment before replying. "In some things. Caber tossing, killing things, including other people, and fixing leaking toilets. But I also think that women are better at comforting the afflicted, honesty, and looking for peaceful solutions to problems that testosterone only makes worse."

"I'm serious," Laura said.

"So am I," he responded. "What each sex is better at doesn't matter a lot. To use a euphemism I dislike, we are differently abled. Men and women aren't like oil and water; they're like bacon and eggs. You can enjoy either one separately, but taken together, the joint experience transcends the individual ones."

She was silent for a moment. "That piece of insight surprises me, Kileen. Normally you tend to think in physical terms. I've noticed that in your writing."

"Aha...Then you admit to reading my books!"

"Only the last one, but I suspect the male tendency to attempt to solve problems physically rather than intellectually is a thread that runs through all of them."

He nodded. "Of course. Males are prisoners of their gonads. Everyone knows that."

"I didn't mean..."

Jack pushed more bark into the flames. It flared briefly, illuminating Laura's sunken eyes and drawn mouth.

She rocked back and forth, hugging her knees tightly. "Okay, I deserved that."

"No," he said, tired of the topic. "To summarize, I don't think that men are superior to women and my book doesn't say that. Let's drop the subject. I'm getting sick of it." He rubbed his shoulders against the kayak to ease an itch...or had it been something crawling down his back? Squashed in any case.

"All right, as long as it's confession time.... I've been married," Laura said at last.

"What!"

"I said I've been married... in graduate school. It was a mistake."

"Ah..."

"Ah, what?"

"Just 'ah.'"

"Go ahead and say it," she demanded.

"Say what"

"That I hate men because I had a failed marriage." She looked away. "That's what you're thinking."

"No, I'm not," he replied. "Okay, I'll tell you something I've never admitted before. I can't get close to anyone who's female. My parents were divorced, and most of my friends are divorced. They screwed up their lives and the lives of their kids. I grew up being shuttled between two people who used me as a weapon to get back at each other."

He shook his head. "We live in a society where we discard the people that we love or thought we loved like last year's calendar. The law's too easy and alimony's too high and people look at divorce the way they look at bankruptcy, a quick fix and a clean slate. Till death us do part? Don't make me laugh." He stirred the fire and looked at her. If he expected a response, it didn't come.

Jack had decided long ago that some things could never be explained—the lyrics to "Send In The Clowns"...why Michigan had gone for a first down on fourth and two against Stanford in the 1970 Rose Bowl...how women's minds work.

"Also," he continued, "I don't understand women. Never have. Their thought processes elude me. I understand one woman, one I know at work. But she thinks like a man." He pushed thoughts of Pat out of his mind.

"Women aren't hard to understand. We're logical. It's men who go off half-cocked and tear up relationships," Lara replied.

The flames crackled and danced, casting distorted shadows behind them.

"Okay, men aren't responsible for all failing relationships," Laura said. "I'm not talking about why my marriage broke up. I *know* why it failed. We were both too wrapped up in ourselves and didn't care a tinker's damn about the other one until it was too late."

She stared into the fire's red and yellow embers. "No, I meant Ashford Sloan, that creep from *Glimpse Magazine*. He came into my seminar, listened to vulnerable women discuss their concerns, even their weaknesses. We trusted him and he lied in that scandal rag. He betrayed our trust." Her voice shook with rage. "How could he do that? You wouldn't do that, would you...pretend to be someone else just to get a story?"

Jack didn't speak. When he did, his words were measured.

"I've done the same sort of thing—but for different reasons. Journalists sometimes pretend to be what they're not. They have to. It would be nice if everyone in the world was honest and forthcoming, but it doesn't turn out that way. Criminals don't want to discuss their crimes, politicians clam up about bribery and corruption, bureaucrats protect their turf and jobs."

She looked away into the darkness, disappointment evident.

"I've never betrayed a trust and flat out lied to sell papers," he continued. "I wouldn't do what Stone did. But I took a job as an orderly in a mental hospital once to find out how the mentally ill were being treated after the state slashed the health budget. I lied on the application form and no one checked my references. I found patients unnecessarily restrained, over-medicated, and ignored because the staff was underpaid and overworked. I wrote about it. And I don't regret it because what I found out changed the way things were done. People were treated better afterward."

"That's different," Laura objected.

"Sure. But it's the same under-handed technique employed to achieve a worthier goal."

He threw the last of the wood on the fire and watched sparks float upward. "I don't know about you, but I've had a full day. I think I'll get some sleep."

"Sleep?" She looked around. "Where?"

He took a branch and began to swing it back and forth along the ground, sweeping aside brush and leaves. "Here. This is your spot. I'll be right next door." He yawned. "You can use the rest room first."

"Rest room?"

He gestured toward thick brush at the edge of the jungle.

"Oh," she said.

Something splashed, disturbing the dark surface of the water. A bird cried. Insects droned just outside the smoky shield of the fire...waiting.

Chapter 35

*Practicing the Golden Rule is not
a sacrifice; it is an investment.*

ANON.

Murky, grayish light seeped through the tangle of mangroves. The first birds stirred, fluttering their wings and greeting the new day with soft, tentative cries. Laura smiled. She nestled in her bed on Sanibel Island, hugging an enormous teddy bear, soft and warm to the touch. Buffy rubbed against one leg. She reached down to pet the cat, and her fingers came in contact with something un-Buffy like. Laura opened her eyes and screamed. First, she found the teddy bear to which she had cuddled up was Jack. One of her arms had been about his waist, her chin resting on a shoulder. Worse, the itch on her leg appeared to be caused by a fat brown leech, gorged with blood—her blood. She screamed again and jumped to her feet. That set off the screeching of howler monkeys in the trees.

"Get it off! Get it off!" she cried, reaching to pull the leech off her leg.

"Don't do that!" Jack knocked her hand away. "Have you got a cigarette?"

She looked at him in disbelief. "Are you mad! Where would I get a cigarette in the jungle? I don't even smoke!"

Half awake, he mumbled, "good point" and got on his hands and knees, pawing the dirt near the fire. As Laura hopped about, trying to shake the leech off, he picked up a dry twig.

"That should do it." Next he pawed through the contents of the large dry bag and pulled out the matches. Lighting one, he ignited the twig, which glowed red and began to burn slowly. Ignoring her protests and flinching, he gently prodded the leech with the smoldering end of the twig. Gradually, the leech relinquished its grip, shrinking from the heat. Finally, it fell away. Laura stepped back and examined the angry red blotch on her leg.

"It's supposed to work better with a cigarette, I guess," he said.

She glared at him. "You guess? You've never done that before? You experimented on me!"

"Don't say thanks, it might go to my head," he grumbled.

She looked at the bloated, loathsome leech on the ground. That was *her* blood swelling it to obscene proportions. She gritted her teeth and resisted the urge to stamp on it.

"Thanks," she said in a low voice.

"What?" Jack pretended not to hear. "What did you say?"

She scratched at a mosquito bite, one of many.

"You heard me."

He grinned. "Okay. Ready for breakfast? We have…" he paused for effect, "one granola bar, flavored with delicious flakes of melted and coagulated chocolate, and a mouthful of yesterday's water." He broke the bar in half and handed the larger piece to her.

Laura started to sit down. "Wait," he warned, "until I check." He walked around their slice of dry land briskly and then sat down himself. "Okay."

"What do you mean okay?"

"No snakes. Sometimes they come out of the water and spend the night on land if there aren't any crocodiles thrashing about."

She looked around nervously. "I don't believe you."

He shrugged. That had been one of the questions he had asked himself last night. Do crocodiles get tired of swimming and haul up on the nearest bank to sleep? Fortunately, he never found out.

Early morning sun filtered through the tops of the trees and lit up their section of the riverbank. "Wait a minute," he said and began rooting around again in the dry sack. "Ah, here it is." He pulled out a small point-and-shoot digital camera, focused on her and pressed the shutter.

"Don't you dare take a picture of me," Laura wailed. She knew how she looked. Her hair hung in limp tangles. Through eyes red-rimmed from the water and smoke, she examined bite marks that had raised welts on her arms and legs. Mud caked her red shorts and sneakers.

"Beauty in the wild is a rare thing," Jack grinned, clicking the shutter again. "I wonder what *Glimpse* would pay for this?"

"I'd kill you first," Laura fumed, reaching for the camera, which he laughingly held out of reach. They both stopped, aware of a new sound, the "whup, whup,whup" of a helicopter passing unseen overhead. Two hours later, they heard an even better sound: the "put, put, put" of a gasoline motor as a boat maneuvered up the slough toward them.

Castillo met them at the dock with apologies, orange juice, and ointment for their bug bites. So did Maria Ramirez and the Channel 4 news team, which beamed an interview back to San Jose by satellite. After the news team had packed up, Jack accepted a clean shirt and pair of pants and went into the marina office to change. Castillo apologized to Laura for not having a change of clothes for her. He did offer a worn shirt, however, which she was glad to exchange for Jack's now-filthy jacket.

"I am so sorry, Miss Sanders... but the weather is unpredictable." Castillo gestured apologetically. Relieved at the rescue, he began calculating just how much he could bill Mari O'Reilly. After all, one new kayak had been lost and another badly damaged. He mentally upgraded the truck to be bought. Leather seats? No. Air conditioning and CD/DVD player... Yes...!

"Please... I just want to get back to the hotel," Laura begged, her eyes blinking in fatigue.

"Of course, of course. Your driver is waiting. You are lucky, you know."

Laura nodded. "I guess so. If my competition hadn't missed the take-out point, too, I'd have spent the night alone." She shuddered at the thought, realizing Jack had shared his food and removed a leech.

Castillo looked surprised. "Oh, no, miss. My son said your friend deliberately paddled past the landing. He pointed his paddle to indicate he intended to continue down the river!"

Laura's shoulders slumped. "Damn," she said softly, looking up the dock toward the shack into which Jack had disappeared.

For Mari, however, it was all finally coming together. After a sleepless night, broken up with periodic trips to the computer to check out CNN online, she had gone to the office, steeling herself for the bad news that both of her Challenge of the Sexes contestants had vanished in the wilds of Costa Rica, where she, fool that she was, had sent them. She could see it now: editorials in the New York Times flailing television in general (and her in particular) for risking innocent lives to boost ratings. Then would follow public expressions of regret, puzzlement, and consternation from the 39th floor. Even her mother would get into the act.

And how would her audience react? Would they boo and jeer? Or… one of Mari's strengths had always been self-confidence. She asked herself: Does Larry King agonize over the path not taken? Would Oprah? Of course not. No guts, no glory. Sure, if the average person were in her shoes he or she might put an "out of the office" message on the telephone system, sneak down the back stairs, shut the window in the limo so the chauffeur's prattle couldn't be heard, and hide away in a condo on Central Park West, ordering meals in from Alfredo's. Not Mari! She'd confront the problem head-on at the next show. She could see it now. She'd wear black, something simple but still sexy. No makeup. Instead, she'd rub her eyes a little until they reddened, perhaps with onion, and everyone would think she'd been crying. Then, in a low voice overwhelmed occasionally by emotion, she'd lead a tribute to the valiant Florida educator and flaky Left Coast writer who had carried the quest for truth (or something) to its ultimate conclusion. As she mentally ran through a possible wardrobe, Cindy burst into the room without knocking.

"They're okay! Rescuers found them in a swamp this morning with nothing more than a few mosquito bites," Cindy babbled. "Dr. Sanders struck something and her kayak overturned. Kileen found her after his boat sprang a leak." She waited expectantly for Mari to display the relief that she herself felt.

"Oh... good..." Mari shifted gears regretfully. She still replayed the tribute in her mind, the one at which she wore the simple but sexy black dress.

She refocused. "Okay, we're back on track with Plan A." She paused as an afterthought hit her. "Did we get any footage of the rescue?"

Cindy shook her head. "No. But a local TV reporter did an interview and NBC picked it."

Mari swore. Wrong network. Oh, well. On the other hand, any press was good press. What a buildup for the presentation of the check for $1 million to Laura Sanders! What killer ratings! Of course, she'd have to persuade the Committee of Seven to dump the final event in the challenge due to the almost-disaster on the river. But Laura Sanders was ahead! "Get me Nancy Ferlman on the telephone," she said Cindy.

Nancy Ferlman turned out to be a tough sell; but Mari argued that since the kayak challenge had ended without result (she thought of saying in an almost dead heat but it didn't seem appropriate), Laura should be declared the winner on points. No, another adventure racing test wasn't possible and might be even more dangerous. No one wanted that, did they? And, like a good salesperson, Mari kept her best argument for last. Hadn't Dr. Sanders won four of the six challenges? Mrs. Ferlman said that she would present Mari's views to the committee. Mari would hear from them after a conference call. One hour later, she did. After voting 4-3 against trying to set up another final event, they declared Laura the winner.

Television networks interrupted daytime programming to report the rescue and later Mari's announcement Laura reigned as winner of the Challenge of the Sexes. The story got extended coverage on the ABC, CBS, NBC, and FOX evening news. It led ESPN's Sports Center, possessing all the elements of a television sports producer's wet dream: Adventure! Competition! Danger! Disaster! Rescue! Victory! Awards! Everything but sex. Print media lagged by several hours (newspapers) or several days (magazines) but made up for it with in-depth coverage. Big, bold headlines read:

The New York Times

> 'Challenge' Racers
> Rescued on River;
> Fla. Prof. Victor

Le Monde

> Elle remporte!

Sydney Morning Herald

> Jungle Bungle!

Newsweek

> Soggy...Safe...Successful!

Variety

> Chick Chills 'Challenge'

Glimpse

> Exclusive!

> Challenge of Sexes
> Pair Escapes From
> 'Big Foot' in Swamp

Outdoor Living

> What Your Survival Kit Should Contain

Popular Mechanics

> Why Waterproofing Your Cell Phone Could Save
> Your Life!

Working Women's Wear

> Classy While Casual in the Tropics? Read on!

And in New York, the little woman bubbled to the top of the Challenge of the Sexes scoreboard for the last time. And just so viewers at home could see the results more easily, Mari had a large arrow added with one word: "Winner!"

Chapter 36

Life is a long lesson in humility.

JAMES M. BARRIE

"You got shafted, man," commiserated Rasheed "Downtown" Jones. "Women will do it to you every time. Now take my ex...." He launched into a lengthy and truly depressing tale. Unlike other Sun employees who had been laid off, Jones had been rehired quickly after a rash of break-ins and vandalism in the newspaper's parking lot. Management had decided paying an additional non-union salary was more cost efficient than paying increased insurance premiums. It was also suggested morale might suffer if employees worried about whether or not their cars were safe, but that objection was dismissed as unimportant until a custom stereo player was stolen from the publisher's BMW.

Other reactions to Jack's loss followed: surprise, sympathy, and, in one case, barely restrained glee. His own reaction differed—relief. He had checked his ego at the door long ago and wanted this thing to go away. Good sport that he was (Jack determined to win *that* battle at least), he sent Laura a telegram: *The best man, woman, person, human being has won. Congratulations.* The words "woman" and "man" had X's drawn through them.

Cindy burst into Mari's office without knocking and threw down copies of New York newspapers on her desk.

Damn! thought Mari. She'd really, really have to talk to Cindy again about that!

"I've got a bunch of calls from TV and newspaper and magazine people who want interviews but can't get in touch with Dr. Sanders and Kileen," Cindy blurted out. "What should I do?"

"Put them through to me," Mari responded. She'd deflect them with stories about how poor Laura and Jack were recovering from their brush with death. She spent an hour fielding calls and then took the elevator to the 39th floor. She took the papers along. It took some persuading, but the suits finally gave her what she wanted: a promise the Challenge of the Sexes finale would be in prime time. They'd be pre-empting the popular series spinoff "CSI, Schenectady," but that wasn't her problem.

Jack enjoyed the flight to New York in first class. After being whisked by limo to a mid-Manhattan hotel, he changed into a dark turtleneck sweater, black leather jacket, and took a cab to the Eugene P. Doyle Theater. As before, Laura was waiting in the Green Room when he walked arrived.

"Hi," she said. She sounded tentative, unsure of his reaction.

"Hi, yourself," replied Jack. "Is life a sea of tranquility again?"

"Mostly," she admitted. "My telephone number's still unlisted. But after tonight, this should be over, right?"

"I sure hope so. All of this attention is going to my head. Of course, I'll miss those gourmet meals in first class and the open bar in limos."

Jack admired the new Laura. She looked poised in a dark blue suit and white blouse. Gone were the granny glasses and long hair. No briefcase and homework, either.

He smiled. My, what a good hair styling and makeup job can do. Maybe I should try it, too. Still, he detected lines under her eyes that hadn't been there before.

"I wanted to thank you for coming to my rescue. The marina owner told me that you went past the takeout point to find me."

"No worries," he said. "That's just part of the service."

She bit her lip. "I don't think so, but thanks."

The door opened and a familiar looking young woman with streaked blonde hair stuck her head in. "Three minutes, folks." She ducked out.

Laura looked at Jack, who appeared relaxed. She wondered if he had been sampling the limo bar on the way over, but she couldn't detect any odor of alcohol.

And then it was show time. When they were ushered onto the stage and sat down, Jack's eyes widened. The warm-up guy wore a tuxedo. Mari looked stunning in a form-fitting fringed white gown, sling-back heels with ankle ties, and gold locket on a matching neck-band. He wished he'd spiffed up and done more than get his gray suit dry cleaned.

"Hi, guys," she said. "We're on in a few minutes. Prime time with a national TV audience! I hope you're recording this at home. Let me know if you need a copy."

Right, thought Jack. I'll give some as Christmas gifts. He noticed the set had been changed. The couch and Mari's desk had been replaced by chairs on which sat the Committee of Seven, ready for *their* 15 minutes of fame. Or so. Actually, they were just props. Only Mari and Laura were going to be in the spotlight if Mari had anything to do with it.

She got down to business. "I'll ask both of you how you feel and what you learned, that sort of thing," Mari said briskly. "Of course, I'll be talking more with Dr. Sanders, Jack."

He nodded. Big surprise there.

"Then Dr. Sanders gets to speak. It would be nice if you mentioned how you hope that your victory is an inspiration to women everywhere, Laura."

Laura's lips tightened.

And then Mari left to check on final details as the clock ticked down.

But if the production values had been upscaled, the audience hadn't. Mari had fought the network's attempt to turn the show into a tux and gown affair like the Academy Awards. She sensed, and the network's demographics people confirmed, that people comfy in jeans, sport shirts, Yankees jackets, and shorts clapped more enthusiastically.

The warm-up guy wrapped up and Mari took center stage. On the audience's large, overhead screen, the camera zoomed in on a beaming Mari. "Good evening and welcome to the end of the Challenge of the Sexes." She went for the earnest look. "When it began, months ago, I said that we'd have our contestants, Dr. Laura Sanders and Jack Kileen back at the end to receive well-deserved recognition."

"Well, here they are!" Mari gestured to Laura and Jack. Applause rolled out of the audience and onto the stage and into millions of homes. (Exactly how many, they'd find out the next day when the overnight Nielsen ratings were available. The network's ads in TV Guide and carefully selected newspapers would hype the numbers, of course.)

"It's been a long, difficult competition to see whether this woman or this man is superior...."

Laura noticed the qualifier. Good.

"And tonight we're going to honor both of them," Mari continued, slipping a little on the earnest meter as the spotlight lingered on Laura. She discussed Laura's and Jack's backgrounds briefly and recapped how the contest began. Next, she introduced the Committee of Seven and explained the contests. And then, just as the studio audience started to get restless, she got to the point.

"But first, we followed our contestants with cameras as they met some of their challenges. Here are some of the highlights.

The studio lights dimmed and new images filled the giant screen. Some sequences were brief. The income tax and computer competitions Jack had won apparently had struck the writers as boring so they were largely ignored; but he suffered through extensive reliving of his disaster bathing the dog. Come to think of it, he *had* noticed a young man with a video camera in the apartment complex that seemed to have been taking pictures. Jack had to laugh at some of the footage, even though it showed him as pretty inept. Other sequences, like the one of his dinner party, had been shot through a window, clear invasions of privacy. He wondered how they could get away with that. Laura fared better although she looked like a klutz practicing paddling in a kayak. He noticed she wasn't laughing.

The tape ended and the lights came up. Interviews followed. Sally and Pat showed up. Neither Laura nor Jack had known they'd be there. Cindy had sworn them to secrecy when arranging their tickets. Each received a check for $1,000 and a gift certificate for a week at a resort in Cancun. Jack had to admit Mari was a skilled interviewer. She drew out a number of humorous anecdotes from them. Pat smiled at Jack as she walked off the stage.

Mari walked over to Laura and Jack. "And now let's hear from our competitors," she said, thrusting the mike at Jack. "Do you still think that men are superior to women?" she said with a laugh.

He recognized one of her trademark tricks, the knife between the ribs delivered with a warm, friendly smile. "I never did," said Jack. He smiled back.

"Have you been kidded much about being beaten by a woman?"

"Sure, by a few men. Most women were too polite to rub it in."

Mari's frown lines appeared. She tightened her grip on the microphone, now a bulb-shaped lance, and pointed it toward Jack aggressively. "Did you notice the two events you won involved physical and technical activities and the four events Dr. Sanders won required more... intellectual skills?"

Jack sensed where *that* was going. "Are you suggesting women are smarter than men or just that I'm stronger and dumber than Dr. Sanders?"

Mari turned to the audience and laughed, but it sounded strained. "Dr. Sanders won the cultural test. Doesn't that show she has the broader knowledge of lots of things? I wonder if that isn't reflective of women in general."

"Who knows? Dr. Sanders is an educator," he replied. "That makes her a professional student. She's far better read than I am—better read than most people, male or female. She may well be smarter if you gave us intelligence tests. That wouldn't surprise me at all." He smiled. "If you and I took the cultural test, Mari. The results might be different."

The muscles in Mari's face tightened but she gave no ground. "So has your opinion of women changed after all this?" A low murmur rose in the audience.

"I don't think so," he said. "I've always had a high opinion of women. My mother was one."

Laughter erupted. Mari started to say something and flushed. This wasn't going the way she wanted.

She turned to Laura. "Dr. Sanders, you seem to have survived your ordeal in the jungle well."

"With a little help," Laura said, glancing at Jack.

Mari decided to shift gears. "What is your feeling of greatest accomplishment?" she asked hurriedly.

Laura ignored her. "Mr. Kileen may not know as much as I do about English novels or history, but he knows when to help a woman in distress. He could have gotten off the river and perhaps won the contest, but he risked his neck by going on and finding me. You can't measure that in points."

Jack gave her his most earnest "aw shucks, it weren't nothin,' mam," look.

"You're too generous, Dr. Sanders," Mari said firmly. "You had the fastest time kayaking. You deserved to win."

Laura would have none of it. "His boat had sprung a leak," she said. "It almost sank, but he went looking for me anyway."

Mari squirmed.

"You know," Laura said slowly, "I enjoyed the competition."

She got an encouraging nod.

"People need to challenge themselves occasionally," Laura continued. "That's hard to do unless you can measure what you're doing against what someone else is doing. For people like me who live in an intellectual womb—college can be that—it's good to get outside once in a while and rub up against the real world."

"The problem," she went on, "is when you confuse winning with achieving, especially if it gives you a distorted view of what you think you've achieved. The biggest victory isn't over someone else; it's over yourself and your limitations. You were right, Mari, when you said "this woman" and "this man" competed; but you were wrong when you said one turned out to be superior. It's not that simple. Someone once told me that men and women are like ham and eggs, okay when taken individually, but far superior when combined. I don't know about the ham and eggs analogy; I wish I could offer a better one. But I agree with the concept. Men and women make a great team—when they can overlook how they're different and accept how they're alike."

Mari received an unpleasant rocket in her ear from the director. "Can the philosophy. Move it along. This is dragging." She started to interrupt, but Laura wouldn't slow down. "I've got some old '40s records at home," she said, "and one of them is by Johnny Mercer. The title is 'Accentuate the Positive.' He sings about 'accentuating the positive' and 'eliminating the negative.' I think that we all need to work on that."

The audience broke into applause. Mari knew better than to try and top that. "We'll be right back," she said, forcing a smile.

She tried. Jack had to give her that. Mari really tried. She asked question after question designed to get Laura to boast about her victories and agree that yes, women really do get rotten treatment from unreasonable, uncaring, chauvinistic men. Laura refused to bite. Finally, Mari introduced the president of the Road Whacker Tire Co., who presented a large green replica of a check for $1 million to Laura. Jack got a check for $5,000 and a certificate good for four new all-weather tires to Jack. Laura said she'd use part of the money to fund scholarships at her university; Jack just smiled. And then it ended. When the cameras winked off and the audience filed out, he offered to buy Laura a drink. She begged off, pleading fatigue, and returned to the hotel. She left the next morning on an early flight.

He never saw her again.

Ch*a*pter 37

*Begin at the beginning and go on
till you come to the end; then stop.*

LEWIS CARROLL

Ah, Christmas in California! It didn't get much better than that. Or not. Jack clapped along with the festive crowd as the mayor of San Francisco sneezed and flipped a switch. The towering Christmas tree in Union Square lit up like … well… like a Christmas tree. His honor, fellow politicians, community activists, and religious leaders, most of whom were at each other's throats the rest of the year, shared a brief moment of camaraderie. Jack decided to skip the caroling and wander over to the Hyatt Hotel to admire the annual display of miniature houses, sleds, trains, skiers, and ice skaters nestled in tiny villages aglitter with mica flakes scattered on cotton. That plus an Irish coffee at the Buena Vista might change his mood. He found it hard to get the holiday spirit when the pavement is bare, even if the panhandlers wear Santa hats and ring bells.

Christmas didn't seem right to him without snow and bracing cold weather. Oh, everyone tried. The stores had window displays with Santa and his elves, and the city festooned lamp poles with wreaths and garlands.

But Jack had grown up in New York State where tingly, frosty Yules—with or without snow—were the norm. Even the Christmas cards he received depressed him, especially the idyllic Currier & Ives reproductions of people all bundled up from the cold, skating on picturesque frozen lakes and riding in horse-drawn sleds. Bah... humbug....

Of course, if he *really* wanted to see snow, he could drive up to Lake Tahoe with thousands of Bay Area skiers who, like lemmings, created moving traffic jams on the highway. At least he had the satisfaction of knowing transplanted Easterners and Midwesterners like himself would get their revenge on New Year's Day. That's when people in snow country would be watching the Rose Bowl game on TV, envying inebriated, shirtless young were basking in the warm Southern California sunshine and smog.

His life had returned to the slow lane. It was safe to go the phone and the mailbox. He had stumbled upon the 3-F Rule: Fame Fades Fast. The Sun's editor had made a rare foray into the newsroom and complimented him on a story he had written about a family that had lost all of its Christmas presents in a house fire. The newspaper's readers had replaced the presents almost overnight. The editor had called him "Jack," and he had called the editor "Jim." Being on a first-name basis with your bosses represented one of the perks of working in the media—feigned equalitarianism. Everyone was equal. Only the paychecks and parking spaces differed.

Back in his apartment, Jack put some Sinatra on the stereo to match his mood. Nothing like listening to Old Blue Eyes sing "Guess I'll Hang My Tears out to Dry" to make you want to go out and get a gun and shoot yourself. Why hang around for Christmas? he brooded. He could be skin diving in Maui and watching the sunset instead of the fog.

Last Saturday, he had driven down to Monterey with a cute blonde flight attendant who had moved into an apartment upstairs. But it didn't work. He couldn't stop thinking of Pat. He had driven back that same night, the flight attendant fuming at his side, not buying his story about unexpectedly having to write a deadline story. Heck, he wouldn't have bought it, either. At least, for the first time in his life, his bank account had a healthy balance. He had added a check for $12,500 from his publisher, an advance for a book on the Challenge of the Sexes. He suspected Laura would be doing a book, too, undoubtedly with a bigger advance. He toyed with the idea of asking if she might be interested in collaborating. They could flip a coin to see whose name came first on the dust jacket.

Nah...He opened a beer, drank half, and poured the rest down the sink. This was silly. He'd call Pat. Jack walked over to the phone and picked it up and started to dial. But then he stopped and put it down.

In Chicago, Larry Clayton began his regular morning meeting of Glimpse department heads by banging his fist on the table. It was a trick he had learned from the publisher. One startled editor dumped his coffee into his lap. "I'm not happy, people," Clayton boomed. "It's the holiday season and we need some story ideas. A miracle would be good, but I'll settle for a nice tearjerker if it's tragic enough. Let's get on it!" After the meeting broke up, he walked out into the newsroom and looked around. He missed that last kid, what was his name? ...Nevasconi!, the one who had bailed to attend law school. Law school! Another talented, aggressive, hungry, creative young reporter who came cheap lured away from creative journalism. And what was the name of the kid before him? It slipped his mind.

Maggie, glass in hand, wandered about her apartment. She had gotten the green plastic tree with the wire arms that folded up from a closet. Adorned by a few small ornaments, it occupied a round coffee table by the window. A few cards stood grouped around it, but the only present under it came from Jack Kileen. She suspected it was a book on hockey. He had given her one last year. She decided to watch a movie on TV she'd recorded, "White Christmas," and then thaw a turkey dinner. Going out would be nice, but restaurants and theaters had gotten anal about smoking. She coughed and took a sip of her bourbon and water.

Cindy grabbed another tissue from the box on her desk, blew into it, and contemplated her Christmas present from Mari. It had been there on her desk when she returned from lunch. She opened it. It contained a box of candy and a Christmas card. Inside the card she read a terse note informing her that as of Jan. 1 she would have the title of administrative assistant—for the same pay. Cindy decided to start on the candy early. She needed a chocolate fix.

Laura didn't look forward to another lonely Christmas. The moon over Miami (or Sanibel Island) lost something when you watched TV and saw snow and ice-skating at Rockefeller Center in New York City. Still, she had to admit her life was on an uptick. Organizations that wanted her to speak now offered fees as well as re-imbursement for expenses. Her classes had wait lists. She had put aside several writing projects for educational journals and bought a pair of in-line skates. One of her students had promised to teach her to skate without a trip to the emergency room.

She had received a Christmas card from Jack Kileen. It contained pictures of her he had taken in the swamp with a promise she'd never see them in *Glimpse* or any other publication. Also, her social life had picked up considerably since the Challenge of the Sexes; however, she wasn't getting anywhere being subtle with Morris Evander, who always seemed glad to see her but never asked for a date. He didn't need a push; he needed an avalanche.

With exams over, most of the students and faculty had departed, and the campus had an eerie, deserted, science fiction-like feel. Evander's office door stood ajar. He sat humming softly, wearing a blue cardigan sweater, playing solitaire on the computer.

She stuck her head in. "Hi, Morris, don't administrators get a break, too?"

He swiveled around in his chair. "Oh, Laura! Ready for the holiday break?"

"Better believe it. I need some down time."

He nodded sympathetically. "You certainly deserve it." He still hadn't adjusted to the new, attractive Laura, the celebrity model.

She decided to cut to the chase. "Morris, if you're going to be in town and don't have other plans, how about joining me for dinner on Christmas Eve?"

He looked unhappy. "I'm sorry, Laura. I was just cleaning up some paperwork. I'm flying to Boston tonight to spend the holiday with my fiancée. You may remember her. Wilma Price? She taught Spanish here for a year. That's when we met."

Laura forced a smile. "Oh... right...Wilma Chase."

Mari didn't look forward to the holidays, either. She could spend it with her aging parents in Ohio. Her father would be in the bag before dinner and probably dribble turkey gravy down his shirt. Her mother would fawn over Mari's sister's new baby and look at Mari reproachfully. Maybe she should plead about having too much work to do and stay in New York. Chip Wilson's departure had set her back again. She had figured him out the first day. He had stayed just long enough to work his contacts and then departed for a job with CNN in London. But at least Cliff Hansen had gotten his, the rat. Apparently working for Jerry Elkins had been tougher than he had expected. Hansen had had a mild infarction (that's what doctors called heart attacks) and was spending the holidays in Riverside General Hospital eating Jell-O and drinking fruit juice. Not that it did *her* any good. So she had put out another call for a temporary director, anticipating the jokes to come. The light on Cindy's line lit and the telephone rang.

"Yes." She checked her watch. Almost time to split.

"I've got three applications for the director's job," wheezed Cindy. She suffered The Holiday Curse, a bad head cold.

"Schedule appointments after the holidays. I don't want to deal with it now." Boy, was that the truth.

Cindy wheezed again. "Okay, but there's one guy here now. Just dropped off the application and résumé. He wants to know if you have a few minutes to talk to him."

"No, I don't..." But she stopped as a shy-looking man holding an overcoat stepped tentatively into her office. He stroked his mustache nervously and smiled engagingly.

"Hello, I'm Ashford Sloan."

Christmas morning broke bright and clear in Union City. A fuzzy green mantle had appeared on the hills after early rains. To the south, Mission Peak displayed a sprinkling of snow the sun would melt by afternoon. Pat had gotten up early to prepare a cinnamon twist coffee cake Jimmy liked. She relaxed with the local newspaper and a second cup of coffee. They had opened their presents on Christmas Eve. The doorbell chimed. Who...? She opened it and blinked in surprise. Jack. He wore a ridiculous Santa's hat, a wide grin, and held a large box. The gift, wrapped in silver paper, had been tied awkwardly.

"Merry Christmas! This is for Jimmy." The box shifted again, and she detected the muffled sound of panting.

She shook her head. "Is that what I think it is?"

"Probably." His eyes held hers. "And I've got another box, much smaller, for you. What's inside it is only as big as your finger."

"Is that what I think it is?" She couldn't trust her voice.

"Why don't you open it and find out?"

She stepped aside and he walked back into her life.

The End

Epilogue

Jack writes a book about his experiences, "Nice Guys Finish Second." After layoffs at The Sun, he joins a public relation firm and becomes an assistant coach on Jimmy's middle school baseball team, the Grover Hill Giants.

Just as she did in the race, **Laura Sanders** beats Jack to press with her book, "Women Can End on Top!" It peaks briefly at No. 14 on the New York Times Best Seller list and winds up on the reading lists of women's studies classes. She never marries.

Mari O'Reilly can't repeat her success with the Challenge of the Sexes, and her show continues to decline in the ratings. After leaving the network, she is occasionally seen on cable TV selling dietary supplements and aids for the incontinent.

After being fired by Mari for writing a tell-all book about the cutthroat world of afternoon television, **Ashford Sloan** becomes a professor of mass media at an Ivy League college. He writes several well-received books about the decline in journalism ethics.

Cliff Hansen is replaced with a stunning young female producer while he's on sick leave. He makes a comeback as the director of reality shows, including "The Absolutely, Positively, Flat Out, Most Disgusting Moments on TV—Part Two."

Jerry Elkins uses his recognition as a TV talk show host to run for Congress on a moral values platform. He is defeated after a photo of him wearing black tights and holding a whip appears on an adult entertainment website.

Denied a promotion to editor-in-chief, **Larry Clayton** quits *Glimpse Magazine* and launches a new publication, *Peek!* It lasts for three issues.

Maggie Bauer retires from the Sun at the mandatory age of 70. She dies alone a year later of lung cancer and cirrhosis of the liver.

The NFL, fearing legislation by Congress, adopts a "don't ask, don't tell" policy toward gay players. **"Cracker" Marion Sally** becomes the league's Director of Player Relationships and conducts well-received sensitivity sessions for teams.

Cindy Martinez runs into her high school honey, Billy Krantz, at a singles bar. After his divorce becomes final, they marry. Her wedding gift to him is a '92 Ford Taurus badly in need of repair.

Figures of the little man and little woman that bobbed up and down registering victory and defeat on the Challenge of the Sexes scoreboard wind up for sale on eBay. There are no bidders.

The End